"Nobody gives away tons of expensive gadgets without getting something in return." Things like this don't happen in Disney movies, let alone real life.

"Fair point." I can picture Nate running a hand through his hair while he thinks things through. After a few seconds he says, "People do strange things for all kinds of reasons, you know. Maybe it's someone who played Santa Claus at the mall this year and decided it was so much fun he didn't want to stop. Or maybe some rich dude learned he has only two months to live and has decided to give his money away to a worthwhile cause."

"You call indulging Jack's every desire worthwhile?"

"No, but getting me a passing physics grade is. Although, now that I'm considering all the options, I realize how short-sighted my choice was."

"Why?" I ask. "Because you don't think your physics teacher can be bribed by a terminally ill rich guy?"

"Everyone has a price, Kaylee. You just have to be willing to push until you figure out what it is. Whoever's behind this website knows that. But it's occurred to me that my request can't be fulfilled for another two and a half weeks. If I'd been more materialistic like Jack and almost everyone else, I'd already have my first order in hand and have moved on to my second. Now, thanks to the rules of the site, I have to wait until the first request is fulfilled before I can ask for anything else."

"By then you won't be able to ask for anything."

"Why not?"

"Because there won't be anyone left to invite to the network."

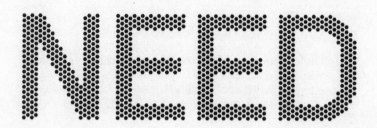

NEED

BY JOELLE CHARBONNEAU

Houghton Mifflin Harcourt
Boston New York

www.hmhco.com

The text was set in Adobe Garamond.

The Library of Congress has cataloged the hardcover
edition as follows:
NEED / Joelle Charbonneau.
p. cm.
Summary: "In this exploration of the dark side of social media, and
government control and manipulation, the teenagers in a small town
are drawn deeper and deeper into a social networking site
that promises to grant their every need—regardless of the
consequences." —Provided by publisher
[1. Social media—Fiction.] I. Title. II. Title: NEED.
PZ7.C37354Naam 2015
[Fic]—dc23
2014034512

ISBN: 978-0-544-41669-7 hardcover
ISBN: 978-0-544-93883-0 paperback

Printed in the United States of America
DOC 10 9 8 7 6 5
4500700411

To my brother, TJ,
also known as AJ, Anthony, Tony, and XJ.
Sorry, but you'll always be TJ to me!

do was invite five qualified friends to join. As soon as they accepted the invitations, presto, the phone was his."

"The world doesn't work that way." At least, my world doesn't. "The site must ask for a credit card or something. No one gives out free cell phones for inviting five people to a new social network."

"This one does." Nate swings back to face the screen. "Trust me, my brother isn't clever enough to make something like this up. And he's not the only one who got stuff. Look at this."

Nate clicks the mouse and shifts the laptop so I can see the screen from where I'm standing behind him. Normally, without glasses, I wouldn't be able to read anything. In this case, I can make out the large red letters in the center of a black box.

```
NETWORK MEMBERS—48
NEEDS PENDING—43
NEEDS FULFILLED—7
```

"So . . ." Nate looks at me with a goofy smile. "What should I ask for? A new bike? A computer?"

"You don't need either of those things."

"What's your point?" Nate shrugs. "Jack didn't really need a phone, but he got one."

"Yeah, but . . ." But what? I'm not exactly sure. There's something about this whole setup that bugs me. Or maybe it's just the question we're asked—*What do you need?* Because I know what need is, and it's not another phone.

Nate gives me an annoyed look and I feel a twinge of guilt.

When Nate heard my mom and brother weren't home, he dropped what he was doing to come over and keep me company. And knowing Nate, he probably had a zillion offers for something more entertaining to do with his night. At some point he's going to realize that and start accepting those invitations. Then what will I do?

So I slide my glasses back on and say, "I guess I'm just surprised your brother sent you an invitation."

"He didn't." Nate flashes a wide grin. "He forgot to log out when he left to meet his friends, and I borrowed his computer and sent an invitation to myself." Nate rolls out his shoulders. "The network assigns a profile name to every user, and as far as I can tell, no one is allowed to say anything on the site that will reveal their identity or to disclose online or in real life whether their need has been fulfilled." He clicks the mouse several times and then points to the screen as he reads: "Doing so violates the terms of use and voids any possible fulfillment of requests in the future."

"But Jack—"

"Yep." Nate laughs. "Jack already violated the terms. He's going to be displeased when he tries to get something else and the NEED fairy godmother gives him the finger. I can't wait."

"You're assuming the people who operate the system know Jack told his friends," I say. "The odds of that occurring have to be pretty low."

"Yeah. What a bummer." Nate lets out a dramatic sigh. "Still, there's always a chance someone will learn about Jack breaking the rules, which is good. It gives me something to dream about when he's being a jerk."

"So, basically, you'll be dreaming about it a lot." I laugh.

"A guy has to have a hobby. We can't all have brothers we actually like and get along with." I see Nate's eyes shift to the framed photograph on my desk of me, Mom, and DJ from this summer. DJ's blond hair shines in the sunlight. His face is filled with delight. Mom and I look happy too, but our brown hair makes us look less bright. Or maybe it's just that I know how much we both wish we were more like DJ.

"Have you heard anything?" Nate asks.

I bite my bottom lip, pull my phone out of my back pocket, and check to make sure I didn't miss a message. Nothing. "Mom took DJ to the ER at All Saints Hospital, and her phone doesn't always get the best reception there. I'm sure she'll update me soon." The tests won't say he's had a relapse. They just can't. He deserves better than that. He deserves better than everything he's gotten up to now. Karma owes him. I'd be there with him now if I'd been allowed to go. Instead, my mother insisted I stay here. Out of the way. Alone.

Nate reaches out and I step toward him. He takes my hand and webs his fingers through mine. No. Not alone. Behind him, I can read the word NEED shining in large red block letters at the top of the computer screen, which is appropriate. Because in my life, Nate is someone I need. Without him, I'm not sure how I would get through nights like this. If he ever finds a serious girlfriend, I'll be sunk.

"So . . ." Nate's voice is once again filled with mischief as he lets go of my hand and swivels toward the desk. "Back to the really important stuff. What should I ask the great and power-ful NEED network for? A car would be nice."

"You live two blocks from school," I say. "You don't *need* a car. Not to mention that you'd have to get a job to pay for gas and insurance."

"Sad but true. And since I'm not interested in hard labor, I'll have to ask for something else." Nate tilts his head to the side. His expression turns serious. "You know what I really need? A B on my physics final. Before break, Mr. Lott told me I have to get at least an eighty percent on that test or I'll fail the class and end up in summer school."

"I don't think the people running NEED can take your final for you."

"No, but whoever created this thing must have skills. He might be able to hack into the system and change my grade. Nothing ventured, nothing gained, right?" Nate types *An A on my physics final* into the box and hits Enter. The message in the box changes. Now it reads: NEED REQUEST BEING VERI-FIED. PLEASE STAND BY. The image of a clock appears.

"I thought you said you needed a B."

"Why settle?" Nate taps his fingers on the wood of my desk as the second hand of the clock on the NEED site travels from twelve to one. Then two. As it travels to the number three, I feel my phone vibrate in my pocket. My stomach lurches. My legs are unsteady as I stand and pull out the phone.

"What does it say?" Nate asks.

I try to breathe, but I can't as I click the Talk button, praying that DJ is okay. Thankfully, my mother doesn't draw things out and tells me in the first sentence that he is. No relapse. He's still sick, but it isn't worse. With every relapse it can get so much worse. So this is good. Still, my voice shakes when I put down the phone and say, "The doctor is going to run one more test, but they think a virus caused the fever. Everything else is stable." For now.

"That's a relief. Hey, I haven't asked in the last week, but your father . . ."

I shake my head. "I still haven't been able to find him. The Christmas card he sent had a Kenosha return address and postmark, but when I called the apartment complex they said they'd never heard of him."

"You'll find him, Kaylee." Nate gets up and puts his arms around me. "If not, we'll convince more people around here to get tested. Someone will step up and help."

I lean into Nate and close my eyes. "I hope so." I used to think so. Then I learned the truth. People say they care, but they just don't give a damn. Not my father. Not the people in this town. Not the school psychologist my mother insists I see to deal with my "issues." No one. Opening my eyes, I see the screen behind Nate change and am grateful for the distraction. "The clock on the site stopped ticking."

Nate's face lights up. He gives me one final squeeze before sliding into the chair in front of the computer screen. "Score. My request has been processed. Now, according to this, I just have to invite six qualified friends to the site and my need will be met. That's easy enough." Nate types my name and email address and hits Send before I can object. He then types five more addresses.

"Who did you just invite?"

"I'm not telling. Unlike Jack, I plan on following the rules." After hitting Log Out, Nate shoves back the chair and stands. "Now, did your mom say when they'll be home?"

"No." The last time I went with DJ and Mom to the ER, it took hours before DJ was discharged. It's like clocks stop working when you step into a hospital. "I doubt it will be any time soon."

"Good." Nate grabs my arm and pulls me toward the door. "That means we still have time to raid the fridge and watch a scary movie before they get back."

"Does it have to be a horror film?" I ask, even though I know the answer. "Can't we watch *Lord of the Rings* for the hundredth time? I won't complain when you say all the dialogue and reenact the fight scenes."

"Tempting, but no." He laughs. "You have to do something nice for me because I came over, and I have my heart set on hearing you shriek like a girl."

"In case you haven't noticed, I am a girl."

"And I've been working hard for the last seven years to not hold it against you." Nate turns and winks. "You get the popcorn. I'll get the soda. It's time to have some fun."

Hannah

HANNAH MAZUR SITS at her desk and pulls the book she was assigned to read over break out of her backpack. She's put it off for the last week and a half, but school starts again on Wednesday, which means she has to get started.

A Tale of Two Cities. Even the title sounds boring. Her teacher swore she wasn't really assigning homework this holiday. She said she was giving everyone the gift of a wonderful story. Yeah, right. If that were the case, there would be a hot guy on the cover.

Since she doesn't want to spend New Year's Eve catching up, Hannah flips to the first page and starts reading. After ten minutes, her eyes glaze over and her brain goes fuzzy. If this is Mrs. Hernandez's idea of a gift, she needs to get out more.

Laughter from downstairs makes Hannah want to get up and see what she's missing, but she can't. Not after telling everyone that she was going upstairs to finish her homework. Her mother will give her "the look," which will inevitably lead to being told she can't go to Logan's New Year's Eve party.

Hannah skims a few more pages and decides to take a break to look at email. After all, reading in small doses will probably make her remember the book better.

She grins as she sees an email from Nate Weakley in her inbox. Maybe this means Nate is finally paying attention. About time he stopped being so into Kaylee Dunham. After her playing-sick routine last year that only proved she needed acting lessons and psychiatric help, Kaylee doesn't deserve Nate. Between that and her getting in people's faces about being tested as a kidney donor, it's no wonder he eventually lost interest. Everyone feels bad that Kaylee's brother could die, but going up to people in the cafeteria in front of everyone and begging them to be tested is just uncool. Hannah hated the way people looked at her, waiting for her response. And, of course, she felt like dirt when she said no. No one said yes, but still. Asking people that way is just mean.

She clicks on the link and laughs at the website. Is Nate playing a joke? If so, she's game. This is a heck of a lot more fun than Charles Dickens.

She thinks about the question.

What do you need?

Hmm . . . CliffsNotes? A great new outfit for the party? Nah. To get Nate's attention she has to be more intriguing than that. And who knows, maybe he'll try to find a way to get her what she wants. If so, she has to make it harder than a trip to the mall. Hannah discards one idea after another until she finally has it.

"I need an extra week of Christmas break."

Heck, her father would be thrilled if that came through. He likes teaching, but even he said this year's break hasn't been long enough. He'd have more time to watch football and play video games with her brothers, and she'd be able to ditch reading this book for another couple of days. It's what her father would call a win-win proposition.

The NEED clock is ticking. When her request is accepted, she puts in the requisite seven email addresses and hits Send.

Kaylee

I'M NOT SURE if an enormous bowl of popcorn drowned in butter, a psychopath chasing people around the woods, and Nate calling me a girl every time I covered my eyes should technically be termed "fun," but it took my mind off things for a while. Nate would say that wasn't his goal. Nate lies.

It's just after midnight when DJ and Mom walk into the house. Nate and I stop talking as we watch them come in. Despite his having been in the cold, DJ's face is pale. But his blue eyes light up when he spots Nate.

"Hey, DJ." Nate holds out his hand, and DJ and he bump fists. "How are you feeling? Kaylee said you and your mom were hanging out in the ER, so I kept her company here." He leans forward and in a loud whisper adds, "I made her watch a slasher flick."

"Aw, man. I wish I had been with you guys." DJ sighs. "There is nothing wrong with me."

"You had a fever," Mom says.

"I have a cold." DJ rolls his eyes. "The doctors said it was no big deal, but Mom made them do a bunch of tests anyway. What a waste."

Maybe. But I still wrap my arms around his slight shoulders and hug him tight. I don't know what I'd do if I lost him.

"Hey." DJ squirms, but not very hard because he loves me. He knows I need this moment. And maybe he needs it too, because the second before he breaks free he hugs me back.

"Cut your sister a break, kid. Her nerves are shot from all the jumping and shrieking. She put on a better show than the actors did." Nate gives me a deliberate look. "If you want to watch it again I'd be happy to come back."

"That would be awesome. Right, Kaylee?" DJ turns toward me as I'm about to say no. And I can't, because I see the fatigue under the excitement and the worry that he tries to pretend he doesn't feel. That soon there may not be movie nights and fun. That the steroids will stop helping. That his kidneys will give out before a new kidney can be found. And I can't bring myself to take away even a single moment of happiness.

"Absolutely," I say. "The sooner the better."

"How about tomorrow?" DJ asks.

Mom shakes her head. "The doctor said you need to rest."

"Actually, Mom," DJ says, grinning, "that's what the doctor told *you*."

"How about this?" Nate says, shrugging into his thick black coat. "You rest tomorrow, and on Friday we'll have a horror movie marathon to celebrate the demise of your cold. You can even pick the first flick."

"Deal."

Mom gives Nate a grateful smile as she tells DJ to get ready for bed. Looking at Nate, she says, "I hope you won't mention DJ's cold to anyone. The last thing he needs is more people gossiping about his health."

"You can count on me, Mrs. D."

"That's great." She gives an absent smile. "Have a good night." Without a glance at me, she hurries after my brother to make sure he actually goes to bed instead of reading comic books by flashlight.

"Thanks," I say, walking Nate to the door.

"You never have to thank me for watching scary movies."

"Not that." I smile, grateful that he once again has the words to make me feel better. "But . . . tonight. Putting up with me. Keeping me sane. Being nice to DJ. You know."

"I know." Nate steps forward and wraps his arms around me for the second time tonight. I think that's a record. I must look pathetic, but at the moment I don't care. I lean into him and breathe in the smell of popcorn and dog, and the faint scent of cigarette smoke that means his mother has fallen off the no-smoking wagon again. For several seconds we just stand there. When we were nine, Nate told me we could do anything as long as we did it together. I think he got the line from a movie. He was a film junkie even then. But wherever he got it, I believed him. And I still believe him, because he's here after all the mistakes I've made and the idiotic things I've done. Because that's what best friends do.

"Call me tomorrow and let me know how you're doing." He gives me one last hug before jamming the purple hat his grandmother knitted for him onto his head. "And don't forget to check your inbox and accept the invitation. You don't want to live with my failing physics grade on your conscience, do you?"

He heads out into the cold and I lock the door after him. Then I watch out the front window as he walks down the driveway I shoveled yesterday to the street. When he reaches it, he turns and waves. I smile, wave back, and watch him trudge out of sight, knowing he'll text me when he gets home because I like hearing he's safe. Nate is crazy and fun and sometimes a touch wild, but he's always forgiving of what he calls my compulsive need to control the world.

Figuring my mother is too tired to come back downstairs, I check to make sure the back door is locked, then head upstairs. There's light under Mom's door, but I don't knock to see if she's still awake. Instead I walk to the next closed door, turn the handle, and squint into the darkness. I don't step inside because I've learned the hard way that I don't want to walk on whatever LEGO are currently scattered across the floor. So I stand in the doorway and watch DJ sleep, grateful his breathing is easy. For tonight he's okay, and for the zillionth time I wish I were different so I could help make him well.

As I close DJ's door, my mother steps out into the hall. "Is everything all right?" she whispers.

"Everything's fine. I just wanted to make sure he didn't need anything before I went to bed. You should get some sleep," I tell her. She has to get up for work in the morning.

"I will. You should go to bed too." Mom frowns and looks down at her hands. "And I know I said you could get some of those driving hours in after I get off work tomorrow, but with DJ's cold, I don't want him going in the car unless he has to and he shouldn't be left home alone . . ."

"Don't worry about it, Mom." I shrug. "It's no big deal." Nate isn't the only one who can lie. "We can do it another time when things are better. Maybe Sunday."

"We'll see."

I've heard those words enough to know that I have a better chance of having a pink pony delivered to my door than getting a driving lesson this weekend. At this rate, I'll earn my license by the time I graduate college. I could get angry, but there are more important things to focus on.

"Mom . . ." I say before I can lose my nerve. "Have you thought any more about hiring a private detective? I could chip in the money Nana and Papa sent me for Christmas. It's not a lot, but it could—"

"I told you no, Kaylee."

I flinch at the anger in her voice, but I don't back down. "But if there's a chance Dad could be a match—"

"If your father was interested in helping your brother, he would never have left in the first place. We've even talked this through with Dr. Jain. I'm handling things. I expect you to let me. Now go to bed."

She goes to her room and closes the door behind her. I hear the click of the lock. My mother has shut me out. Again. And really, why should tonight be any different? I could force the issue and demand she talk to me, but that would only wake up DJ. That wouldn't help anything.

I ball my hands into fists and stare at the door, foolishly waiting for her to change her mind. For once, I want her to understand. Yes, Craigslist wasn't smart. Lying about a cash reward for anyone who got tested and was a match wasn't just a bad idea, it was illegal. Something I didn't realize when I did it.

But I was desperate. I've done so many things out of desperation to help. And so far, instead of saving DJ's life, I've screwed up everything about my own.

I change into a pair of flannel pants and a T-shirt and am climbing into bed when I hear my phone vibrate. Nate. He's texting to say he arrived home and is hoping I am sitting at my desk, helping him secure a better future with an improved grade.

I text back that I wouldn't dare limit the possibilities for his life. Then I hop out of bed and walk over to my laptop. A few keystrokes and I click on the email with the header "Nate Weakley has invited you to NEED."

CONGRATULATIONS. YOU HAVE BEEN INVITED
TO NEED—THE NEWEST, INVITATION-ONLY
SOCIAL MEDIA SITE FOR NOTTAWA HIGH SCHOOL
STUDENTS. JOIN YOUR FRIENDS IN DISCOVERING
HOW MUCH BETTER LIFE CAN BE WHEN YOU ARE
PRESENTED WITH AN ANONYMOUS WAY TO EXPRESS
YOUR THOUGHTS AND ARE GIVEN THE TOOLS TO
GET THE THINGS YOU NEED.

I didn't realize the site was only for NHS students. That's strange. But now that I know, I push my chair back from the desk and think twice about clicking on the link below the sales pitch. While I don't like most of the people from my high school, and I don't associate with them unless I can't avoid it, accepting their online friendship requests is basically a requirement. Why they bother to send those requests is beyond me, but it seems like the more someone dislikes a person, the more they want to have contact on the Internet. Up until now, I've ignored anything they post, especially when it seems like they're baiting me into a response.

Most of the kids at my school are jerks. A few got tested when I put posters up and began passing out flyers about the kidney donation process before class. Three that I know of out of hundreds. The rest stopped meeting my eyes in the hall. Even the teachers looked the other way, so I fought back. I fought for my brother. Nate says I shouldn't take their name-calling personally. He says everyone hates feeling like a coward for not wanting to be tested. And instead of admitting it, they attack the person who has forced them to acknowledge to themselves that they're afraid.

Maybe he's right. It's hard to separate what they've done out of embarrassment from what I've done out of anger. I'm to blame for a lot, but not for everything. The rest is on them. Which is why I avoid dealing with them online as much as possible. Why bother if I don't have to? Then again, unlike all the others, this site wants its members to be anonymous. The network doesn't want anyone to know who's lurking behind the profiles. No one will know I'm a member. I know I'm trying to talk myself into joining because I don't want to disappoint Nate, and deep down I have to admit that I'm curious to see how my classmates and former friends interact online when they don't know who they're talking to and when they're certain their parents or other adults in the community aren't watching.

Biting my lip, I roll my chair back to the desk and click the link with my mouse.

Welcome to NEED appears on the screen.

PLEASE ENTER YOUR NAME AND CLICK THE BOX
TO CONFIRM YOU ARE A STUDENT CURRENTLY
ENROLLED IN NOTTAWA HIGH SCHOOL.

I follow the instructions and hit Enter. A new screen appears giving me my site identification number, D106; congratulating me on becoming a part of NEED; and inviting me to customize my home page. There are lots of options for adding wallpaper, changing my avatar to one of the hundreds of colorful images in the NEED database, and choosing links to the Need Exchange page, where members can message each other. I click around the site for a few minutes, trying to decipher its purpose, and end up on the page that Nate showed me earlier.

I read the boldface words again.

> **WANT:** A DESIRE TO POSSESS OR DO
> SOMETHING. A WISH.
> **NEED:** SOMETHING REQUIRED BECAUSE IT
> IS ESSENTIAL. SOMETHING VERY IMPORTANT
> THAT YOU CANNOT LIVE WITHOUT.
> WHAT DO YOU *NEED?*

I stare at the question and the blinking cursor in the box below it and think of my mother telling me she doesn't have time for me, again. Of the way she locked the door to keep me out. Is she concerned about DJ? Yes. Should she be? Absolutely. Nephrotic syndrome is scary. Incredibly scary, even in the best of circumstances. Is Mom upset that I keep pressing the issue of searching for Dad? Of course. But I can hear more than concern and frustration behind her words. I see it in her eyes every time she thinks I'm not watching. It doesn't matter that I didn't hesitate before offering to be a donor for my brother. It doesn't matter that I asked the doctors to test me anyway even though my blood type isn't a match. It only matters that when my mother sees me, she sees herself. Someone not quite good enough to save DJ. And, as hard as I've tried, I can't find the person who can.

I wipe tears from my cheek with my T-shirt and take a deep breath. Crying is stupid. And I hate feeling stupid.

WHAT DO YOU *NEED?*

The red words on the screen are seductive. Do I believe someone sitting behind a computer creating a website for high school students can help me? Do I believe that whoever created this site really wants to make my life better?

No. I'm not that naive. But in the darkness, I find myself wanting to believe there is someone who cares. Someone who opens the door to me instead of bolting it shut. So, under the question that asks what I need, I type:

I NEED A KIDNEY FOR MY BROTHER.

And I press Enter.

The minute my finger hits the key, I want to take back the request. How dumb can I be? The site is anonymous now, but even so, other members will know this request came from me. They'll all laugh at me. Great.

The same message I saw when Nate made his request flashes:

NEED REQUEST BEING VERIFIED. PLEASE STAND BY. Followed by a red ticking clock. I watch the second hand crawl and wait for the site to send a reply.

Tick. Tick. Tick.

With each passing second, I feel more foolish. Ten minutes go by and the clock is still ticking. Huh. Maybe my screen is frozen. I shut down the browser and log on again to NEED. The clock reappears. The hands are still moving, and I start to wonder if the response Nate received was sent by a live operator. If so, the person behind the system is either long asleep or completely baffled as to how to reply. I did ask for something that would immediately identify me as the user. Maybe breaking the rules means I won't be able to request anything else.

Well, if the person who's running NEED is asleep or has decided to put my account in limbo, there's no point waiting for whatever message is on its way. But instead of closing my laptop, I turn it so I can see the screen from bed before slipping under the covers. Just before I drift off to sleep, I squint across the room and see the site clock vanish.

I put my glasses back on, lean forward, and read: YOUR NEED REQUEST HAS BEEN PROCESSED. WE WILL DO OUR BEST TO SEE THAT YOUR NEED IS MET.

My last thought before drifting off to sleep is that I wasn't asked to invite my friends. Either the system experienced a glitch or the person who sent the reply was too kind to say what I already know. That NEED and the powers behind it can't help me. No matter what the site tells me or anyone says, my family is well and totally screwed.

NETWORK MEMBERS—89
NEEDS PENDING—78
NEEDS FULFILLED—15

Sydney

SYDNEY CAREFULLY CLOSES the front door so he doesn't wake anyone, and lets the heat inside the house seep into his frozen body and fingers. The weather report he watched on Monday said this week is going to be warmer than last.

Yeah, right.

Of course, the weatherman can afford to be wrong. He isn't the one freezing his ass off. And the guy sure as hell isn't going to get kicked off TV. Which just goes to show how unfair life is. If only Sydney's father had gone into meteorology instead of leaving a computer security job in the city to run his own real estate company. Although, to be fair, for a while it had been good. At least, that's what everyone says. Then the bubble burst and, with it, his family. Hooray for the American dream, where everyone can get screwed if they work hard enough. And his mother wonders why he isn't all hot and bothered to go to college for a computer science degree or take the military recruiters up on their promises of a meaningful career in communications or some other crap like that. Since he didn't apply to colleges, the school counselor asked him not to dismiss the G.I. Joe thing out of hand. So he hasn't told them yet to take a walk. Working for the government has perks, according to his dad, since there are always jobs to be had. Makes sense, since the government prints its own money. But while showing off his shooting skill has appeal, taking orders for the rest of his life doesn't. He does that enough now, although that's about to change. At eighteen his real life is beginning, and he plans on making the most of it.

Now that he can almost feel his ears again, Sydney peels off his gloves, blows hot air onto his hands and flexes his fingers. Better. They're still stiff, but at least he can move them.

He slides his backpack off his shoulder, puts it on the bench next to the front door, and takes a seat beside it. It takes three tries to yank off his boots, but finally his feet are free. Thank God. A warm shower will thaw them out. Quickly, he stores his boots and coat so his mom won't ream him in the morning. The deer hanging behind the boat in the garage will probably cut him some slack, but he figures he should bank that good-will. A guy never knows when he might need a "Get Out of Jail Free" card. Especially given what's coming.

Grabbing his backpack, he heads through the quiet house and down into the basement. He wants a shower and some sleep, but he's still wired. He needs to unwind a little first.

After blowing on his hands again, he powers up his laptop. While he waits for the Start screen to appear, he unzips his backpack and pulls out his grandfather's old hunting knife. He reaches back in for a cleaning cloth, and — though he already cleaned the blood off the knife in the garage — wipes the serrated blade the way his grandfather taught him. Carefully, he places the knife in his desk drawer, locks it, and slips the key into the small box he's mounted under the bottom of the desk. He doesn't want anyone to accidentally hurt themselves. That would suck, and things suck bad enough as it is.

Now that his laptop is booted up, he plugs in his password and gets to work. Typing fast he goes through several screens, and smiles. Very cool. This whole networking site is intriguing. And he decides he doesn't mind taking a few orders when there's something interesting going on. He leans back in his chair and flexes the fingers that are finally warm and tries to decide what he needs.

The answer is easy. Money. And isn't that always the answer? Now he just has to figure out how much.

Kaylee

"GUESS WHAT TIME IT IS?" I call down the hall.

"Bite me," DJ yells back. "I'm not taking my temperature again."

"Wanna bet?" I snag the thermometer off the kitchen counter and head to the living room, where my brother is sprawled on the couch in front of the TV. "Mom's going to be calling in five minutes to check in."

"Tell her I'm fine." A car skids and crashes in high definition.

"She's going to ask if you have a fever."

"Mom needs to get a grip." DJ lets out a dramatic sigh. "I didn't have a fever the last four times she asked you to check. I think we can officially give it up for dead and move on."

"It's not that simple." The hospital tests showed no relapse —yet. With his immune system so compromised, it wouldn't take much to threaten that status. Each time a patient experiences a nephrotic syndrome relapse, the prognosis is scarier.

There's a greater chance of fluid retention. Pneumonia. Clots. Additional kidney damage. For DJ the next relapse could mean complete kidney failure. If we don't have a donor by then . . .

"Yes." DJ sits up and turns toward me. He doesn't look at the TV as a car explodes. "It is that simple. But it sure feels as if you and Mom are more interested in proving that I'm dying instead of fighting off a cold. I expect that from Mom. It's what she does. But you're supposed to be on my side."

"I am on your side, and you're not dying," I say, wishing my stomach didn't twist as I speak. "I'm not going to let that happen."

"There's nothing you can do to stop it, Kaylee. I wish you could. Then I wouldn't have to be scared. And I'm tired of being scared." In his eyes I see the little boy I used to play blocks with who cried when he stacked them too high and they fell down. And I see the fear that he's so good at hiding because he wants to forget that there's a chance his immune system will give out. He deserves to forget and be happy. Even if it's just for a few hours.

I tuck the thermometer in my pocket, lie down on the floor next to the couch, and say, "Do you mind if I watch the movie with you?"

"Okay. You didn't miss much. Just the bad guys taking money from the other bad guys, and that guy chasing them in the car is a suspected cop who thinks he killed his partner and hasn't been able to forgive himself. Only, he didn't kill him and I think the partner is working with the bad guys, but we haven't gotten there yet." A truck rams a car off the road and there's another explosion as some guy jumps out of the truck and fires his gun. I haven't a clue what's happening, but it doesn't matter because I'm not really watching. I'm listening to DJ cheer and watching him bounce up and down when the good guy finally confronts the partner who supposedly was dead.

The house phone rings and I have no problem lying to Mom about taking DJ's temperature. Because DJ wants normal.

Not long after the first movie has ended and a second one begins—because apparently every bad action flick needs a sequel—I notice that my brother has fallen asleep on the couch next to me. I place a blanket over DJ and then lie down next to him and brush his hair off his face.

While he sleeps, I watch and wish. Finally, when it looks like he might wake up, I stand and go up to my bedroom so he doesn't have to feel embarrassed about his big sister watching over his sleep like he's a baby or something.

I shuffle through the folders in my desk drawer, ignoring the paper on top. I know I should toss it. It only proves how terrible people can be. Like I really need a reminder of that. But I leave it there as I pull a list of names out from underneath it, hoping that at least a few of these people are more compassionate than those I have contacted in the past. The list is comprised of all the people I can think of who might know where my father is. Fifteen have lines drawn through them, which is disheartening. When I made the list, the names at the top were my best hopes. Shows how much I know. So far, only one of them, Mr. Bryski, has admitted to hearing from my father since he left for a fishing trip last spring.

The doctors told us from the beginning that a close family member with the same blood type would make the best donor for DJ. Family donors have the highest probability of making a six-point match, which would give DJ's body the best shot at accepting the new organ. As far as I am concerned, Dad is going to be that donor whether he likes it or not. No matter what my mother says, he owes us that much.

I log on to the email account I created for this project and check in with Mr. Bryski to see if he's heard anything else from my father. He promised to keep me updated, but I trust nobody. Not even him, which is why when I finish the email I don't sign my name. He probably thinks he's talking to my mother. Most of the people I contact this way do. I selected my email address specifically with that misdirection in mind. People like making assumptions, and for once it's working in my favor.

I send six more emails and then start making phone calls to hotels in the Kenosha area and surrounding towns. There are dozens, so every day I call a different group of them. The people who answer the phone aren't allowed to give out guest names, but occasionally I find myself speaking with a receptionist or concierge who feels sorry for a girl who is looking for her missing father, or who thinks I might be willing to pay for assistance. I don't really believe that any of these people will lead me to my dad. No one has stepped up so far, no matter what I've tried. But since promising money on Craigslist is out and my attempt to steal medical records from the school to help me target potential donors landed me in therapy, looking for a needle in a haystack is better than my mother's plan—which from what I can tell consists of doing nothing.

At least, that's what I attempt to remember as the man on the phone cuts me off with a tirade about prank calls and hangs up. And I try not to think what it says about me that this is what I've come to expect.

I make a few more phone calls and then one by one search the social media sites for my father's name. As always, I feel a twinge of disappointment when I come up empty. Dad never liked to spend his time in front of a computer screen, which made it easier for him to disappear from our lives. The police might be able to find him. The courts can search too, if Mom decides to file for child support. But so far she refuses to pursue either route, insisting that she knows best and that Dad can't help us. I've tried to get DJ to push her because she can't say no to him, but he avoids talking about Dad. I know he thinks it's his fault that Dad left. Just three weeks after learning that DJ's most recent relapse had damaged his kidneys to the extent that he would soon be in desperate need of a transplant, Dad was gone. He certainly knows how to kick someone when they're down.

Since my attempts to find my father are going nowhere fast, I take a break and log on to my normal email account. Wow. Twenty-three unread messages.

VICKI BOCKNICK HAS INVITED YOU TO NEED.
QUINCY HANSON HAS INVITED YOU TO NEED.
MARTYN UDDEN HAS INVITED YOU TO NEED.
JOSE ALVARADO HAS INVITED YOU TO NEED.
VERA PETZEL HAS INVITED YOU TO NEED.

One after another. All invitations to NEED. All since I went to bed fourteen hours ago. And most of the people who sent these emails aren't what I'd call friends. Why would they bother to invite me?

I click on the NEED bookmark I created, log on, and read the main screen twice when it appears. Either I wasn't paying attention yesterday or this page is new. Line after line of need requests.

COMPUTERS
PHONES
CLOTHES
CARS
JEWELRY
SKIS
AN EXTRA WEEK OF WINTER BREAK

There must be over a hundred requests. Under each one is a comment box where network users can click either Need or Want and add an anonymous comment. Some requests have a star, and judging by the congratulatory remarks beneath them, I figure it signifies the ones that have already been fulfilled.

Some requests have dozens of comments. Others, which must be the newest, have only a few. The messages range from *I need that too* and *I should have said that* to *Are you kidding? You need a life.* Most of the needs are generic enough or expressed so often that it would be nearly impossible for anyone to figure out who posted them. But mine won't be. And I can only imagine the comments I've gotten, especially since the people behind them get to be anonymous.

I tell myself that I don't care. That after all the insults and snide comments and dismissiveness from my peers, I am immune to anything they do or say. But clearly I'm not, because my insides curl as I scroll down through the requests and comments, looking for mine. Only, I don't find it.

I go back to the top and scroll through again. I see Nate's request for his physics final grade followed by a bunch of snarky comments, but my request isn't there. Whoever is in charge of NEED must have decided to remove my post because it was too outlandish or because it gave away my identity.

Relief fills me until I click on my profile page. Under my assigned user ID are the words:

NEED REQUESTS SUBMITTED:

KIDNEY FOR BROTHER—WAITING FOR FULFILLMENT

Nothing else. No comment box. No mean quips or snarky remarks. But wait. At the bottom of the page is an asterisk followed by a message that wasn't there before.

*THIS PROFILE PAGE IS CURRENTLY HIDDEN FROM OTHER NETWORK MEMBERS.

No one will see what I've asked for.

Why? I click off my profile page and on another member's request for a new pair of skis. Immediately, the screen changes and I can see the member's anonymous profile, personalized with a big, yellow smiley face background. The request status is *Waiting for fulfillment,* and there is no asterisked message at the bottom.

The network must have locked my page to protect my identity. After all, who else at our high school would ask for a kidney? I'm safe from additional ridicule . . . for now. But what if that changes? Almost every social media site I've been a part of has rolled out updates. The number of users on this network is growing fast. What happens if NEED stops being anonymous and my profile becomes viewable to all members? The comments about my being pushed over the edge by a deadbeat father and an almost-dead brother won't just be whispered in hallways. They'll be printed in capital letters on my screen and on the screens of everyone in my high school. Some will defend me. Not everyone thinks I'm an attention whore using my family problems to get sympathy. But those who do will be relentless when they stumble across my NEED profile. They've done it on other social media sites. They'll do it here. I should never have gone on this site.

If I have to sit around waiting for the site to revoke my anonymity, I might totally lose it. I have to delete my account. And I have to do it now.

There's no Delete feature on my profile page, so I click on the home page and look for a My Account tab or a way to navigate to Settings. Or maybe a Privacy button? Something. Anything. There has to be a way to get rid of this account. Only, no matter how many places I click on, I can't find a way to wipe my profile from the system. I must be missing something.

Desperate, I pick up the phone and call Nate.

"Hey," Nate says. "I was just going to call you. How's DJ doing today?"

"Better. Frustrated that Mom keeps calling to see if his fever is back. The usual."

Nate laughs. "Well, usual is better than unusual. Whenever things get unusual at your place all hell breaks loose. So, this is good."

"I hadn't thought of it that way."

"That's why you keep me around. To do your thinking for you. Speaking of that, I had an idea about how we can get more people around here to get tested as a possible donor."

Nate might actually be able to swing getting more people tested. While his family ignores him because he lacks athletic prowess, at school he's considered very cool. But I doubt even he has the ability to convince our classmates or their parents to undergo elective surgery to help someone else.

"Anyone who likes DJ or our family enough to donate one of their kidneys already went through the process." It was a pitifully small number. A few family friends. A couple of my dad's co-workers. And Nate. Turns out his blood type is right, but none of the six antigens in the tissue typing is correct. His kidney has a high risk of being rejected by DJ's body, which means Nate isn't a match. Just like me. So I faked my own illness to spend time in the nurse's office and check blood types of fellow students in the hope I could target the ones who were most likely to be a match. I thought it was a good idea. I was wrong.

"Yeah, but what about all the people who don't know you? You appealed to this town, which is not only small, but filled with a lot of small-minded, self-important jerks. I know you have issues with social media because people are idiots, but not everyone on the Internet is as simple-minded as the people we go to school with. A good social media campaign could build awareness and maybe encourage other people outside of this community to get tested. You just need something to make the campaign go viral. I've been working on something I think could get people fired up. It just takes one to be a match."

And that one has to be willing to go through the rest of his life with only one kidney. Most people aren't that selfless without getting paid for it. My mother will also hate the public aspect of this idea, but I don't really care. Maybe if she hates it enough she'll actually do something to help find my father. "Let me talk to DJ and see what he thinks." Before Nate can push, I say, "Speaking of social media, I can't find a way to delete my NEED account."

"Why would you want to do that? I've been playing around with the site most of the day. It's really wild."

"Wild how?"

"Well, to start with, the person who put this thing together is an evil genius. From what I can tell, the site went live three days ago. When I sent myself the invitation yesterday, there were only 26 users. It's up to 407 now. Make that 410. I've gotten almost sixty email invitations to join since this morning. I finally had to put a status up on my other social media accounts telling everyone I was a member and that they should send requests elsewhere. I'm guessing by tomorrow everyone from school who checked their email will be on NEED."

I click on the NEED Network Statistics screen.

```
NETWORK MEMBERS—410
NEEDS PENDING—398
NEEDS FULFILLED—48
```

"The almighty Jack's already had his second request fulfilled. He told Mom that he ordered a slide board with the gift card he got from our grandmother, but I checked out the box it was delivered in after he pitched it. No label or postage. Just his name written in black block letters. I doubt Mom believes him, but of course she'd never question her team captain son."

"What's a slide board?" I ask.

"Some sort of agility workout thing. He and his football friends are trying it out in the family room now. If you need a laugh, you should come over and watch. They're all tripping over themselves and pretending they meant to do it."

I type *slide board* into Google and hit Enter. Wow. Depending on the brand, those boards range from $250 to $500. New phones could cost just as much. NEED has shelled out a lot of money just on Jack's requests. And his were only two of the forty-eight requests that have already been fulfilled.

"Where's the money coming from?" I interrupt whatever Jack-bashing story Nate is telling this time.

"What money?"

"The money being used to buy the slide board and all the other things people are asking for."

"Why does it matter?"

"Because nobody gives away tons of expensive gadgets without getting something in return." Things like this don't happen in Disney movies, let alone real life.

"Fair point." I can picture Nate running a hand through his hair while he thinks things through. After a few seconds he says, "People do strange things for all kinds of reasons, you know. Maybe it's someone who played Santa Claus at the mall this year and decided it was so much fun he didn't want to stop. Or maybe some rich dude learned he has only two months to live and has decided to give his money away to a worthwhile cause."

"You call indulging Jack's every desire worthwhile?"

"No, but getting me a passing physics grade is. Although, now that I'm considering all the options, I realize how short-sighted my choice was."

"Why?" I ask. "Because you don't think your physics teacher can be bribed by a terminally ill rich guy?"

"Everyone has a price, Kaylee. You just have to be willing to push until you figure out what it is. Whoever's behind this website knows that. But it's occurred to me that my request can't be fulfilled for another two and a half weeks. If I'd been more materialistic like Jack and almost everyone else, I'd already have my first order in hand and have moved on to my second. Now, thanks to the rules of the site, I have to wait until the first request is fulfilled before I can ask for anything else."

"By then you won't be able to ask for anything."

"Why not?"

"Because there won't be anyone left to invite to the network." I click on the screen and see the member number has risen to 424. "That's the catch. Right? You invite people on to the site and get your need fulfilled? Once everyone has joined, the whole thing will be over."

"I don't think so," Nate says. The mocking humor is gone. "Think about it. Whoever's behind this wants all of us on the site. They set the bar low so it's easy for the user to leap over and get their reward. That's not going to last much longer.

Now that the network is up and running, I'm guessing they'll raise the price from a couple of emails to something more."

"Like what?" I ask.

The silence stretches for what seems like forever until finally Nate says, "I don't know, but I doubt we'll have to wait very long to find out."

Gina

THIS ROYALLY SUCKS.

Gina shoves back her chair and scowls at the screen. How can she invite twelve friends on to this dumb site if everyone who's eligible is already on it? And how is it that she ended up one of the last to be invited? That should never happen. She's always the first to know about everything—parties, breakups, hookups. So, how *did* this happen?

When Gina reamed her best friend about never having sent her an email, Michelle said it was because she assumed Gina had already been invited by someone else. Which makes sense, but still. There's no way she's going to be the only one of her friends who doesn't receive her NEED request. Thanks to the anonymity of the site, no one will actually know she hasn't been granted a request yet, but it's the principle of the matter. Gina Ferguson is always on the cutting edge of trends. If NEED is the next big thing, she's not only going to be a part of it, she's going to stand out from the rest.

Of course, for that to happen, the site has to cooperate.

Taking a deep breath, Gina rolls her chair back toward the desk and clicks on her profile page, which includes not only an irritating identification code she can't change, but updates on her request.

NEED REQUESTS SUBMITTED:

CONCERT TICKETS TO SEE BLONDFIRE—WAITING FOR FULFILLMENT REQUIREMENT TO BE MET.

12 QUALIFIED USER REQUESTS REQUIRED.

1 QUALIFIED USER HAS ACCEPTED YOUR INVITATION.

(ALL OUTSTANDING INVITATIONS HAVE BEEN SENT TO CURRENT USERS. WE ENCOURAGE YOU TO TRY AGAIN OR CLICK HERE TO RESET THE FULFILLMENT REQUIREMENT.)

One. How is that possible? She sent invites to everyone from her world history, English, and statistics classes. She can barely recognize most of them by sight let alone by name. They aren't part of the popular crowd, so how did they get on NEED before her?

This is so annoying.

Wait.

Gina reads the message again and lets out a sigh of relief.

Ethan

ETHAN CLOSES HIS LAPTOP and picks up the page he printed. He doesn't want to get the instructions wrong. Not if it means not getting the new computer he needs. The graphics on his current one suck. And the processor speed . . . No wonder he keeps getting his butt kicked in Mercenary of War. But the one NEED will give him after this will have him at the top of the mercenary leaderboard in no time. Maybe it isn't the nicest thing to do, but in the grand scheme of things it isn't that big a deal. Essentially, Ethan tells himself, he's playing a harmless joke.

Okay, maybe not all that harmless, but it's not like anyone's going to be seriously hurt or anything. And the heroes in Mercenary of War often have to participate in quests they don't really believe in. It's the only way to gain the experience and fame necessary to move up in the ranks. He's just doing what his character would do. And when it's over he'll be rewarded. No one can find fault with that. And if his mom asks about the computer, well, he'll just say he earned enough money to buy it. Technically, that isn't a lie. Because NEED will be paying for the job it asked Ethan to do. His first real-life mercenary commission.

But first things first. Time to go walk Shadow and scout out the area. A mercenary always does reconnaissance before performing an assignment. It's the only way to guarantee success. And if he brings Shadow along, no one will wonder what he's doing taking a walk in the cold. It's a perfect cover. As long as it works.

Bryan

Standing on the corner of Prairie and Ridge Streets near the streetlight, Bryan VanMeter looks down at the box in his hand. He shivers as a blast of cold wind whips his scarf around. He's seen the familiar white and green box with the "Made with love" stamp in his own house dozens of times. For special occasions, his mother always orders a cake from Mrs. Lollipolous's bakery. Which is good, because his mother is a terrible cook.

But this isn't big enough to be a cake box, and he didn't get it from the bakery. It was waiting for him where the message said it would be—in the fiction section of the library, on the bottom shelf behind the books by authors whose last names start with the letter *K*. Now all he has to do is deliver it to Amanda Highland's house, take a photograph of it sitting on her doorstep, and post the picture on the NEED message board to prove the task has been completed. Nothing to it.

But just thinking of Amanda makes his neck start to sweat.

He still has no idea how he let his friends convince him to asking her out for New Year's Eve. How idiotic could he be?

She said no.

Of course she did. Amanda's beautiful. She's athletic. And mysterious. Or at least as mysterious as a person can be in this town. It's not like there are tons of people here. No wonder he noticed Amanda when she moved to Nottawa a year and a half ago. Unlike most of the popular girls, she rarely dates, and she spends her lunch hour in the school library. That's why Bryan allowed himself to be convinced she might say yes when he asked her to go with him to the movies on New Year's Eve. They have the library and a love of books in common, which isn't exactly a mainstream passion. He should know. Even his friends make fun of the amount he reads.

He kicks at a chunk of ice on the sidewalk as he remembers the way Amanda tried to let him down nicely. But she should have come up with a better excuse, because no one with half a brain would believe that Amanda's parents don't allow her to go to the movies. Even the strictest parents aren't that insane. It wouldn't be so bad if his friends hadn't spread the story. But they did, and now everyone knows Amanda turned him down. The last thing he wants is to be seen near her house and appear even more pathetic.

He thinks about untying the string and looking inside despite his instructions not to open the box. But he doesn't, because his fingers are too cold. At least, that's what he tells himself.

He turns and walks down the block toward Amanda's house, which is awash with Christmas lights. Her parents really go all out with the holiday theme. Bryan hurries to the front door, places the box on the holiday welcome mat, and pulls out his phone.

His fingers shake as he pushes the Camera button, and it takes three tries before he is able to snap a photo. Inside he hears a girl laugh. Amanda. He knows that laugh well. He used to dream about it. It used to make him happy. Now he pictures her laughing when she told her friends about him asking her out. How he thought he was good enough.

It's that laugh that makes his hands stop trembling, along with the thought of getting the prescription his parents said isn't necessary. He's tired of being the nice guy with acne who girls turn to for homework help. His doctor said there's a good chance the treatment will stop the breakouts. Then everything will change for the better.

Bryan doesn't consider looking in the box again before he turns and walks away. And when he feels a stab of worry at what might be contained inside as he posts a picture of the box on the website, he tells himself that if the box helps make Amanda sorry for lying to him, it's no less than she deserves.

Lynn

"DID YOU ASK for something yet?"

"I'm just about ready to do it now." Lynn puts her cell on speakerphone so she can type while she talks to Hannah. Hannah can balance her phone against her shoulder while doing almost anything, which is a skill Lynn hasn't mastered. "What do you think I should ask for?"

Hannah's laugh comes over the speaker. "How about a date for New Year's Eve so you can show Logan that you're totally over him?"

Lynn stares at the phone.

"Hey, are you there? I didn't mean to upset you or anything. I mean, you're over Logan, aren't you?"

"Of course I am," says Lynn, though she's not. Being dumped sucked. Having everyone at school know she had been dumped sucked even more. "But I don't want to show up at the party with just anyone, or it'll make me look desperate."

"You're right. So what are you going to ask for?"

"I don't know," Lynn says. She still doesn't know by the time Hannah hangs up, because Amanda is calling. What does she need? Not much. Making Logan regret breaking up with her would be nice, but how juvenile is that? If a guy doesn't want her, well, she has enough self-respect not to want him anymore.

Technically, she doesn't need anything. But as she scrolls down the list of other people's requests, Lynn sees something she wants too.

I need a later curfew time on New Year's Eve.

If it's later than Logan's, so much the better. Although she doubts anyone can convince her father that a later curfew is a good idea. He believes in rules and regulations, and curfew falls into both those categories. Still, it would be nice if he changed his mind.

Lynn smiles when she sees the message that her request has been accepted, but frowns as she keeps reading:

TO OBTAIN YOUR REQUEST, TAKE A PHOTOGRAPH
OF THE FIRST PAGE OF YOUR FATHER'S MILITARY
MEDICAL RECORD AND HIS DOG TAGS AND POST
IT ON THE MESSAGE BOARD TO CONFIRM YOU
COMPLETED THE TASK.

Dad's dog tags hang from a clip on the corkboard in his office. His medical records are probably in the filing cabinet along with everything else he needs when he goes to the VA hospital to have his leg adjusted. Lynn can hear Hannah tell her to go ahead and take the photograph. It's no big deal. The only people seeing it are their friends. It's not like everyone doesn't already know that Lynn's dad has a prosthetic leg.

And maybe they do. But there's no way she's going to put her father's personal information on the Internet for everyone to see. Those papers include his Social Security and driver's license numbers. His blood type. No way. Her father trusts her. No website or curfew is worth screwing with that. So she shuts down her computer and forgets about the request. If her friends want to pull mindless pranks and screw around online, they can. Logan probably will. But Lynn . . . well, she has better things to do.

NETWORK MEMBERS—532
NEEDS PENDING—520
NEEDS FULFILLED—58

Kaylee

I SIT UP IN BED. My heart is pounding hard as I fumble for the lamp switch and blink when the room floods with light.

No one is here. Nothing makes a sound.

The clock on the end table next to the photograph of my father reads 2:08 a.m. I must have had a bad dream, although normally I can remember whatever awakened me. DJ used to be the one plagued by nightmares. But something changed after he was diagnosed. Suddenly, the ghosts and goblins that haunted his dreams didn't scare him anymore. DJ hasn't had a nightmare since the doctor's visit that changed our lives. I had one that very night.

It was my father who came in to comfort me, explaining that I was having nightmares because I'd discovered monsters that were real. Disease and the prospect of death were far scarier than any boogeyman. After a while, I learned not to cry out when I woke up, and he thought the bad dreams had stopped.

Or maybe he didn't. Maybe he just understood that I needed to prove to myself that I could deal with the fear on my own. Until the day he walked out the door to go on that fishing trip and never came back, I thought he loved me. I was wrong about that. Who knows what else I was wrong about? Probably everything.

I hold my breath and listen to the silence. No creaking floorboards to alert me that my mother is once again hovering outside my brother's door or is going outside to sneak a smoke. No high-pitched whine of the old TV in my brother's room that tells me he is wearing headphones to watch some late-night action flick. Everything is quiet, just as it should be.

I turn off the lights and am burrowed under the blankets when I hear a scraping sound. There it is again. My heart kicks hard in my chest. The sound gets louder. I sit up and try to figure out where it's coming from. Outdoors.

Wait. That isn't a scraping sound. It's shoveling. Someone is shoveling snow.

I roll my eyes and think about what Nate would say about my reaction to an industrious neighbor keeping his driveway clear. No doubt he'd call me a bunch of girly names and then do his impression of me shrieking and covering my face. Needless to say, I don't plan on telling him about this. I live in Wisconsin. You'd think I'd be used to the sounds of snow removal. Especially since I've had to do most of it this year. With DJ's health and Mom's work schedule, shoveling the driveway has fallen to me. I've even put a weather app on my phone so I know when the snow is coming. Maybe that's why the shoveling startled me. We aren't supposed to get any snow until the weekend. Not that I'm surprised the app got it wrong, but now I won't be able to sleep in. After the way Mom shut me out, I want to let her just deal with the snow herself. But I won't. Not because I'm nice, but because I refuse to sink to her level.

I put on my glasses, walk to the window, and turn the blinds so I can see how hard the snow is coming down. It's not. I look down at the backyard below my window and once again hear the sound of a shovel hitting ice and snow. Why would someone be shoveling when there isn't any new snow?

I start to go back to bed, then change my mind. There's no way I'll sleep. Not while I'm wondering what's going on. I glance at my mother's closed bedroom door and am careful not to make a sound as I tiptoe by. There's no point in freaking Mom out unless there's really a reason.

When I reach the bottom of the stairs, I make a beeline for the living room window. The snow is reflecting the moon, and makes the front yard bright enough to see that there's nothing unusual out there. Shaking my head, I start to turn. That's when I see something move. A shadow at the edge of the yard by the large tree near the street. Not a shadow. A man, and he's holding a shovel. The shovel he must have used to dig the hole in the snow at his feet. And when he puts the shovel down and throws something in the hole, I don't think. I run to the front door, fumble with the locks, and throw it open.

"Hey."

The guy starts, then reaches down, grabs his shovel, and runs. By the time I pull on my boots and race out into the cold he's almost all the way down the block. I run onto the street to try to see which way he will go next.

He looks back at me as he reaches the end of the block. I

can't make out his face. Only that his coat is black and his hat is green and yellow. Then he bolts to the left onto Beloit Street and disappears from view.

I wrap my arms around myself as the frigid wind whips my hair. I grit my teeth and walk slowly toward the tree and the hole that he dug in the snow. A hole that is shaped like a rectangle. And now that I am closer I can see what he threw inside.

A rectangular cardboard box with writing on the top.

Get a clue. No one wants to help. You might as well just go ahead and die.

The box is supposed to be a coffin. The hole is a grave. And the note . . .

Suddenly it hurts to breathe. The wind stings my face as I read the words again. Words that can only be meant for my brother.

Anger builds and claws to get out. I need to move. I have to destroy the note and the hole so DJ never sees it. I have to do something. But all I can do is wrap my arms tighter around my body and rock back and forth as I stare at the cardboard coffin.

How could someone do this? How?

The snap of a twig makes me jump. I spin around to see if someone is behind me. No one is there, but that doesn't stop the fear that cuts through the horror and makes me run through the snow. Back to the house. Inside, where it's safe.

I close the door and start to shake. I'm so cold. So scared. So shocked that anyone could be this cruel. It feels like forever before I stop shivering. When I do, I stand, grab the first coat I find in the closet, and wrap myself in it. Then I do the only other thing I can think of. I dial the police on my cell as I go upstairs to wake my mom.

Two officers arrive. One of them looks familiar, and when he introduces himself to Mom, I realize his son, Logan Shepens, is in my class. Not that we're friends or anything.

Mom makes coffee for the police and herself, and hot chocolate for me, and repeatedly reminds us all to keep our voices down while Officers Shepens and Klein discuss what has happened. They want to talk with my brother, too, but Mom asks that DJ be allowed to sleep as long as possible. She shut his door after I woke her and is still worried about him fighting his cold. I'm not sure what difference an extra hour or two of sleep is going to make. Learning about the snowy grave and the message inside is going to hurt no matter when he finds out about it. But I don't question her. What's the point?

I hold a mug of hot chocolate in my hands, wondering if I'll ever feel warm again, and I answer the officers' questions. What time did I wake up? Why did I go outside? Did I recognize the person who dug the hole in the snow? Is there anyone I can think of who is angry with our family or has said anything negative about DJ's illness? The last question I don't answer.

"Ms. Dunham?"

I look down at my drink, wishing I hadn't gotten out of bed. That people weren't so mean.

"Kaylee." My mother's voice is quiet, but I hear the tension. "Answer the officer's question. Do you know someone who would want to hurt DJ?"

There's an accusation in her voice. As if this is my fault. It's the same tone she used when she told me the test results. I wasn't a match. I couldn't save my brother. I was useless.

"Kaylee." This time Officer Shepens asks.

And I answer. "Not exactly. But I got an email." I glance at my mother. "When I learned I wasn't eligible to be DJ's donor, I started looking for my father."

My mother's lips form into a tight line. Disapproval and anger shine in her eyes. During one of our fights, she forbade me to look for Dad. I promised I wouldn't, though I've never understood why she is so insistent about this, and neither does anyone else. I don't understand why she won't go to any lengths to help DJ. She always says we can survive without my father and that she will find another donor. But it doesn't make sense, and she hasn't. So I did. We both lied. And now she knows.

I squeeze the mug between my hands, trying to ignore the way everything inside me tenses and my eyes burn. Taking a deep breath, I say, "I've been sending emails to everyone I can think of who knows my father, hoping one of his friends has heard from him. A couple days ago, I got a message from someone. If you wait a minute, I'll go get it."

Before the police or my mother can object, I jump out of my chair and run up the stairs to my room. When I received the email, I printed it out. Why? I'm not sure. Part of me wanted to make copies and put it up all over town. That way he'd feel as bad as he'd made me feel. Instead, I put it in my top desk drawer.

I touch my brother's door as I hurry past it, and when I walk into the kitchen I don't hesitate. I hand the paper to Officer Shepens and feel my mother's stare boring into me as he reads the words I'll never forget.

Get a clue. I don't want to help you track down Mel and he doesn't want to be found. Find someone else to harass because I don't care if the kid dies.

The email is from the account of Richard Ward. A bowling

and fishing buddy of my father's, local Boy Scout leader, and deacon of our church. He's also the owner of the drugstore in the center of town.

Officer Shepens reads the note, looks up at me, and passes it to his partner. "Richard Ward sent that to you?"

"I use a different email address for the emails about my father." I turn and look at my mother. "He probably thought he was sending the message to you." Which makes it worse.

My mother's jaw tightens when Officer Klein hands her the printed email, and she doesn't say a word as they question me about the messages leading up to this one. There are two. The first when I asked if Mr. Ward had had any word from my father since he left town. The second a week later when I didn't get a response to the first one. And then this one that made me want to scream and throw things and pull my brother close and protect him from everything bad.

"This sounds more like a kid's prank than something a grown man would do. Do you think the man in the green and yellow hat looked like Richard Ward? Or could it have been someone else?" Officer Shepens asks.

"Of course it was him," my mother snaps. "How much more evidence do you need? He even used the same words."

Which is why I recalled the email when the police asked. But now that I'm thinking things through, I'm not sure. "The man looked bigger than Mr. Ward." Or maybe his coat was bulky and that's why, as much as I want to, I can't picture my father's friend holding the shovel. The idea that someone else might hate us enough to write that message makes me shiver.

Officer Shepens checks his watch and tells my mom there's no point in waking DJ now. They'll come back later to speak to him, and will pay visits to the neighbors to see if anyone saw the man with the shovel. Until then, we should keep our doors locked and call the police at any sign of trouble.

Mom thanks them for their time and asks if there's any chance they would be willing to fill in the hole in the yard before they leave. "I'd like to keep this as quiet as possible. With everything that's happened in the last year . . ." She casts a glance at me and sighs as she looks back at the officers. "I'm sure you understand."

"Of course," Officer Shepens says. "We can—"

"I'll do it," I interrupt. "I want to do it." That way if any of our neighbors look out the window, they won't wonder what the Nottawa Police Department is doing digging in our front yard. Not that it will stop the news from getting out, but it might spread more slowly. Mom should approve of that.

The police don't object, so I put on my boots as they leave. Mom looks at me for several long moments. I wait for her to yell or ask if we can talk or tell me she understands why I decided to try to find my father.

"Make sure you wear your gloves," she says. Then she turns and walks away.

I stand in the kitchen for several minutes, surrounded by reminders of the family we used to be. The scarred wooden table and chairs. The stonework vase my mother bought from a local artist, filled with Popsicle sticks and paper flowers DJ made in school. Report cards and pictures on the fridge. I wish we could go back. To before. When I hear a door close upstairs, I put on my coat and go to the garage to get a shovel.

The neighborhood is quiet. The only sound is the crunch of my boots in the snow as I walk across the front yard. The box with the message is gone. The police must have taken it with them as evidence.

I drop my shovel and pull out my phone. The snow shines bright as I click a photo. The police have pictures. They told my mother we could ask for copies if we needed them, but this one is just for me. To remind me that people can't be depended on to be kind. No matter what Nate believes, no one is going to step up and offer to donate a kidney to DJ. If I want my brother to live, I'll have to find a way to save him myself.

NETWORK MEMBERS—632
NEEDS PENDING—628
NEEDS FULFILLED—108

Yvonne

"YVONNE, WHAT ARE YOU doing here? You asked for today off."

Yvonne jumps as Mrs. Lollipolous comes out from the kitchen in the back of the bakery. She gives her boss a friendly wave. "I know, but my family's plans fell through and I knew you were going to be really busy getting ready for this weekend. So, I thought I'd see if you still wanted me to help out."

A relieved grin spreads across Mrs. L.'s flushed face. "You are a godsend, Yvonne. Marta called in sick, and Ricky and I are too busy in back doing the wedding cakes for this weekend to pack all the orders and also man the front of the store." Mrs. L. wipes her hands on her flour-coated apron and nods. "I'd love you to handle things out here for a couple of hours, but only if you're sure you want to. You work so hard at school and here and I know how much you wanted a day off."

"I want to work. Honest, Mrs. L." Yvonne resists the childish urge to cross her fingers behind her back and adds, "There's nowhere else I'd rather be today."

"What would we do without you? I should go out and thank your mother for changing her plans and making our lives easier."

"No. You can't!" Yvonne almost shouts before Mrs. L. can walk toward the door. "Mom went to the drugstore. I told her I'd call her there if you didn't need me."

It could be true. After all, her family can't afford cell phones. They can barely afford their landline. But Yvonne can tell Mrs. L. has heard the lie in her voice. She wants to apologize and explain, but she can't. She's not allowed to explain. All she can do is shift from foot to foot as Mrs. L. watches her with narrowed eyes.

Please don't be mad. Please don't fire me for one mistake. Please.

Mrs. L. sighs and pats the shoulder of Yvonne's faded, slightly too small brown winter coat. "Well, I guess I'll just have to thank her later with several loaves of bread and some of those sticky buns your sisters love so much. Ricky just made a big batch, even though we don't have orders for half of them. Why don't I pack some up now so they don't dry out before you bring them home? And maybe a few other surprises, too."

Relief is followed by guilt. Yvonne's throat is tight and her eyes sting when she says, "Thanks, Mrs. L."

Mrs. L. gives her a warm, sympathetic smile. "It's my pleasure. What good is running a bakery if you don't get to feed the ones you care for?" They both jump as a pan clatters in the back and Ricky shouts something in Italian. "I'd better get back there before he destroys the kitchen. Let me know if you need help. I'm coming! You'd better not have dropped my meringues!"

Yvonne takes off her coat, grateful that Mrs. L. left before the guilt got the best of her. She knows her boss thinks her family's finances are the reason Yvonne chose to come in to work. For once, being the responsible girl who never gets into trouble has paid off.

She hates lying to Mrs. L., but what she said isn't that far from the truth. Although this money isn't for her family. It's for her. College applications are expensive, and some of the schools recommend personal interviews on campus. There are hardship waivers, but her parents have already said they don't want to use those. They have their pride, and Yvonne wants them to keep it. But she'd also like to apply to more than the two schools they can afford.

And this one thing she has to do is kind of strange, but not bad.

Mouth dry, muscles tight and jumpy, Yvonne walks over to the door to the kitchen and peeks through the small glass window to make sure Mrs. L. and Ricky aren't headed up front. Then she walks to the register and pulls out the old-fashioned handwritten order book that Mrs. L. refuses to give up. Quickly, she writes yesterday's date in the top corner and an order for seventeen chocolate chunk cookies with ground peanuts. Next to the order goes the name Kaylee Dunham. Filled. Paid in full. Picked up.

She files it with yesterday's orders and closes the drawer. With a quick glance toward the kitchen to make sure her actions went unnoticed, Yvonne puts the whole thing out of her mind and gets to work filling orders. After all, it's just a piece of paper. What's the harm?

Sameena

SAMEENA JUMPS as the dogs next door bark. The lead on the mechanical pencil snaps.

Hell. Sameena throws down the pencil and wants to cry. She wants to be out with friends or skiing or doing what everyone else in her school is doing right now. Instead, her parents insist she has to be at her desk doing homework. Like she has been every single day since school let out.

Crumpling the paper, she throws it into the already overflowing wastebasket next to her desk. This is supposed to be winter break. English might not be her first language, but even when she started learning it she understood that "break" means the same thing as "vacation." Maybe instead of giving her teachers homemade cards for the holiday, she should have given them a dictionary, because the stack of work on her desk makes it clear they have forgotten the definition.

"Sameena, are you ready for me to check your work?" Her father's voice makes her wince. She wishes she were done. Her cousins would be done by now. They are the smart ones. *But I'm the one that my parents ended up with and I can't concentrate with those dogs barking. I wish they would stop. Then maybe I'd be able to hear myself think.*

"Sameena?" The door opens and her father steps inside. "Are you ready?"

She blinks back the tears and gives her father a bright smile. "I'm still working. I want to do some of the extra-credit problems, too. Just to see if I can."

"Of course you can, Sameena." He doesn't smile back. "You simply need to apply yourself. If you worked more and spent less time sleeping in, listening to music, and talking to your friends on the computer you would already have your homework done."

"I am working, Daddy." Every day. All day. Even when her parents think she's turned out the lights and is long asleep. And still nothing makes sense.

"Good. I expect to see a four-point-oh on your report card this semester. You need it after last year. You can't expect to get in to a top college if you don't have top grades."

The door closes, punctuating the pronouncement. Not that she needs a lecture. She knows. She should; she hears it every day. How she has to work. Has to be smart. But she's not.

Sameena picks up the pencil and starts again. The dogs' barking gets louder as she frantically erases. The equation won't balance. She closes her eyes. Takes a deep breath and starts one more time. The lead snaps again as one of the dogs howls.

She crumples the paper, throws it to the floor, and tries to concentrate. All she has to do is concentrate and she'll be able to finish this assignment. Her father won't be upset. She won't have to tell him that she's not smart. That she's in the wrong-level classes. That her teachers know it. They know he always fixes her homework. Everyone knows.

Those damn dogs. If they would just stop barking. She could concentrate. She'd be better.

"Stop."

Breathe.

"Stop."

Concentrate.

A tear drips onto the page as she erases again, wishing there was a way to make the noise stop. Those dogs just need to stop. Maybe that website will help her figure out a way.

Amanda

"YOU SAID YOU WERE GOING to wear the blue sweater, Amanda."

Amanda hops onto one of the kitchen island stools and smiles at her mother, who is wearing a Green Bay Packers sweatshirt. "Aunt Mary sent this to me for Christmas. I thought maybe you could take a picture of me wearing it tonight at the party so she knows how much I like it."

"That's a wonderful idea." Her mother puts down the knife she is using to cut vegetables for the party and comes around the island to give Amanda a hug. "There are days I find it hard to believe you aren't in pigtails anymore. But when you do something like this, I realize what an amazing young woman you've become."

Amanda grimaces. She hates when her mother says things like this—because she isn't amazing. When her mother suggested she wear the heavy, chunky-knit blue sweater, Amanda only pretended to agree with the choice, knowing full well she was going to wear the lower-cut, more flattering red one her aunt had sent.

Not that the blue one isn't okay. It is. Just not for her sixteenth birthday party. Sixteen is supposed to be special. She's supposed to feel more like an adult. Less like a child. So far that hasn't happened, but at least Amanda has avoided fighting about the sweater. She hates making people feel bad. Which is why she can't get Bryan out of her mind.

She hurt him. And she hadn't meant to. But she was so surprised when he called. She didn't even know he had her cell number. If she'd had time to think, she could have come up with an excuse that would have let him down gently. Instead, she told the truth, which is so strange it might as well be a lie.

"Are you okay, honey?"

Amanda looks up. Her mother is looking at her with concern.

"I'm fine, Mom." She smiles to prove it. "I guess I'm just nervous about tonight. We've been planning the party for so long, I'm worried it won't go well."

"It doesn't have to be perfect as long as you have fun." Her mother wipes her hands on a towel and brushes back a lock of blond hair that in length and color is just like Amanda's. "I'm going to go upstairs and hop into the shower. Do you want a snack or something before I disappear for a while?"

"Go shower, Mom. I can get my own snack if I need one. I think I'm old enough to handle that." She laughs.

"Okay." Her mom tucks the towel on the oven door and gives Amanda one of those weepy looks that makes her wish she had worn the blue sweater. "But there are all sorts of crackers and munchies in the cupboard if you change your mind."

"Thanks."

When her mother disappears, Amanda grabs a bottle of water from the fridge and tries to decide what to do about Bryan. Someone posted on the new networking site that he needs to figure out what he did to make a certain girl dislike him. That has to have been Bryan. How awful is that?

Even if she explains why her mother won't let her go to the movie theater, he might not believe her. Not many people here in Nottawa know about her peanut allergy. Her decision, which means this whole thing with Bryan is her fault. Her mother made such a big deal about her allergy when she was younger. It was embarrassing. Worse, kids started blaming her when they couldn't bring homemade cupcakes or cookies in to class for their birthdays. Which meant no one wanted to be her friend. So when they moved here almost two years ago, she and her mother came to an agreement. She would follow Mom's rules about her allergy in secret, as crazy as they sometimes were, and Amanda could live her life without feeling like a freak.

Maybe inviting Bryan to the party is the answer. If he comes, she can explain why the movie theater in town is off-limits. If they didn't roast peanuts, her mother probably wouldn't have a problem, but since they do . . .

Sighing, Amanda starts to open the cupboard and notices a green and white bakery box sitting on the far end of the counter next to a pile of mail. She grins and tosses her hair as she flips open the lid. Chocolate chunk cookies. Her favorite. And a note. "Happy birthday, Amanda. Celebrate with sweets made just for you."

Mrs. Lollipolous has a second kitchen where she bakes both gluten-free and peanut-free cookies and cakes. Mom must have ordered these as a surprise and forgot to hide them. Which means Amanda really shouldn't eat one.

Amanda counts the cookies. There are seventeen. One too many for a sweet sixteen party. Someone counted wrong. Well, she'll just fix that.

She snags a cookie, closes the lid, slides the box back into the corner, and peeks down the hall to make sure Mom is upstairs. Yep. The shower is running. And since her mother takes epic showers, Amanda has time to enjoy every bite. Then she'll call Bryan. Because it's the right thing to do. And besides, despite the acne, he is kind of cute and really nice.

After two bites she knows.

Her throat tightens. The cookie drops to the floor as she starts to cough. Eyes watering, Amanda stumbles to the counter and fumbles to pull out the drawer where her mother keeps the EpiPen.

Where is it? It has to be here.

She tries to call out to her mother but nothing comes out. Her throat is too tight. She can't breathe.

There. Her fingers curl around the pen.

Everything gets fuzzy as she unbuttons her pants so she can give herself a shot. She puts the pen on her thigh, but loses her balance before she can push the injector.

She barely notices when she hits her head on the corner of the drawer. The world has already gone black.

NETWORK MEMBERS—657
NEEDS PENDING—652
NEEDS FULFILLED—109

Kaylee

"Hey." My door opens and Nate pokes his head inside. "What gives around here? When your mom let me in, you would've thought I was here for a funeral instead of movie night. Where's DJ?"

Ugh. I forgot about movie night. Not a surprise, considering how bad today has been.

I put aside *The Grapes of Wrath*, which I haven't been able to concentrate on anyway, and swing my legs over the side of my bed. "DJ's locked himself in his room." My mother has been trying to coax him into opening the door for most of the day. After the third time, I told her to take the door off the hinges, but she insists DJ needs his space and will come out when he's ready. While I'm worried about my brother, I can't help but be glad he's kept the door locked. Now Mom knows what it feels like.

"What happened?" Nate asks. "Did they get into a fight? I thought that was more your thing."

I scowl. "It's been a rough day. There was an 'incident' this morning." Incident. The mild-mannered word the cops are using to describe what basically amounts to someone wishing DJ would drop dead.

"What kind of incident?"

I pick up my phone, pull up the photograph I took this morning, and hold it out to show Nate. "Someone dug a grave in the snow and left a message essentially telling DJ it was for him."

"Are you kidding?" Nate grabs my phone and stares at the photograph. "Who the hell would do something like that?"

I shrug. "I'm surprised you haven't heard about it. We've gotten so many calls my mom finally decided to take the phone off the hook."

The police paid a visit to Richard Ward at the drugstore and word spread. Fast. I'm spreading rumors. I'm blaming someone without evidence. I'm causing drama. Again.

I called Nate not long after the police came back to talk to DJ, but didn't leave a message. He always calls back when he sees he missed one of my calls. When he didn't this time, I figured it was his way of saying he'd had enough of my problems. I was hurt, but I didn't blame him. Much.

Nate shakes his head, still staring at the image of the grave beneath the tree. "Today was Obligatory Holiday Visit to Obscure Relatives Day. Dad's still pissed about Jack's new iPhone, so we all had to leave our phones behind. I was going to call when I got back, but I got distracted by the whole thing with Amanda."

"What about Amanda?" Now I'm the one who's confused.

"You haven't heard?" He glances up. "Amanda's in the hospital. Her sweet sixteen party was supposed to be tonight, so people were sending texts to let everyone who had been invited know."

Which explains why I haven't heard. I wasn't invited. And, of course, Nate was.

"What happened to her?" I ask, telling myself it doesn't matter that Amanda didn't invite me. Just because she actually cared enough to ask me how my brother was doing and promised to get tested as a donor doesn't make us best friends or anything.

"Between the rumors that she was poisoned by her mother and that someone came in and beat her up, it's hard to say. I'm putting my money on whatever explanation is behind door number three." Nate looks back down at my phone and frowns. "Although after seeing this picture, I'm thinking maybe those theories aren't that crazy."

"Amanda's mother wouldn't poison her, and there's no way someone would break into her house and beat her up."

"Yesterday, I would have said there was no way someone would dig a hole in your yard and put a threatening note for DJ in it." Nate hands my phone back to me.

Fair point. Still . . . "Instead of jumping to conclusions, why don't you check with your network of informants and see if anyone knows how Amanda is doing." I've seen DJ hooked up to beeping machines far too many times to wish that on anyone, let alone Amanda. "Everyone is probably exaggerating how bad it is, but it would be nice to know for sure."

"If you insist." Nate pulls out his own phone and starts dialing. After the first three calls, I tell Nate I'm going downstairs to get us something to drink. It's one thing to know my best friend is more popular than me; it's another thing to hear him talking about parties and ski trips I haven't been asked to be a part of.

Not that I want to go. After all the sideways glances, unkind comments, and horrible messages I've received, I'd rather spend my time alone than with most of the people who attend my school. Not that I really have a choice. No one invites me to group events anymore. But Nate is always invited. Most days, I can pretend that Nate will always choose me over those offers. But I know the truth. Nothing lasts forever. I survived my dad's abandonment. When Nate goes too, I'm not sure what I'll do.

I reach the bottom of the stairs and hear the sound of one of Mom's cooking shows coming from the family room. Careful not to step on the creaky middle floorboard, I go to the kitchen, grab two sodas, and hurry back up to my room. Bullet dodged.

Nate's finishing a call when I walk in. "Amanda is definitely in the hospital. She had an allergic reaction to peanuts, went into some kind of shock, and hit her head when she passed out and fell. Her mother found her unconscious in the kitchen and called the paramedics."

That sounds bad. "But she's going to be okay, right?"

Nate shrugs. "The last Megan heard, Amanda is still unconscious, but it sounds like the doctors are optimistic. She promised to keep me posted." After putting his phone away, Nate slips his arm through mine and says, "While we wait for news, why don't I get DJ to come out of his room so we can start movie night." He picks up his drink and flashes a smile that makes the dark cloud over this day fade. "You didn't think I was going to let you off the zombie and slasher hook that easy, did you? Let's get this party started."

Ethan

FINALLY. CONFIRMATION that Ethan has fulfilled his part of the bargain with NEED. His computer will be delivered tomorrow. All Ethan has to do now is make sure the shed out back is unlocked. Which is perfect, since he can wait until his parents go out before retrieving the box. The fewer questions his mom and dad ask, the better. And by this time tomorrow, he'll be dodging assassins and taking out targets in high def. It's too bad the computer isn't going to arrive tonight. Because his current one has already crashed twice. And right in the middle of a level. Which blows wide.

Normally, he'd be really pissed at having to start the level over. Today, he doesn't mind so much. The new computer is part of it. But for the first time, lighting up enemy targets and knifing people in the back aren't that exciting. Because they aren't real. This morning—digging the hole, running to avoid being caught, and sneaking back inside his house without making a sound—he had a chance to be like the characters he loves. He'd been given a mission and he had carried it out.

Just thinking about it gives him a massive rush. Was he scared when Kaylee yelled and started to chase him? Hell, yeah. But that's okay. Being scared is part of the deal. The mercenary trainer says that those with no fear are the ones who get sloppy. Sloppy means you get dead or get caught. He was neither, which means he won the level. The thrill of success gave him a buzz that lasted most of the day. When his friend Logan Shepens called and told him his father had to go out early because of a vandalism report, it was hard to separate fear from excitement. What an awesome high. He didn't know a person could feel that alive.

Only now, the high is gone and the game he's playing online doesn't seem that interesting. Not when he knows how much more exciting it is to perform missions for real.

Ethan tries to concentrate on the target on his screen, but gives up, shuts down the game mid-level, and logs on to NEED. When he gets to the request page, he rereads the prompt and frowns. What should he ask for this time? He could request computer software or maybe a new iPod, but that isn't what he really wants. No. Those things are ordinary. Boring. And he is done with boring. He's been boring all his life. People expect him to be boring. Hell, he expects himself to be dull and uninteresting. But he doesn't want to be. He wants the rush he felt today. He wants the excitement of being a real-life Mercenary of War. He wants to be interesting and different, just like his characters. No . . . he doesn't just want it. He needs it. But what the hell can he ask for that will give him that?

He turns the problem over in his head for several minutes. Then he types: *I need another mission. The more dangerous the better.*

Honesty is always the best policy.

He pictures himself racing down icy streets, leaving explosions and chaos behind him. Then he presses Enter.

YOUR REQUEST IS BEING PROCESSED.

He smiles.

NETWORK MEMBERS—690
NEEDS PENDING—686
NEEDS FULFILLED—122

Kaylee

MOVIE NIGHT IS a hit with DJ. Less so with me, since I seem to jump and squeal more than usual with each scary sequence. The man in our yard and Amanda's 'accident' have put me on edge.

But I'm glad that when DJ goes to bed, he is smiling and laughing and leaves his door unlocked. Nate's magic works again. Mom, having assured herself that DJ doesn't have a fever or isn't huddled in tears, has long since turned in, so Nate helps me turn off the lights and straighten up.

"DJ seems like he's doing okay, all things considered," Nate says, as he puts the empty popcorn bowl in the sink.

I nod. "He's gotten good at getting back up after being knocked down." A skill I could learn from him, because the shock and upset I felt earlier that day have segued into a white-hot rage. At whoever did this. At my father, who could have stayed and prevented it. And at myself. Because if Richard Ward is behind the hole in the yard, I, too, am to blame. "Nate." I jam my hands into my back pockets. "Do you think it was my emails about my father that caused this?"

"What? No."

His denial is emphatic, but the guilt I've been holding at bay breaks free and threatens to overwhelm me. "If I had listened to my mom and trusted her to handle finding a donor—"

"Kaylee, this isn't your fault." Nate grabs my hand and squeezes so tight that it hurts. "No matter what you've done, there's nothing wrong with trying to save your brother's life. Anyone who says different is lying. Trust me, you're one of the best people I know."

"Right. You don't need to lie to make me feel better."

"I'm not." Nate loosens his grip but doesn't let go of my hand. "You've always put other people's needs in front of your own. You never even stopped to consider if the surgery would hurt or what it would mean for you to live your entire life without one of your kidneys. The minute you heard DJ needed a transplant, you volunteered. No questions asked."

"He's my brother."

"If it had been me or someone else in this town, you would have still volunteered. Remember Kristen Rothchild's ninth birthday party?"

"Vaguely." It happened over seven years ago.

"Well, I remember that more kids showed up than were supposed to and Kristen's mom was short a cupcake. You realized the problem before she did and said you didn't want one."

"I must have been full."

He shakes his head. "You didn't want one of the other kids

to be upset, so you fixed it. That was the day I decided I wanted to be your best friend, and I bribed you with half of my chocolate cupcake."

"I remember now. It was vanilla."

"If it had been vanilla, I would have given you the entire thing. Who needs vanilla cake?" Nate grins, but his eyes are dead serious when they meet mine. "My point is, the only person to blame for what happened in your yard is the jerk who dug the hole. Not the person who sold him the shovel. Not your father for having such crappy taste in friends. Not you for trying to help your brother. The person who, for whatever reason, made a choice and dug that hole. He'll have to live with the consequences. And who knows. Maybe it'll turn out to be a good thing."

I flinch and yank free of Nate's grasp. "I can't imagine how."

"Think about it." Nate folds his arms across his chest. "This kind of story gets people fired up. People are going to talk. They'll be angry at someone picking on a sick kid, especially a kid like DJ who gets good grades, is nice to everyone, and has never gotten into trouble. This is the kind of story that people share on social media and that makes everyone want to help. If we play our cards right, DJ's story could go viral."

"That would be great, but I kind of doubt it."

"Don't be so pessimistic. It's not a good look for you." Nate holds up a hand before I can make a comeback. "Don't take my word for it. Look at how fast NEED spread. A few people were invited on to the site. They were asked to invite five more, who then invited six. Four days ago, no one we know had ever heard of NEED. Today, everyone we go to school with is talking about it. This story with DJ is going to spread in the same way. And if one person gets tested for every twenty who hear about it, we'll have a great chance of finding a donor before things get really bad."

"That sounds wonderful," I say, swallowing down my fear. "But I don't think I'll give up looking for my father."

"I didn't say you should. How about I come over on Sunday and help you make phone calls? We can borrow my mom's car and drive to the condo complex that the Christmas card was sent from. We'll flash your dad's picture around like one of those black-and-white-movie PIs. Maybe someone will remember something."

"I don't have my driver's license yet, and you're busy that day. Remember? You told Megan you'd see her on Sunday."

"You should know by now that I never go to the stuff I say yes to. You'd think people would stop asking me, but for some reason they never do."

Nate's grin disappears and his expression turns solemn. "As far as I can tell, you're the only one who can count on me to do most of what I say. You're the only one who has ever mattered enough for me to bother to be a nice guy. Why do you think that is?"

I feel hot and cold and nervous as Nate looks at me. It's as if everything depends on the answer I give. But I'm not sure what answer he wants or if I have the courage to give it. So I take the easy way out and shrug, as if this is just another one of his crazy ideas. "I don't know."

My heart pounds faster.

Nate stares at me. Then he nods and steps away. "I know you don't. Sometimes I don't either. I guess it must have something to do with that chocolate cupcake. I have a few things

I have to do tomorrow, but I'll be here bright and early on Sunday to help you search for your dad. If you need anything before then, let me know." He grabs his jacket off the back of the kitchen chair and slips into it as I follow him to the front door. Hand on the knob, he turns. "Kaylee . . ."

I wrap my arms tight around myself as his eyes study my face. Shifting my feet, I try not to worry as he looks as if he's trying to decide how to say what it is he wants to say. When several seconds pass and he still hasn't said anything, I ask, "Yes?"

He opens his mouth but then shakes his head. "Nothing. Just . . . after what happened this morning and what happened to Amanda, I want you to promise me that you'll be careful. Okay?"

"Sure." It's not like we live in a war zone, as creepy as this morning's incident was. "I promise."

"Good." Nate flips his scarf around his neck with a flourish. "Because while I make an excellent sidekick, I'd be a terrible hero. And we all know how much I hate being bad at things."

And with that parting salvo, he opens the door and is gone, leaving me feeling jittery and unsettled. Which is why, when I go up to my room, I slide into my desk chair and fire up my computer instead of going to bed. No one has replied to the emails I sent yesterday. Either they've been too busy to check their inboxes or they just don't care.

I log on to Facebook and search for news of Amanda. There are lots of posts on her page. People praying that she gets well. Requests for updates on her condition. Stuff Nate told me about and more. Much more. About ten posts down I see a message from Amanda's aunt asking that everyone pray for her niece, followed by lots of comments sending hugs and prayers, along with a few people saying they never knew Amanda had such a bad allergy. Me neither, and I have to wonder how someone with such a severe allergy ate a cookie containing nuts in her own home. Unless her mother just missed reading a label, like some of the comments suggest.

Still, I can't help thinking how strange this whole thing is. In grade school, we couldn't bring homemade cookies or cupcakes into the building because of the risk to kids who had food allergies. And the kids who had the allergies were careful about checking labels on anything they considered eating. While I don't know her well, I would bet that Amanda is the cautious type. Unless she was trying to kill herself, which seems like a stretch, considering she was getting ready for a party. I can't imagine her eating something without first looking at the ingredients. I just hope the reaction wasn't as bad as the posts on her page make it sound, because hospitals suck. DJ could give a dissertation on the subject. Maybe if Nate knows what he's talking about, my brother might get a chance to not see them so often in the future.

Nate.

He's rarely serious, and I know he had more that he wanted to say. So why didn't he say it? Is he worried that I'll blame him if his plan doesn't work? Or is he thinking that our friendship could develop into something more? And if he does want us to be more than friends, would that put what we have now at risk? I don't know. I hope Nate won't bring it up again so I don't have to make that choice. At least, not until my father is found and DJ is better.

Since I don't want to think about the intensity of Nate's

stare, I focus on his plan for DJ and sign in to NEED. If we're going to mimic the outreach this site has, I should probably look at it again. I click on my profile page and I let out a huge sigh of relief as I see that no one has discovered it yet. Or if they have, they haven't left any comments under my need request. At least one good thing has happened today.

I click on the various tabs and try to imagine what Nate is thinking about for the viral campaign. He wants to use a picture of today's vandalism, which makes me uneasy, even though I understand his reasoning. The most popular posts on social media sites always have pictures. Even here on the NEED message board, there are lots of photos, of shoes, iPads, new phones. Some of the photos document the rewards that NEED has bestowed. Others are of items they're hoping to request in the future.

Then I see it, and I feel as if I've been punched in the gut. The tree. The hole. Our house. Our nightmare. But only part of it. Because the makeshift coffin is missing. Wait. No. It isn't.

I lean in closer to the screen. At the bottom right corner of the photograph, I can see the edge of the box and a shovel sitting on the snow. This photograph is from before the box was put into the grave, and must have been taken by the person who dug that hole. A person who belongs to NEED.

I click on the profile of the person who posted the photo. L592. Crap. I forgot that NEED doesn't let users post identifying information. Maybe the cops can subpoena the site and get the user's name and other data. Since I really don't want to have the police come to the door and wake up DJ or my mother, I decide to wait on that until morning and instead try to see if there's a way I can figure out who the user is on my own. The only thing I have to help is the pending need request: a Michael Kors purse.

What?

That can't be right. I didn't see the person's face, but I'm sure it wasn't a girl. And maybe it's sexist of me, but I can't see any guy in my high school interested in carrying around a purse. Could NEED be so intent on anonymity that they are mixing up what we see on people's profile pages? They blocked mine, but they can't do that for everyone without causing suspicion. That makes me realize that unless someone brags, it's almost impossible to learn who committed what act for which request.

I go back to the message board. Maybe there are comments on the photograph that can give me a clue to the poster's identity. But as I scroll down, another photograph makes me pause.

It's a picture of someone's front door, decorated for the holiday. But it's not the cheerful wreath and lights that make my breath catch. At the bottom of the door is a holiday mat with the words WELCOME TO THE HIGHLANDS' printed on it, and on the mat is a green and white bakery box.

It's a photo of Amanda Highland's house.

Dread grows inside me as I pick up my phone and dial Nate so he can tell me if what I'm seeing is what I think it is. Unless I'm totally out of my mind, someone who belongs to NEED delivered the peanut-laden cookies in that box. They are the reason Amanda could soon be dead.

Bryan

No. No. No. No. No.

Bryan's computer screen shines bright in the dark room. Amanda's face smiles out at him as he reads the posts from her friends and family. Dismay. Horror. Prayers. Love.

Because of him.

No. This isn't his fault. He doesn't even know what was in the box he delivered. And if it was the cookies that caused the allergic reaction, Bryan isn't the one who chose to give them to her. Someone else is to blame. He's a victim. Just like Amanda. Except he's sitting in his room safe and sound and she's in a coma, fighting for her life.

He gags as his stomach cramps. Sweat breaks out on his forehead and saliva fills his mouth. He's going to be sick.

He makes it to the bathroom just in time. Even after his stomach is empty, his body heaves as if trying to push out the guilt. Because no matter how much he wants to believe this isn't his fault, it is. He knows it is.

His stomach cramps again. His legs tremble. He has no idea how long he sits on the bathroom floor. It feels like hours have passed when his legs are strong enough to stand. He brushes his teeth and splashes cold water on his face. When he looks up from the sink, he stares at the acne that he hates so much.

The house is quiet when Bryan walks back to his room. His mother must not have heard him getting sick, which is a miracle because she almost always wakes up when something is wrong with him or his brothers and sisters. She says mothers have a sixth sense. Not tonight.

Mostly he's glad his mom is asleep, but part of him wishes she weren't. With Amanda's face filling the screen, he'd tell her about NEED and the delivery he made. How deep in his heart he knew when putting the box on her doorstep that he was do-ing something bad.

His eyes are heavy, but he doesn't get into bed. Instead he sits in front of the computer, reading the updates as they scroll by. The updates become less frequent as the hours pass. Still he sits in front of the monitor. Watching. Waiting. Hoping.

Which is why, when a new post appears at four thirty in the morning, Bryan is awake to read it.

My niece, Amanda, has gone to heaven. She brought us sixteen years of joy and is gone too soon. How could this happen? I just don't understand.

There are no tears as Bryan reads the message again and again. His fingers hover over the keys. He wants to say he is sorry. He wants to give Amanda's aunt an explanation. But he knows that won't help. Because, no matter the reason, Amanda is dead.

He is cold and empty when he reaches for his mouse and

logs on to NEED. He doesn't read the message board to see if someone has found the picture he posted earlier. That doesn't matter. Neither does the message on his page that says his NEED request has been delivered to the mailbox for him to retrieve. Only one thing matters now.

"What do you *need?*" the site asks.

I need a gun.

Enter.

NETWORK MEMBERS—689
NEEDS PENDING—685
NEEDS FULFILLED—144

Kaylee

NIGHTMARES HAUNT ME. Dreams of my brother in an icy grave. My mother screaming that it's all my fault. Me screaming as my father steps over a collapsed, unmoving Amanda and strides out the door.

Amanda.

I jolt awake. Sunlight streams through the blinds as I squint at my clock. Eight a.m. It's Saturday. Mom is probably awake, but she'll let my brother and me sleep as late as we want, since it's winter break. I start to lie back down, then remember Amanda's lifeless face in my dreams and the photo I saw posted on NEED. Sliding out of bed, I turn on my laptop to look for an update on her condition.

After my brother's diagnosis, his deteriorating condition, and my father's abandonment, I thought nothing could shock me anymore. I was wrong.

I read the words Amanda's aunt Mary wrote several times before they finally sink in. Then I scroll back up and read the other posts. Despite the early hour, there are dozens of messages expressing shock. Horror. Despair. And there will be more as the day goes on. Almost all the messages offer condolences to the family and prayers. I start to add mine, but stop before I hit Enter.

Why bother? Nothing I say, or anyone else says, will do any good, because no matter how much anyone wishes it could be different, Amanda is gone.

I want to cry. Amanda was nice. I didn't know her well, but I knew enough to understand that she wasn't like everyone else. She didn't obsess over boyfriends and phones and the hot new music group. She didn't roll her eyes at people and make them feel idiotic for expressing an opinion or being different. Maybe if I had been more open, we could have been friends. It's stupid, but part of me always thought she wanted to be. And now it can never happen.

Tears burn the backs of my eyes and clog my throat, but not a single drop falls, because as I read the posts lamenting such a terrible accident, I feel something so much more than sadness and despair. I feel fear. Icy, heart-stopping fear. The photo I saw on NEED last night makes me think Amanda's death isn't the accident nearly everyone believes it to be.

NEED killed Amanda. Or someone who participates in NEED did. Maybe it wasn't intentional and was just a sick joke gone awry. Maybe someone thought Amanda would recognize the danger the cookies posed. If she had, she'd now be alive and wondering if whoever sent her the cookies understood they were lethal.

My fingers shake as I grab my phone and dial Nate's number. Voicemail. Just like last night when I first saw the photo and tried to reach him. He must have turned the ringer to silent when he went to bed and is still asleep. Otherwise he would have gotten my middle-of-the-night message and would have called. After the beep, I try to tell him about Amanda's death, but all I can get out before hanging up is "Call me. Please."

Clutching the phone in my hands, I think of Amanda, then of the hole in our yard and my brother's white face as my mother explained what had happened. DJ's first question was "Why?" and despite Nate's horror movie marathon, I know the incident haunted DJ throughout the day and into his dreams. Just as it did me.

Could that be the purpose of NEED? To cause this fear and uncertainty?

I shake my head and imagine Nate telling me that I'm being dramatic. That I'm overreacting. And really, a social media site created just to strike fear into the hearts of Nottawa High School students does seem nuts. As I'm sure Nate would ask, why bother? What could be accomplished by sowing that kind of fear here in Nottawa, Wisconsin? It's not like the kids who go to our high school are anything special.

Still . . .

I click off of Amanda's page and log on to NEED. Quickly, I scan through the various links and photos on the message board until I find the one I'm looking for. The one of Amanda's front stoop and the bakery box. Maybe it's just a coincidence that this photo was posted on the day that Amanda died, but even if I could make myself believe that, the photograph of the icy grave in my front yard would convince me otherwise.

I don't know how or why, but somehow NEED is connected to both. There's just no other explanation, and because NEED is anonymous, I can't figure out who did what on my own. The cops should be able to do what I can't. So I punch in the number. But my finger hovers over the Call button as I think about what the cops might say. What everyone else will say when they hear that based solely on a couple of pictures I found posted online, I'm accusing a website, at least indirectly, of killing someone everyone loved and hurting my own family.

Drama queen.

Attention seeker.

Crazy.

Or, as I heard my school therapist, Dr. Jain, explain to my mother, I have a desperate need to compensate for my father's defection and brother's illness with actions based in a reality of my own making.

I don't. I'm not. I know I'm not. I've done stupid things to get attention for DJ. So stupid, but I didn't know what else to do. I told lies. Lots of them. They didn't help. They only made things go from bad to worse. Will calling the cops now do more of the same? Or will they understand that I'm telling the truth?

Almost everyone in this town aside from DJ and Nate has called me names or used me as an example of a good girl who took a turn for the misguided. I've already gotten online messages calling me out for Officer Shepens questioning Mr. Ward. If I call the police again and report the activity on NEED and no one believes me, there will be worse. I'll be a target for attacking something that everyone who attends Nottawa High

School belongs to. Even if I'm right, everyone will hate me for shutting down a site that has given so many of them things they want.

I shouldn't care. A good person should never consider how people will react when something important is at stake. Amanda is dead. Other lives could be on the line.

But I'm not a good person. Nate might think I am, but my hesitation tells me he's wrong. Because I'm tired of being alone. Of hearing Nate talk about invitations he doesn't care about getting and pretending that I don't care either. Pretending I don't wonder what life would be like if DJ hadn't gotten sick. If my father hadn't left. If my mother had been a match for DJ. If I had been. I won't stop fighting for my brother. I only have to remember the way he looked lying asleep on the living room floor to find the courage to protect him at any cost. But still, I worry that everything I have done and all that I am thinking of doing now will ultimately hurt him more than it will help. If kids from school start picking on him because of me, I don't know what I'll do. They won't do it in public, but online they could attack from behind their screens, where no one is really watching. Not really. And then what?

I watch the screen fade to black and rub the edge of my cell phone with my thumb, wishing Nate would get out of bed and listen to his messages. If he calls the police, no one will condemn me. That thought fills me with guilt, because it's the thinking of a coward. Something I've accused everyone in town of being who didn't get tested as a potential donor. How many times have I yelled at Dr. Jain that they're all too scared to do the right thing? I've said that the ability to save a life should mean more than any of their fears.

NEED

Shouldn't it be the same for me? Or have I been lying to myself?

I dial Nate's number again. No answer. For the first time since we were kids, he isn't there when I really need him. As I wait for the beep, I realize I could postpone calling the cops until I talk to Nate. But I know that waiting isn't an option. A life is more important than my fear, and someone else might get hurt before Nate rolls out of bed. And if I am being completely honest, I'm forced to admit that there is another reason. I want Nate to keep thinking I'm the person he believes I am, even though that person doesn't really exist.

This time when I leave a message, my voice is steady. "Nate, if you wake up in the next few minutes, throw on some clothes and come over to my house. I'm calling the cops. I think someone on NEED killed Amanda."

Before I can lose my nerve, I hit End and then dial the Nottawa Police Department. It rings several times and I almost hang up. But before I do, a woman's voice answers and asks me how she can help.

For some reason, the question catches me off-guard. For a moment I just sit without moving, trying to decide what to say.

"Hello? Hello, is anyone there? If this is a prank call, I—"

"No." I wince at the desperation and panic in my voice. "I'm here. This isn't a prank. I promise. Is Officer Shepens there?"

"Officer Shepens isn't available at the moment. Is this a police matter? If so, I am happy to take a report and contact the officer on duty. If not, it might be best to contact Officer Shepens at his home. This is not an appropriate line to contact officers for personal—"

"This is a police matter. Honest." Crap. I'm screwing everything up and I haven't even started to talk about the problem. "Officer Shepens came to my house yesterday. I called because someone dug a hole in my front yard and . . ." I swallow down the bile that rises when I think of the cardboard coffin and the message written on it. ". . . left a disturbing note about my brother."

"The Dunham residence. Correct?"

Am I imagining the edge that I hear in her voice?

When I confirm she asks, "Do you have additional information to add to your original statement?"

Yes. No. Well, not to just anyone. "Is Officer Shepens working today?" I ask. "I'd be more comfortable talking to him. He said I should call if I thought of anything new." Okay, he didn't exactly say that, but he was here. He saw what someone did to our yard and will recognize the photo on the NEED message board. He should, since he took one just like it.

The woman on the phone clearly isn't happy, but she finally agrees to put me on hold while she contacts Officer Shepens. Down the hall in my house I hear the shower shut off. My mother is definitely awake.

"Officer Shepens will be by to take your statement within the next half-hour. Please don't go anywhere until he arrives."

I assure her that I won't leave the house, and I hang up. Pots and pans clank in the kitchen below, telling me that Mom has decided to cook breakfast. Probably waffles, because they're DJ's favorite. I watch the NEED message board as I pull on a pair of jeans and an oversize, fraying blue sweater that I typically keep stashed in the back of my closet. I snuck the sweater from a box of my father's clothes before my mother put it in storage. Normally, I don't wear it outside my room because I don't want to upset DJ. But I tell myself that today he has waffles to make him feel better. This is all I have. Despite Dad leaving us, the sweater still smells like him. Or maybe I just imagine it does. Either way, the hint of aftershave and wool makes me remember how he made me feel like I could face anything.

And when the doorbell rings and my mother's angry voice calls for me to come downstairs, I am glad for the reminder as I grab my laptop and prepare to face what's ahead.

Gina

DENIED? HOW COULD her request be denied? She did exactly what the site asked her to do.

Okay. Maybe not exactly what it said. But she shouldn't be penalized for taking creative license. After all, who could blame her for giving the note a little extra panache? Maybe the bright red lipstick print and the extra line about being turned on by keeping their little secret weren't part of the instructions, but clearly the note was designed to upset the Frey family's perfect little world. Getting revenge and concert tickets all in one fabulous package—how awesome that should have been.

Except it isn't, because NEED doesn't understand or appreciate dramatic flair. And she's being punished for its lack of vision. That's just plain wrong. Especially since she already told some of her friends that she'd gotten the tickets from NEED. After hearing about Dani's new camera and Jeanine's professional makeup artist's kit, Gina wasn't going to admit she hadn't received anything yet. So she swore them to secrecy (yeah, right), since they aren't supposed to tell others what they received, and told them about the tickets. The way they looked when they heard about the passes—jaws dropped, eyes wide and filled with envy—made waiting in the freezing cold for Luke's dad to leave the house totally worthwhile. She even parked way down the street and slouched in the seat so no one would see her. Her friends hadn't had to sit in the cold and they didn't slip on ice and almost break an ankle walking up Luke's driveway to deliver a dumb note. They didn't do anything . . . not really . . . to earn their rewards. She did, and now everyone is expecting her to go to that concert. If she doesn't go, they'll all think she lied. Her reputation will be ruined.

No way in hell is that going to happen. NEED doesn't know who it's dealing with, but Gina isn't one to accept defeat. Especially not when her reputation is on the line. She's going to get those tickets if it's the last thing she does.

Brushing a piece of her dark hair out of her eyes, Gina rereads the infuriating message.

YOUR NEED REQUEST HAS BEEN DENIED DUE TO INCORRECT COMPLETION OF YOUR FULFILLMENT REQUIREMENT. IF YOU CHOOSE TO RESUBMIT, CAREFULLY READ AND FOLLOW ANY INSTRUCTIONS PROVIDED TO ENSURE YOUR NEED REQUEST IS GRANTED.

Gina grits her teeth and wants to scream, but catches herself before she does. Her little sister is probably listening at the door, just waiting to run to Mom and tell her that something is wrong. It's her sister's fault that Mom and Dad are upset. She borrowed the car to deliver NEED's note, and they wouldn't have noticed the car was gone or insisted that she give back the extra set of keys if Krissy hadn't tattled. Sisters really suck.

So does this idiotic website. But Gina isn't going to let it beat her. No one beats her.

Taking a deep breath, Gina places her cursor in the request field. She frowns at the chip on one of her newly polished nails and starts to type, trying to decide if she should ask for something even more glamorous. Maybe add a limo to take her to the concert.

With a smug smile, Gina adds the car to her request, re-reads what she typed to ensure there's no miscommunication (since NEED has already demonstrated it has issues with making itself clear), and when she declares the message perfect, hits Send. Take that, NEED. Now when she gets this request granted, she'll be able to tell her friends that she secured two gifts from the site: the tickets and the limo. They'll be totally jealous they're stuck with ordinary things while Gina gets to live like a star.

The NEED clock ticks away and Gina pushes back from her desk and walks over to her dresser to snag her pink polish. Might as well touch up her nail while she's waiting for the site to respond.

Damn. It isn't just one nail that's chipped. It's two. If Gina's parents weren't so stubborn, she wouldn't have to live here and drive two towns over to get a decent manicure. She touches up her nails, carefully replaces the cap on the pink polish so she doesn't spill it, and then notices the monitor. The clock is gone.

Her NEED request must have been accepted. Good. Now she can do whatever it asks and no one will ever know . . .

Wait. She reads the message on the screen three times to make sure it says what she thinks it does. Are they kidding?

"Gina. It's time to go."

Ugh. She forgot. Her mother is taking her and her sister to Kenosha so they can spend their Christmas money at the outlet stores. After the whole car thing, it's a miracle her mother hasn't canceled.

"I'll be there in a minute," Gina yells, then reads the red lettering again.

"You have thirty seconds, or we're leaving without you."

"Okay!" Gina stands up, grabs her purse, and casts one last look at the screen before hurrying toward the door. She's glad to have an excuse not to have to make a decision yet. Because while Gina is normally up for taking a razor to someone's reputation, she's never had to destroy a life. Are concert tickets and a limo worth it? Is it worth it to one-up her friends and maintain her reputation?

For the first time, Gina wishes she were a better person. A better person would say no.

```
NETWORK MEMBERS—689
NEEDS PENDING—684
NEEDS FULFILLED—165
```

Kaylee

My mother is waiting for me at the bottom of the stairs. She glances at the laptop I hold to my chest. "Officer Shepens says you called the police station this morning. I told him he had to be mistaken."

Her dark hair is pulled back, which makes her face look strained. Tired. More disappointed. I didn't think that was possible. A small corner inside me, the part that wishes for her approval more than anything, wants to agree with her. To say there is a mistake. That there's no reason for me to call the police without telling her about it before the cops arrive at the door.

Down the hall, I can see Officer Shepens standing near the kitchen table. His back is to us, but I'm pretty sure he is trying to take in every word we say. I would be.

"I called and asked to talk to Officer Shepens since he was here yesterday. There's something I think he needs to know."

I walk around my mother and head toward the kitchen.

Officer Shepens turns the minute I step through the doorway. Yeah—he was listening all right. Good. Despite the way my cheeks heat, I'm glad he isn't just phoning it in. NEED is smart. It'll take someone smarter to shut it down.

"Thanks for coming," I say, setting my laptop on the table.

He nods, unzips his black jacket, and pulls a small notebook from an inside pocket. "You made it sound pretty important. Do both of you want to take a seat?"

My mother reaches around me for her cup of coffee and then offers Officer Shepens one. He thanks her for the coffee and pulls out the chair directly opposite from where I have sat down. Without waiting for my mom to sit, I say, "Amanda Highland died a few hours ago. I came across something that makes me believe her death was caused by the same thing that's responsible for what happened in our yard yesterday morning."

"Oh my God." I jump as my mother's coffee cup clatters to the counter. "Did she confront someone while they vandalized her house?"

"No." I cut my mom off before she can start imagining all the awful things that could have happened. "Someone gave her cookies. She ate one and had an allergic reaction that killed her. Isn't that what happened, Officer Shepens?"

I assume he's heard.

With an unreadable expression, he studies me over the rim of his cup. "Amanda Highland died this morning from anaphylaxis."

"That poor family." Mom sags against the countertop. "When I think about what they must be going through . . ."

It's easy for us to imagine what it's like to lose someone. To have that hole in the fabric of a family. We live with that every day, and without a donor we could lose one more. Amanda's family must be in hell.

"Wait." Mom shakes her head. "I don't understand why you called the police about this." The sadness and concern in her face are replaced by an expression that makes everything inside me go still. "It's terrible that a girl died, but I don't see how an allergic reaction could have anything to do with DJ and what happened here."

"Kaylee must have seen or heard something that made her believe the two are connected. Right, Kaylee?" Officer Shepens says calmly.

I rub the palms of my hands on my jeans and swallow down the hurt. I shouldn't care. I should be used it. But I'm not. I hate that I'm not.

"There's this website."

"A website?" My mother sighs. "Kaylee . . ."

Officer Shepens holds up a hand. "Tell me about the website, Kaylee."

I keep my eyes on Officer Shepens and say, "It's new. The site is called NEED and it's only for Nottawa High School students, but no one is supposed to say what their profile name is or post information that gives away their identity." Officer Shepens frowns, and inside I cringe. I'm explaining this wrong. So I try again. "The website asks the users to tell it what they need. Once the request is accepted, the site gives you a task to perform in order to get what you asked for. And there's this message board where people can post links to things they want or post pictures and comment on them. One of the pictures was of the hole in our yard. And there was another with a bakery box sitting on Amanda's front porch. I—"

"Kaylee, let me make sure I'm understanding you." Officer Shepens rests his elbows on the table. "You're saying there's a website with photos of your front yard and of Amanda's house?"

"Not her house," I answer him. "The front stoop. There was a green and white bakery box sitting next to the front door. And the photo of our yard was taken before I ran outside. The box hadn't been put into the hole yet. And—"

"And you realize this is hard to believe." Officer Shepens's voice is kind, but his words turn me cold. "Unless you can show us what you're talking about . . ."

"I can." I open the cover of my laptop as the doorbell rings. "I can prove that I'm not making this up."

"Hey. Is someone here?" DJ's voice calls from upstairs.

Yes, but I don't care. I type in the password as my mother goes to see who's at the door.

"Hey, Mom. Who's here?"

My desktop appears and I click on my Web browser.

Footsteps pound on the stairs.

"Is Kaylee around?" Nate's voice calls from the front door. "I got a message from her and thought I should come over."

"Here," I say as I click on the bookmark for NEED and turn the screen around to face Officer Shepens.

"Hey, Nate! Are we going to watch movies again today? That would be awesome. Wow . . . what are the police doing here? Did something else happen?"

"Nothing happened," my mother snaps. "Nate isn't staying and you, DJ, are going back upstairs."

DJ yells at Mom that Nate has every right to be here. Nate

apologizes for not calling to make sure it was okay for him to come over. He says my name. But I say nothing as I wait for Officer Shepens's reaction. When he frowns, I turn the screen back around and try to understand what I'm seeing.

The Internet connection is still working.

The Web address is correct.

But the screen is black.

NEED is gone.

Sydney

"I'LL BE THERE in a minute, Dad." Get a grip. It's not like there's any hurry. Sydney's dad insists they salt the sidewalks and driveways for the properties he represents every weekend.

"Opportunities can be lost if you aren't paying attention. You never know when a prospective buyer is going to drive by and call for a closer look."

"Never" is right. So far it has never happened. But every Saturday morning they have to go out and make sure each house is ready for the phantom people who will want to see it. His dad says it's good business. His dad is wrong. Good business pays money, and as far as Sydney can tell, his dad hasn't pulled a paycheck since early December. But Sydney has.

Reaching into his back pocket, he pulls out the envelope he found under a pile of boards near the shed. Just where NEED said it would be. Five hundred dollars. Not a bad payday for the job Sydney was asked to do. More should be on its way, now that he's finished the most recent assignment, and more after that if things work out the way he hopes.

Sydney shuts down his computer and stashes the envelope of cash in the drawer along with his knife.

"Come on, Sydney," his dad calls. "Time is money."

Yes. Yes, it is. Sydney smiles as he locks the drawer. Unlike his dad, he plans on making money. Lots of it. No matter what it takes.

Hannah

HANNAH SWIPES THE BOTTOM of her nose with the back of her hand and looks around for the Kleenex she just had. Where did it go?

There. She picks up the crumpled tissue and checks her cell phone just in case. Nate still hasn't returned her call. Calling his house today was a terrible move. He must think so too; otherwise he would have texted an apology for missing her call, or called her back.

Something.

Anything.

Unless Jack didn't give Nate the message. She should have called Nate's cell phone, of course, but she was too upset to pay attention to what number she had dialed until Jack picked up. If only she'd hung up then. But Nate and Jack sound a lot alike on the phone, and she had poured her heart out about how life is short, and she didn't want to regret not telling him how she felt, before Jack interrupted and filled her in on her mistake.

How mortifying. And now if she dials Nate's cell and Jack already told him about the first call, she'll look desperate on top of looking like an airhead. She wishes she could take it back. She was an idiot to call after learning about Amanda's death. But the shock and the sadness made her think about how much she wanted to be with Nate.

And how lame is it that her first thought wasn't for Amanda and the life she'll never lead, or for her family, who have to be so devastated? Instead, she focused on herself. No wonder Nate isn't interested. Why would any guy want a girl who can't grieve for a friend without freaking out about the inadequacies of her own life?

She needs a do-over. Or a rock to crawl under. She doesn't want to face Nate or anyone else right now. School next week is going to suck, and not just because she hasn't been able to force herself to read that stupid book.

Ah. There she goes again. Thinking of herself. Still . . . she can't help but wonder if NEED can actually make her request come true. A school cancellation would solve her problem, at least for a while. Maybe there's an update or something on the website. If nothing else, it gives her something to think about besides how foolish she was this morning.

Wiping her nose again, she sits down at her computer and logs on, trying not to think about how she basically threw herself at Nate's feet and begged him to go out with her. She clicks the NEED bookmark on her toolbar a second time. A third. What the hell? She tosses the tissue in the trash can and goes in search of another computer, because after everything she's already lost today, she can't possibly lose the hope NEED was giving her, too.

Kaylee

IT'S GONE.

"I don't understand." I type the address in just in case the bookmark link is broken and hit Enter. Nothing. "The site was working this morning."

"What site? What's going on?" DJ asks.

"This isn't right." I check the Internet connection and click on several other sites. Everything is working. Except NEED. "This doesn't make any sense."

"DJ, go upstairs," my mother orders. "Kaylee, I'm going to call Dr. Jain."

"Why does Kaylee need to talk to Dr. Jain?" DJ asks. His eyes narrow at Officer Shepens at the table. "And why are the police here? Did something else happen? What happened, Kaylee?" He turns to me because he knows I'll answer him.

But Mom answers first. "Nothing happened." My mother shoots me a look that warns me to keep my mouth shut. I am not to mention Amanda or anything that could upset my brother. "Kaylee overreacted and made a mistake calling Officer Shepens. Isn't that right, Kaylee?"

Her tone makes it clear that I had better agree or else.

"I'm sorry, Mom." But I'm not. I'm angry, and I'm doing everything I can to not show it as I turn back to the screen. "The website was working this morning. It's real. So is everything I've said. This isn't like what happened after Dad left." I'm not faking illness or telling everyone that my father is dead or offering rewards to strangers that I never intend to fulfill. "NEED is real. Nate's seen it." My words trip over themselves as I turn to Nate, desperate to have someone explain that I'm not crazy. I've never been crazy. "He's the one who sent me an invitation to be a part of the network."

For a moment there is only silence.

"Nate." Officer Shepens pushes back his chair and stands up. "You've seen the website Kaylee told us about?"

"Yeah." Nate sticks his hands in his back pockets, then glances at my brother. "DJ, before I forget, I wanted to grab that comic you were telling me about last night. Can you get it for me?"

My mother nods and moves toward DJ. "I think that's a great idea—"

"I'm not leaving." DJ shakes off my mother's attempt to lead him from the room. "If this has anything to do with what happened in our front yard yesterday, I have the right to hear it."

Nate looks at my mother. When she remains quiet, he says, "The website is what Kaylee said. It riffs on the other social media sites out there. But instead of asking about how you feel or what's happening in your life it asks what you need. Right, Kaylee?"

"Right," I say. "And unlike the other websites, this one asks you to do things in exchange for getting what you said you wanted."

"Like what?" Officer Shepens asks.

"Nate was asked to invite a bunch of friends to the site. That's why he sent me the invitation. Here . . ." I walk around Officer Shepens, go to my email, and let out a sigh of relief. Nate's email is still there. Proof that NEED is real. "This is the email I received when he invited me."

My mother takes DJ's arm to hold him back as Officer Shepens reads the email, then asks, "Do you mind if I send myself a copy of this?"

"Go ahead." While he hits Forward, I tell him that there were only about a hundred users when I first logged on and that by the next day just about everyone was on the site. "That's when I think people started getting asked to do things other than sending emails in order to get what they requested." I describe the photos and explain that the site assigns anonymous profile names so there is no way to tell who is posting what.

Officer Shepens frowns. "And you think the site asked people to dig the hole in your yard and deliver cookies to Amanda?" When I nod he asks, "Have you heard of anyone performing those kinds of tasks to get rewards? Maybe some of your friends?"

"No." Other than Nate, I don't have any real friends. Not anymore.

"How about you, Nate?" Officer Shepens shifts his gaze. "Have you been asked to do anything unusual by this website?"

"No, sir, but I got invited early on and I haven't really talked about the site with anyone other than Kaylee. The site asks people not to talk about it."

Officer Shepens nods. "And have you seen the photographs Kaylee described to us?"

I hold my breath as Nate looks at me, because I don't know the answer.

"Well, there are lots of photographs," Nate says. "People keep posting pictures of phones or movie stars or crazy things they want. It's hard to keep track."

"So you haven't seen them."

"No." Nate looks away as Officer Shepens's phone beeps. "But if Kaylee says she saw them, I believe her."

"I'm sure you do." The phone beeps again. Officer Shepens pulls it out and looks at the display. "I have to take this. This is Shepens," he says as he walks toward the front door.

"Talk about the wrong day to sleep in." Nate takes a step toward me. "I guess I should have looked harder at the posts on the message board when I got home last night, but pictures of shoes and links for thousand-dollar sunglasses don't really turn me on. After a couple of minutes, I logged off and went to bed."

"It's okay," I say. Although I'm certain it's not okay. And by the expression Officer Shepens wears as he returns, I'm pretty sure nothing is.

"I apologize, but I have to go." Officer Shepens slides his phone back into his pocket and zips up his jacket.

"Wait." I take a step forward. "You can't go. Not yet. What about Amanda and her family and DJ and everyone on that social media site? You can't leave and do nothing."

The desperation I've kept at bay breaks free. I shake off the hand that reaches for me. My mother? Nate? DJ? I don't care.

"Kaylee, I plan on checking on the site. I do," Officer Shepens tells me. "But I have to go. There are more important things going on right now than what you think you might have seen . . ."

Might have seen. The words bounce in my head and I go still. Whatever else he says about not filing the report until there is tangible evidence is lost in the haze of that one sentence.

He doesn't believe me.

I look to my mother as she thanks him for keeping this situation quiet.

"I'm not crazy," I whisper as Office Shepens walks back toward the front door. I say it again louder as I hurry after him. "The site is real. The photographs are real."

He is halfway out the door when he turns back and says that he believes I'm telling the truth as I know it. That he won't forget what I've said, but that as much as he would like to stay and discuss the matter further, he really has to go.

Officer Shepens looks like he wants to say more. Instead, he digs into his other pocket, pulls out his card, and hands it to me. He tells me to call if I need anything. His eyes meet mine just before he heads out the door, and for a moment I'm sure I recognize something I see every day when I look in the mirror. Or maybe I just think I see it because it's what I am feeling right now as I stand in the open doorway watching him drive away.

Fear.

Ethan

HE HEARS THE SIREN and smiles. At any moment the car will come over the hill. The lights will flash like they do in the movies when something bad happens. And this was bad. As bad as he could make it.

He knows he should be far away by now. A real mercenary doesn't stay around to admire his work. He goes in, gets his hands dirty, gets out, and cleans up without being seen.

Hanging around after the job is done is a sure-fire way to lose rank in the game. Only a beginner makes that mistake.

But this isn't about improving a rank or rising in fame on the scoreboard. This is real. What he did is real. The screams of "Oh my God" that clawed the cold morning air as he ran through the yards and into the woods were real. And wonderful.

So what if he threw up after he finished? He was professional enough to leave the scene before hurling. Next time he won't eat breakfast beforehand. There's no breakfast on the premission checklist. Weapons and maps, yes. Food, no.

Ethan smiles again. Maybe after he gets out of high school he can join the CIA or FBI or the NSA. They should be able to use a guy with his skills. He could jet from one state to another or country to country, getting paid to covertly eliminate threats. Yeah, that sounds like a perfect use of his talent. He'll have to start looking into how those agencies recruit. Maybe ask his dad to take him to the gun range to work on his shooting. It's never too early to start planning for the future. At least, that's what his parents always say.

He shifts his position behind the bush where he's hiding as the siren gets louder until finally the car flies by. Okay, it didn't go nearly as fast as he thought it should. But faster than any cop around here would normally drive. That will have to suffice. For now.

He picks up his mission supply bag and wishes he could see everyone's face when they read the note he's been charged to leave behind.

I told you that you'd be sorry.

He notices a streak of red—a piece of evidence—that he left on the icy ground where he was kneeling, and kicks some snow over it. Then he heads toward home with a spring in his step. If they aren't sorry now, he has a feeling NEED will make sure they will be very, very soon.

Kaylee

I DON'T WAIT for breakfast or for my mother to tell me that
we have to talk or to announce whatever consequences might
result from Officer Shepens's visit. As soon as I close the front
door I hurry back to the kitchen, grab my laptop, and run upstairs. My mother yells for me to stop. But I don't. Why would
I? It's not like she's going to come after me. She has DJ to worry
about.

After shutting the door to my room, I set my laptop back
on the desk and try the Web address again and again and again.
Still nothing.

I want to scream. Where did it go?

"Hey." The door swings open and Nate walks in carrying a
plate filled with waffles and two forks. "You okay? Your mom
sent me up here to check on you."

"Really?" I study his face, see the dare-you-to-call-me-on-it
look in his eyes, and the flicker of hope his words sparked in
me dies.

"I also let her know you really aren't making this website up.

She didn't want to talk about it while your brother was around, which I understand, but I figured with everything that happened in the past she might want a little more reassurance. You know?"

Yeah. I know. No matter how much I've wanted a fresh start and a second chance, I haven't gotten it. And I'm continuing to pay the price. And maybe so will DJ if NEED is behind Amanda's death and the horrible prank that's been played on him.

"So." Nate puts down the plate of waffles next to the laptop. "Are you okay?"

It's been so long since I've been okay, I don't know what it feels like anymore. "I'm not the one who's dead, so I guess I'm mostly fine." I don't want him to see the hurt I feel. Because really, it isn't important. Especially not when I think of Amanda and DJ and NEED. What do my feelings matter in the middle of all that?

I click on the bookmark again and come up with the same blank screen.

"The website is still down?" Nate asks, stabbing a waffle quarter.

"Yeah. Don't you think that's weird?"

"Websites go down all the time," Nate says through a mouthful of waffle.

"I know, but normally there would be an error message or something saying that the server is down or that the site has been removed. Wouldn't there be?" That's what happens when the school server gets overloaded or one of my brother's online games gets interrupted. You see a note about a system update or a broken link. Here there's nothing. "And the timing bugs me. What are the odds that there's a glitch or someone decided to pull down the site at the same time Officer Shepens arrived?"

Nate offers me the waffle on his fork, but I shake my head.

Nate shoves the piece into his mouth and shrugs. "Coincidences happen all the time."

"But . . ."

"But." Nate holds up an empty fork. "You seeing photos of a bakery box on Amanda's front step and the grave in your yard takes this way beyond coincidence."

"You believe me." Relief and desperate joy fill me. As do tears. I blink them back as Nate frowns.

"Of course I believe you. You must be more freaked than I thought. Kaylee . . ." He holds out a hand and waits for me to take it. And I do. His warm fingers close over mine and he tugs me to my feet. "We're a team. Period. I wasn't there for you the way I should have been last year."

I shake my head. "What are you talking about? I would never have made it through my dad's leaving and DJ's illness without you."

"You'd have made it. You're stronger than you know. I don't have your bravery."

"You're friends with me. That's pretty brave." Popular guy stays friends with unhinged girl. That sounds pretty darn heroic to me.

I try to pull my hand away, but Nate only tightens his grip. "No, it isn't. I just understand you."

He does. Aside from my mother, Dr. Jain, the school nurse, and the principal, Nate is the only one who has heard the truth.

And maybe more important, he has kept my secret. The teachers still think I made myself sick out of concern for DJ after he was first diagnosed. Imaginary migraines and forcing myself to throw up weren't symptoms of lack of sleep and stress. They were methods of getting sent to the nurse's office, where I might be able to gain access to information about my classmates' blood types.

"Hey." There's that thing in his expression again that makes my breath catch. He's still the Nate I've always known. Dependable. Irreverent. Essential. But the flicker in his eyes suggests something more. "We'll get through this like we always do. Together."

I stop trying to pull my hand away and allow him to web his fingers through mine. The connection pushes back some of my anxiety. Anxiety of another kind fills me as Nate leans toward me. His eyes search my face as if looking for an answer to a question—one that I haven't wanted to think about and certainly don't have an answer for. All I know is that I don't want to lose Nate.

He smells of waffles. He puts a hand on my cheek and I can't help but lean into his touch. It comforts even as it terrifies. I stand stiff and awkward and feeling like an idiot as his mouth brushes over mine. The touch is so quick and light that I can almost believe I imagined it. But the flutter in my gut and the way Nate is drawing me close again belie that thought. Only this time, I know I can't just stand there. Nate won't let me. I have to make a choice.

"Yo, Kaylee." DJ's voice calls a second before my door swings open. The warning gives me enough time to jerk back. Away from the choice I'm not sure I'm ready to make. My brother doesn't seem to notice my discomfort or Nate's frown as he makes a beeline for my laptop. "Did the website go back up? Did anyone else . . ."

Die.

The unspoken word hangs in the air.

"The site is still down." Nate puts an arm around DJ and says, "Who knows, the people behind it might have run out of money for all the gifts they've been giving and decided to shut it down for good. Which is probably for the best, although I kind of wish I'd requested a leather jacket or a snowmobile. Now I'll never get what I asked for unless I convince our school shrink that I'm too emotionally distressed to take the physics exam. She likes me, though. It might work."

Following Nate's lead, I keep my tone light. "Fat chance. You'll have to actually study for your final instead of counting on someone hacking into the system and cheating for you."

"You asked the website to cheat?" DJ asks, clearly torn between shock at Nate's dishonesty and awe.

"I was asking for assistance in raising my grade," Nate clarifies.

"That's cheating." DJ isn't fooled. "You're too smart to cheat."

"What's smarter—spending hours studying to take a test in a subject you'll never use again or finding a way to bypass all the studying and still come out looking like a genius?" Nate smiles. "Sometimes being smart is about getting the desired result without having to do something you hate in order to get it."

"That's the kind of thinking that makes NEED so successful," I say. "People don't want to earn enough money or put in the work to get what they want. They're looking for an easy way out and NEED gives it to them. The person who delivered the cookies to Amanda probably thought it was a birthday gift or some minor prank. They thought they were getting something for nothing. They were wrong."

"Yeah." Nate nods. "But what if . . ."

"DJ, what are you doing up there?" Mom yells.

"Ugh." DJ frowns and turns to me. "I forgot. Mom told me you have to come downstairs so you can talk. I'm supposed to ask Nate to keep me company so he doesn't get in the way. Mom wants to talk to you alone."

"Great." Me and Mom talking alone is never a good thing.

"She's not mad, Kaylee. After you left, Nate talked to her. That made a difference," DJ says brightly. "She's not angry or upset like all the other times. Mom's on your side."

I'm not sure I share his optimism. Too much has happened for me to believe the mother who was so suspicious of me is now my champion. But it would be nice.

Nate doesn't suffer from my skepticism as he cheerfully announces, "It sounds like my work here is done. I probably should get home before my mother realizes I'm not around to empty the dishwasher. DJ, tell your mom Kaylee's on her way. I just have one last thing I want to talk to her about."

DJ doesn't look happy to be shooed away, but he goes out of the room yelling to our mother.

Nate turns to me when DJ is out of earshot. "I'll keep checking to see if the website goes up. As long as it stays offline, nothing else bad can happen."

"Unless people got their assignments last night or early this morning and don't realize the site has gone down."

"Leave it to you to find the black lining. But you're right, which means I'll just have to make sure everyone has heard the site went down. If there's no reward there's no reason to act on whatever task NEED handed out." Nate gives my hand a squeeze. "Don't worry about DJ. He's going to be fine."

With one last check to make sure NEED is still offline, I yell to my mother that I'll be there in a minute, and I walk Nate downstairs to the front door.

"If I learn anything, I'll give you a call." He leans forward and I hold my breath as he kisses me on the cheek. "Good luck, but I don't think you'll need it."

With a smile that makes my heart tilt, he disappears out into the cold. Once the door closes, I go in search of my mother, feeling more confident than I have in a long time. DJ still needs a transplant, but maybe with Nate's and my mother's help . . .

I walk into the living room and stop in my tracks when I see my mother isn't alone. Standing in the middle of the room, talking with her in hushed tones, is Dr. Amelia Jain.

When she spots me, Dr. Jain steps forward. "Hello, Kaylee. It's good to see you. I hope you don't mind, but your mother called because she thinks there's a problem and she wanted my help."

I do mind, because I know a setup when I see one. DJ and Nate are wrong. My mother doesn't believe NEED exists. The problem Dr. Jain is here to deal with is me.

Sameena

SAMEENA STANDS AT the window of her room. When her parents decided to move to Nottawa they let her help pick their new house. She fell in love with this place when she saw the second-story corner room. Its big windows face the woods that edge their backyard. The woods seem magical, especially in winter when they glisten with ice and snow. Usually, she barely glances out the window that faces Mrs. Markham's fenced-in yard where those barking beagles live. But today she can't stop looking.

The screams woke her. Last night, Sameena finally let her father look over her homework. It was late, but he insisted on helping her fix the incorrect answers. It took hours. There were so many of them, and no matter how many times he explained the solutions, she still didn't understand.

He said it was because she was tired. And she was. She thanked him and got into bed, but the dogs were still barking.

And barking.

And barking.

She just wanted them to be quiet. She even opened the window when she saw Mrs. Markham come outside to check on her pups and yell that the dogs needed to stop.

And they had.

Oh help. They had.

Red streaks on the snow. So much red against the packed-down white where the dogs had run yesterday. Sameena concentrates on the slashes of crimson. She doesn't want to think about the hacked-up bodies near the red snow. Bodies that won't bother her with their barking anymore.

Which is terrible to think. She's terrible. She didn't want this to happen. She never meant this.

Or did she? What else could she have meant when she typed her request and hit Enter? What else could she have intended to get when she took the jelly jar filled with change off the top shelf of Mr. Nelson's workbench and stashed it in the back seat of the car down the block?

She just wanted the dogs to stop barking so she could concentrate.

But as she sees Mrs. Markham weeping, Sameena swears she still can hear the dogs. They're still barking. Maybe they'll never stop.

DEAR NEED NETWORK MEMBER,
    WE APOLOGIZE FOR THE UNEXPECTED
DISRUPTION OF THE NEED WEBSITE. OUR SERVER
AND SYSTEMS HAVE BEEN UPGRADED TO SERVE YOU
BETTER. CLICK ON THE LINK BELOW TO ACCESS
THE NEW, IMPROVED WEBSITE. WE LOOK FORWARD
TO ONCE AGAIN HELPING YOU ACQUIRE ALL THE
THINGS YOU NEED.
    THANK YOU FOR YOUR PATIENCE.
    THE NEED TEAM

SYSTEM REBOOTING
SERVICE RESTORED
NETWORK MEMBERS—688
NEEDS PENDING—687
NEEDS FULFILLED—200
WHAT DO YOU *NEED?*

Kaylee

MY MOTHER STANDS SILENT. Unmoving. Arms crossed over her chest. Not looking at me. Even though we're in the same room, it's as if a locked door stands between us. And suddenly, I wish it did. Because then I wouldn't see her expression. I could lie to myself and say that she would open the door if she saw how much pain I'm in. I need her now more than ever, but instead it is the diminutive, dark-haired Dr. Jain who offers me a warm smile and a kind word.

"I asked your mother if we could sit and talk in here. I thought we'd all be more comfortable. Don't you?"

No. But I nod anyway because I don't know what else to do.

Dr. Jain takes a seat on our faded blue sofa, and pats the spot next to her. When I stay standing, she lets out a small sigh, but she doesn't tell me to sit. "Your mother is concerned about you, Kaylee."

I doubt it. She's concerned about DJ, although I don't think pointing out the difference will help my cause. So I keep my mouth shut—a defense I probably haven't used often enough. Had I chosen to keep quiet and not call the police I wouldn't be in this position now. Something to remember for next time.

"Your mother says that you're taking Amanda Highland's death hard."

My mother stares at a spot on the carpet.

"I think everyone in town is taking Amanda's death hard," I say. "It shouldn't have happened."

Dr. Jain nods slowly in response. "You're right. Everyone who knew Amanda or her family will be struggling to understand why such a vibrant young woman is now gone. But as far as I know, none of those people have contacted the police to claim Amanda was murdered."

I keep my mouth shut.

"And from what I understand," Dr. Jain continues in a patient, soothing voice, "you also made the assertion that the same source you accuse of murder is also responsible for vandalizing your front yard and taunting your brother."

Since she has said nothing I disagree with, I remain silent. My mother lets out a frustrated huff, but Dr. Jain appears unfazed. Not a surprise. In the half-dozen sessions I've had with her, she never seems flustered or caught off-guard. The woman is unshakable. I wish I had her skill.

Shifting on the couch, Dr. Jain picks up a small, stone-etched vase filled with evergreen branches and turns it in her hands. "The holidays have probably been difficult for you. I know how hard it is to be without people you love at these times. Especially people who leave and don't give you a choice in the matter. The first year after my husband asked for a divorce was incredibly difficult. It's hard to feel better when you're surrounded by memories. I used to live not far from here when I was married. Moving to Maryland after my husband walked out helped me heal. New place. New space. New goals for my life. You don't have that. You're surrounded by reminders. No one can fault you for being upset."

"I'm not upset about my father," I say. I used to be, but there are bigger worries right now than how I feel about my dad not sending a Christmas gift.

Dr. Jain makes a "hmm" sound. "I know you're also concerned about your brother's illness. You've done a valiant job of keeping your brother's health concerns in everyone's thoughts, but the holidays distract people from even the most worthy causes. I suppose it is understandable that you would go to such lengths to remind the community of the problems he faces."

"What?" I go over her words again to see if I misheard. The way she sits there makes me doubt myself. But no. While her tone is laced with sympathy, her words cut deep. As does the way my mother nods in agreement. "You think I called the police and faked the website to help get DJ a kidney?"

"I checked into the website on my way over here. The students I've talked to confirm that it was real, but insist it was simplistic and already declining in popularity when the creator took it down. As for the rest . . ." Dr. Jain frowns. "Kaylee, I'm certain your intentions were good, but scaring your brother by digging a hole in your yard and—"

"Wait. Just wait." Panic washes over me. They actually believe . . . They believe I . . . that I . . . I can't think and I need to think. I can't run or they'll believe I really am guilty. I can't . . .

"Kaylee." My mother's voice snaps me back to reality. "If you'll just admit what you've done, Dr. Jain can help you."

"I haven't done anything." My voice shakes even as I square my shoulders and lift my chin. "This isn't like what happened after Dad left. Then I told people Dad died but my mom didn't want anyone to know." Because hearing about Dad's death would upset DJ. People believed it. I thought they might also believe that since Dad was the only possible donor they would take pity on us for yet another tragedy in our lives and step forward to help. "This is different. I am not the problem here. I don't know who is, but if someone doesn't listen, I think a whole lot worse is going to happen."

"Stop, Kaylee," my mother snaps. "Just stop and listen to yourself. I know you're upset that DJ gets so much attention and you want to be the hero—"

"No. You stop!" I yell. "This isn't about me wanting attention or being a hero. Someone threatened DJ, Mom. Someone dug a grave in our yard and scared the hell out of him. Whatever you believe about me, you can't believe I'd do that." If she does, I don't know what I'll do.

My heart marks the passing seconds as I stare at my mother. I feel helpless as her eyes meet mine. The steel in them—a barrier against me—makes my legs tremble. I ball my hands into fists and promise myself I won't cry. Then I see something flicker in her expression. Doubt.

"I don't believe it, Kaylee." The words are barely a whisper, but they are enough. No matter what our problems, my mother doesn't hate me that much.

She takes a step forward. "I don't know what is going on, but you wouldn't do anything to intentionally hurt your brother. Still . . ."

The hope inside me withers at the word.

". . . I can't completely take your words at face value. You understand why?"

I hate it, but I understand. "But this is different."

"Every situation is different." Dr. Jain stands. "That's why this kind of discussion is so important. When you do something wrong, it's best to acknowledge that action. The truth is always difficult to face and has repercussions, but it's better than the alternative. A bad choice made and not confessed can lead to another that covers it up and then another. With each step off the path it is harder to come back, and it can lead to places no one intended. You both have experienced this first-hand. Which is why it's only natural that your mother doubts your words and your actions. It's hard not to doubt them, Kaylee, especially when what you're saying seems so farfetched." She purses her lips and digs into her pocket for her cell.

I stand there waiting as Dr. Jain speaks into the phone, wishing Mom and I were the only ones in the room. Maybe then I could explain what's happening. Maybe . . .

"I'm sorry, but I have to get going." Dr. Jain slides the phone back into her pants pocket. "Amanda Highland's family is struggling, and I've been asked to see if I can help. Here." She holds out a business card. "I know you have my work number, Kaylee, but this is my private one. If anything happens and you need to talk to someone, please call. It doesn't matter what time. Day or night. I will also reach out to the Nottawa Police Department so they'll contact me if there are any more concerns. I'm invested in you and your journey, Kaylee. I'm invested in your family. I hope you know that."

I stare at the card in her hand. My instinct is to refuse it. After what she just said about me, it's not like I'm going to call her. But as I am about to turn away, I notice the hope in my mother's expression. So, for her, I take the card, ignore the pleased smile on Dr. Jain's face, and shove the card deep into my pocket next to the one given to me by Officer Shepens.

I watch my mother walk Dr. Jain out. My mother looks so grateful as she says something too quiet for me to hear. Dr. Jain lowers her voice as she puts on a long red coat, but it stills carries to where I stand. "I agree. DJ is fragile. Removing him from the situation until it stabilizes is a good idea. Don't second-guess yourself or feel guilty. When Kaylee is ready to face the consequences of her actions, you'll help her too. And rest assured I'll be keeping an eye on the situation."

Her words fan my anger. I stare at her, with her perfectly groomed black hair and expertly made-up face, touching my mother's shoulder. She looks so concerned. My mother looks so sad. All of it due to me. Because they think I'm crazy.

When my mother returns to the living room, I keep my eyes locked on the vase Dr. Jain seemed to admire, pretending not to see the wary way she approaches me.

"Kaylee, I know you're upset that I called Dr. Jain. But I didn't know what else to do. I'm scared."

She pauses. Then, "Kaylee," she repeats, taking another step. But she stops, leaving a gap between us. "I don't know what's going on with you and this website, and with the grave in our front yard and that girl's death, but I'm worried. With

DJ still recovering from his recent illness and everything else that's going on, I've decided we're going to leave town. Aunt Susan has been asking us to visit. I'm going to call her and tell her we're coming today."

"What?" Leave. Today. Leave it all behind. NEED. The ridicule. Amanda's death. Everything that has happened and whatever is going to happen next. Because something will. And I'm glad I won't be here to see it. I tried my best to end the network. What happens next won't be my fault. "Okay," I say, feeling the hum of anxiety inside me fade. "I'll go pack."

"There's no need for you to pack." Mom's shoulders straighten as she looks me square in the eyes. "DJ and I are going alone. His doctor told me he has to avoid stress."

I take a step back and bite my lip.

Me. I'm the stress she thinks my brother needs to avoid.

I can't speak. I can't breathe. I thought I felt alone before. Wrong again.

"I'll take DJ to Aunt Susan's today and stay over with him tonight to make sure he's settled. Tomorrow, I'll come back and we can talk. Dr. Jain thinks having some time alone to think about the things you've done will be good for you."

"You don't believe me." There are more important things to talk about, but for some reason those are the only words that come out.

"I don't know what to believe." The words bring tears to her eyes and I wish I could turn back time to when we were whole. Before DJ got sick and Dad left. Before she stopped wanting to love me and I tried my hardest to stop caring. But as much as I want to hate her, I can't. "After everything that's happened, it's hard to know," she adds.

My fault. Maybe not all of it, but most of it. Had I not lied about my father, the emails, and the Craigslist posting, or faked illness after illness in order to gain access to the school medical files, I wouldn't be in this position now. No one believes the child who cries wolf. Not even her mother.

"You're leaving me."

"DJ—"

"I know DJ needs to be protected. He needs to be safe. But what about me?" Please, don't leave me behind.

"Kaylee, you have to understand—"

"Oh, I do. DJ comes first. DJ always comes first. What about me?"

"DJ is sick. And if it weren't for you he might already have a donor. But you had to cause problems and make us outcasts in this town. Instead of letting me handle things, you wanted to be a hero and you made things so much worse. By making everything public and allowing our actions to be scrutinized, you've demonstrated that you can't be trusted. Because of that, it's been impossible for me to do the things I need to do."

"What things?" She has to be lying. She's been doing nothing to help. Nothing. "What did you need to do and why didn't you tell me what you were doing?" If she is telling the truth, she should have told me her plans.

"If you stay home and stay out of trouble while I'm gone, I'll discuss it with you tomorrow. No more stunts for attention or calls to the police. I need you to show me that you can be trusted . . . Otherwise, we might have to take other steps."

"Steps? What steps?"

"Dr. Jain thinks there are some treatments that could help you. I'm hoping that you'll show both of us that they won't be necessary, and now is a good time to start." She sighs. "Stay home. Stay out of trouble, and we'll talk about everything when I get back. Okay?"

Okay? No. Nothing is okay. My mother is leaving me behind. Not as a punishment, but because she thinks I'm a danger to my brother. It's NEED that scared him. NEED could inflict more harm. I clench my hands at my sides and think about what it would be like if DJ were here and something worse did happen. He'll be safer if he's taken away from here. No matter what my mother thinks, I want him safe. Because of that, I don't cry or scream or demand to be taken with them. DJ matters to me, too, which is why I choke out, "Sure, Mom."

"Good." She turns and walks out of the room without a backward glance. My legs tremble and I sink to the floor, too numb to cry. To be angry. To be anything. My mother is leaving me behind, which shouldn't surprise me, because didn't she do that long ago? This just makes it official.

I hear my brother yell that he can't find his high-tops and he needs them. Mom yells back at him to look in his closet and to hurry because she wants to get on the road as soon as possible. My phone dings and I automatically pull it out of my pocket even though I don't care what the message says.

But when I read Nate's text, I do care, and I'm no longer angry and hurt. I'm scared.

Bryan

IT'S BACK. NEED is back. Why did it have to come back? It was gone. It should be gone.

Bryan had been relieved when it suddenly disappeared. It felt like a sign. It seemed as if someone was telling him that a gun wasn't the answer. With NEED gone, no one would ever have to know about the box he delivered or his reason for doing it.

Now the site is up and running again and the picture he posted is available for all to see. Everyone will know because he can't delete it. He hits Delete again, hoping for a different result, and cringes as the same message box appears.

THIS ACTION CANNOT BE COMPLETED. ALL
UPLOADS AND POSTS TO THE NEED NETWORK ARE
THE PROPERTY OF NEED ACCORDING TO THE TERMS
AND CONDITIONS OF THE SITE.

There is no going back.
He scrolls through the posts. Most are brainless, silly, or

both. Of course, his mother would tell him not to throw stones since his own house is made of glass. She's always saying things like that. But the brainless, silly posts aren't the only things on the site. There's the picture he posted of Amanda's doorstep that he is powerless to erase. The photo of what looks like a grave in the snow. The driver's license and birth certificate of someone named Marcus Jameson. Pictures of suggestive and even sexually graphic notes and barely veiled threats. And one photo that he can't look away from because of the blood. So much blood.

A few people commented on that one.

This is just nasty.

Blood is awesome. I hope you rubbed it all over you.

Is this supposed to scare me? Because I know it isn't real. Duh.

Sick! You're sick and I can't believe we go to the same school. When I find out who you are I'm going to punch you in the face.

You need to watch more horror films. This is the worst fake blood ever.

Yeah—this is totally a fake. Ugh. Someone needs to get a life.

But it isn't fake. He can't tell exactly what died, but something did. Like Amanda. Only he didn't mean to kill her. He didn't. He didn't know. Whoever did this knew. That makes it worse than what he did. And it's certainly worse than what he still has to do.

Bryan clicks back to his profile page and reads the fulfillment requirement one more time. He knows he doesn't have to do it. Not unless he really wants the gun.

Does he?

He thinks of putting the gun in his mouth and pulling the trigger. He's not brave enough to do it another way. He hates blood and pain and he's not sure he could make himself take more than a couple of pills before losing his nerve. But with a gun—maybe. He might have the courage to pull the trigger. No more feeling like he's not good enough. No more wishing his parents would understand. No more living with Amanda's death and the things that led up to it.

He can always change his mind. Can't he? And if he does, he'll have the gun for protection. He thinks about the blood in the photograph. Real. Totally real. There is a good chance that someone he knows did that. What will happen if that same person is sent here to his house and he doesn't have a means of defending himself and his family?

Somewhere inside, he knows he should tell his parents. But to do that he will have to confess to his part in Amanda's death. They might not believe he didn't intend to kill her. They'll hate him. They'll call the police. He'll be arrested and everyone will know.

He can't let them know. Because once they know what he's done they'll hate him just as much as he hates himself. And living with that will be worse than living with Amanda's death.

"Bryan, honey?" The door opens. He closes the laptop lid as his mother enters. She gives him one of those smiles that are designed to cover her worry. "I just wanted to see how you're doing. You know . . . after this morning."

When she came to tell him breakfast was ready, she found him looking at the messages on Amanda's Facebook page. He told her that Amanda had died and his mother held him while he cried. He'd thought about telling her more, but he chickened out. He can't tell her now, either. He is such a coward.

"I'm still trying to accept what happened."

His mom walks over and puts her hands on his shoulders. "Amanda's death is a shock to the whole town. You don't get over those kinds of things right away. Especially not when the person matters to you."

She did matter. It was because she did that he's willing to do what he's now been asked to do.

His mom presses a kiss to the top of his head and gives his shoulders a squeeze. "We're downstairs if you need us. Just remember, something like this takes time to deal with. Give yourself time."

"How much time?" Bryan asks. Because he can't imagine a time when the heavy darkness will lift.

His mom brushes her hand against his cheek. "It's different for everyone. But when you're sad and the walls feel like they're closing in, I want you to remember that the only way to get out of the tunnel is through it. You'll get through this, Bryan." And with a quiet "I love you" and a reminder that he's welcome to join his family downstairs, she slips into the hall and closes the door behind her.

Bryan's heart pounds loudly as he replays in his mind the events of the last twenty-four hours and the words his mother just spoke. To get to the end of this tunnel, he has to go through it. Which means there is only one path for him to take.

Slowly, Bryan reopens the lid of his laptop, types in his password, and rereads the instructions. He makes several phone calls to friends to gather some information. And he realizes that while being a nerd has made him a social outcast, it now will be an advantage. No one will anticipate what he's about to do.

NETWORK MEMBERS—688
NEEDS PENDING—684
NEEDS FULFILLED—210

Kaylee

I CLUTCH MY PHONE as I say goodbye to my brother, who is both excited to be visiting Aunt Susan and bummed that I'm not going too. The moment he told my mother he wouldn't leave if I didn't come almost broke me in two. And because I love him more than anything, I said Nate would keep me company until they returned. But I try to catch my mother's eye because I want to talk to her without DJ knowing. I have to.

"But what if the person who dug the hole in the snow comes back while we're gone?" DJ asks, picking up his duffel bag.

"They're not going to," I say, trying to sound more sure than I feel. Because they might and I don't want to be here if that happens.

"Don't worry, honey," my mother says, handing my brother his coat. "I'll be texting Kaylee every hour to make sure she's okay. And you can text her too, if it makes you feel better. Deal?"

He thinks about it and then smiles. "Deal."

Mom grabs her coat and tells DJ to get in the car. He lets me hug him before disappearing outside. When the door closes behind him, I say, "Mom, please let me come with you. I promise I won't cause trouble or say anything that will upset DJ, but—"

"We talked about this, Kaylee. You said you'd stay here."

"But something has happened since then. The website . . . If you'll just wait for one minute I can prove that I'm telling the truth. Just one minute. Please." I don't wait for her to agree. I race up the stairs and grab my laptop, hoping that Nate isn't wrong and that the website is back up. Or . . .

"Kaylee, we're going. You can show me tomorrow," she yells as I race down the hall and the stairs. I hear a door slam.

"Mom. Wait! Please." I hear the garage door open, and in another moment the car engine is running. They're about to leave.

I race to the front door and jerk it open, still holding my laptop, as my mom backs the car out of the garage. As I start to yell for her not to go, DJ rolls down his window and waves. "Don't forget to text me!"

I look at his face and the words of protest die on my lips. DJ is what matters.

"I won't," I say, forcing myself to lift my free arm and wave.

"Say hi to Nate for me," DJ yells as the car disappears down the street. I walk back into the house, go to my room, and put the laptop back on the desk. I want to feel safe. It's been forever since I felt safe. Whatever medication or treatment Dr. Jain might want to prescribe won't help with that, but getting rid of NEED will at least be a start. Because if I don't expose

NEED and what it is doing to this town, my mother will always think I was lying and I might never feel safe again. It's the only way.

I mistype my password three times before slowing down enough to log on. The email Nate told me about sits in my inbox. No. There are two. The first message, with the new link to NEED, was sent to everyone on the network. The second . . . is only for me.

DEAR KAYLEE,
    WE HAVE BECOME AWARE THAT YOU HAVE
VIOLATED PART THREE OF THE TERMS AND
CONDITIONS OF YOUR NEED MEMBERSHIP. YOUR
CALL TO THE NOTTAWA POLICE DEPARTMENT
THIS MORNING AND YOUR DISCUSSION OF THE
WEBSITE WITH NONMEMBERS IS UNACCEPTABLE
AND MAKES YOU SUBJECT TO TERMINATION,
IN REGARD BOTH TO YOUR MEMBERSHIP AND TO
PENDING NEED REQUESTS. HOWEVER, SINCE YOUR
NEED REQUEST IS CURRENTLY IN THE PROCESS
OF BEING FULFILLED AND THERE IS NO CERTAIN
METHOD OF TERMINATING THAT FULFILLMENT, WE
ARE NOT GOING TO CANCEL YOUR MEMBERSHIP
AT THIS TIME. BUT WE ARE WATCHING.
ANOTHER VIOLATION OF THE MEMBERSHIP TERMS
AND CONDITIONS WILL RESULT IN REMOVING
THE ABILITY TO VIOLATE THAT AGREEMENT—
PERMANENTLY.
    WE HOPE YOU WILL NOT GIVE US CAUSE TO

ENFORCE THIS PENALTY. IT IS NOT WHAT WE
WANT. HOWEVER, AS WE ALL KNOW, THERE IS A
DIFFERENCE BETWEEN A WANT AND A NEED.
    REGARDS,
    THE NEED TEAM

Shivering, I wrap my arms around myself and read the words again. Even though I know what term it is that I violated, I click on the new NEED site link and search for the exact wording.

3. WE RESPECT YOUR RIGHT TO ANONYMITY AND
WE EXPECT YOU TO DO THE SAME FOR US AND
OTHERS.

- YOU WILL NOT POST CONTENT OR TAKE ANY AC-
  TION THAT LEADS TO YOUR OWN PROFILE IDEN-
  TIFICATION OR THE IDENTIFICATION OF AN-
  OTHER'S PROFILE.
- ALL POSTS BECOME THE PROPERTY OF NEED AND
  CAN BE DELETED AT OUR DISCRETION.
- IF YOU VIOLATE THE ANONYMITY OF THIS SITE
  TO ANYONE WHO DOES NOT BELONG TO NEED,
  YOUR ACCOUNT IS SUBJECT TO TERMINATION.
- ANY REPORTS OF ANONYMITY VIOLATIONS OF
  AN INDIVIDUAL PROFILE OR THE SITE ITSELF
  WILL BE INVESTIGATED AND IMMEDIATE ACTION
  TAKEN.
- IF WE DISABLE YOUR PROFILE OR DEEM YOU IN

VIOLATION OF THE ANONYMITY CLAUSE THERE
IS NO APPEAL. ACCOUNTS ONCE TERMINATED
ARE TERMINATED PERMANENTLY.

Permanently.

That word fills me with dread.

I scroll up to the top of the Terms and Conditions and read all of them.

Privacy is important to NEED. That is clear by the time I am done reading all ten sections. Not just privacy for users but for NEED itself. Equally clear is the message that it owns all content. That rule is cloaked in nonthreatening terms, but if you read carefully, you can see that the network can lay claim to everything a user adds to the site. That is sinister enough, but the final term is the most telling.

10. ALL USERS OF NEED ARE RESPONSIBLE
FOR THEIR OWN ACTIONS. NEED FULFILLMENT
REQUESTS ARE NOT MANDATORY. NO USER
WILL BE COMPELLED TO PERFORM ANY ACT
WITH WHICH THEY FEEL UNCOMFORTABLE. BY
ACCEPTING MEMBERSHIP AND AGREEING TO THESE
CONDITIONS, THE NEED USER ABSOLVES THE
NEED NETWORK AND OPERATORS FROM ANY AND ALL
RESPONSIBILITY FOR ACTIONS TAKEN OUTSIDE
OF THE NEED NETWORK. THE ONLY PERSON
RESPONSIBLE FOR YOUR ACTIONS IS YOU.

When I created my account, I didn't read the Terms and Conditions. I just clicked the button that said I accepted them.

After all, aren't they always the same? Does anyone ever read them? Clearly not, since all the people I go to school with joined this site. I have to wonder if they would have cared even if they had read the so-called fine print. With Nate pushing me to join and the anonymity the site dangled, I would have still accepted.

I'm startled when my cell phone signals I have a text. Since my mother has only been gone for ten minutes, I assume it's Nate telling me he's going to be late. But the message is from a number I don't recognize and when I read it, I know why.

The Terms and Conditions are clear, Kaylee. We'll be watching.

"Hey."

I scream. I can't help it. The sound rips from my throat and I push back my chair and spring to my feet even as I recognize the voice. Nate.

"What the hell?" I yell. "Why didn't you knock or ring the bell or something?"

"Sorry," Nate says, even though his smirk says he isn't. "I tried the bell. It didn't work, and I figured if you were up here you couldn't hear me knocking, either. Since your message said DJ and your mom left and I knew you were around somewhere, I used the spare key. And I have to tell you, I'm glad I did. That scream was awesome. Better than any of the movies we've watched."

I'm being threatened by NEED and Nate is casting me as the girl who gets axed in a horror film. This is just perfect.

"Hey." Nate tucks his hands in his jacket pockets and his smile fades. "I really am sorry I freaked you out. I should have texted you to let you know I was here. I wasn't thinking. Are you okay? Did something else happen? Is someone else . . . hurt?"

"No." At least, I don't think so. I could be wrong, though. Something scary might just have been posted on NEED's message board. "But there's this."

I pull up the email and then shift to the side so Nate can sit down and read it. When he's done, I hand him my phone with the text message.

"This is whacked. DJ and your mother left town, didn't they?"

I nod, not admitting that staying wasn't my choice.

"Well then, there's nothing that NEED can do to them now. That's one less thing to worry about."

"Maybe." I want to believe that my not being with them will keep DJ safe. Otherwise, I've been abandoned for no reason.

"You're still worried about DJ?"

"Wouldn't you be if he were your brother?"

"If Jack was in danger of getting roughed up I'd make popcorn and ask for a front-row seat. Or maybe not." Nate pulls off his knitted hat and throws it on my bed. "Jack wasn't his normal, arrogant self today. He even apologized after bumping into me as I was leaving to come here. Something must have gotten into him."

"Something like NEED?" I ask. "Do you think the site asked him to do something he's not comfortable with?"

Nate laughs. "It would take a lot to make my brother uncomfortable."

"Like what?"

The amusement fades. "Jack isn't all that concerned about other people's feelings. Not when they get in the way of something he wants. It would have to be something pretty major to make him act squirrelly."

I think of the cookies that killed Amanda. Did the person who put them at her door know how deadly the gift was? I doubt it. Nate's right. His brother gets off on being a big shot and making other people feel small. If he's having second thoughts about the fulfillment request he was given . . .

"I should call Officer Shepens again."

"Do you think he'll listen to you? This morning didn't exactly go well. And now you know NEED really is watching. You don't want to do something to tick them off if you aren't certain the cops are going to help."

"The site is up and running again."

"And who knows how long that will last. It went down once already. The last thing you want is to call Officer Shepens and have the site go down again. You need to have some way of proving what NEED is doing, and I have an idea." Nate shrugs out of his coat. "Do you mind if I use your laptop for a sec?"

I get out of the way as Nate slides behind the keyboard.

Clicking from one screen to the next, he explains, "Jack is being weird and the chances are good that he's been given a NEED fulfillment request he's not wild about. If we can find out what that request is and report it, Officer Shepens can monitor my brother and catch him in the act. We'll be able to expose NEED, bust my brother, and prove that we're telling the truth all in one fell swoop. And since I used my brother's account to send myself an invite, I know his profile code. He uses the same password for everything he does online. I'll just log on as Jack, go to his profile page, and . . . What the hell is this?"

A message box with red block writing appears on the screen.

THE ACCOUNT YOU ARE ATTEMPTING TO LOG ON
TO IS NOT AUTHORIZED FOR THIS IP ADDRESS.
TO ACCESS NEED, USE THE VALID ACCOUNT
INFORMATION THAT WAS CREATED ON THIS
COMPUTER. IF YOU FEEL YOU HAVE RECEIVED
THIS MESSAGE IN ERROR, CONTACT THE NEED
TEAM AND WE WILL ATTEMPT TO ASSIST YOU.

"I don't get it." Nate closes the message box and returns to the Login screen. Less than a minute later the same error message is displayed and Nate turns to face me. "I just tried to log on to my account but it won't let me. I was able to get into my account from this computer before. They must have updated the system when it was down earlier."

"Why?" I read the message again, wishing I knew computers better. Mostly, I use them to surf the Internet, do my homework, and answer email. "IP address. That's like a serial number or something?"

"Sort of," Nate says as he pulls out his phone and taps on the screen. "Except a serial number is just for ID purposes. Depending on what kind it is, it can identify the owner or where the computer was manufactured, but that's about it. An IP address not only gives information about what kind of machine it is, but when you're on the Web, people can use an IP to track the computer to its physical address. Oh hell. Look." He holds out his phone so I can see the same message from my monitor displayed on the small screen. "I can't log on to NEED from my phone. It looks like they've updated the system to only allow users to connect from the device the account was created on. That's just weird. Most social media sites want users to be able to access their account and post from any location. That's how NEED operated before."

But no longer. Maybe because NEED isn't about social interaction. At least, not the kind we're used to. It's about something different. I don't know what that is, but whatever its purpose, I'm pretty sure the change in login and the new inability to see other users' profiles is a way to hide whatever is coming.

"Can you move for a minute?" I ask. "I want to log back on to my account."

Letting out a frustrated sigh, Nate pushes back the chair and stands, giving me room to sit. I type my account information and password. When the NEED screen appears, I scroll down the message board, looking for anything that might give a clue as to what's going on.

The picture of the bakery box on Amanda's front step is missing. So is the one of our front yard. But there are others. Photographs of a broken mailbox, a snow-covered shed, and a car tire that is well and truly flat. Each photograph must represent some act that a NEED member performed, but it's impossible to say what effects the acts might have had or who was behind them, so I keep scrolling until I suddenly stop.

Blood.

"That can't possibly be real?" Nate asks, leaning over my shoulder. "Can it?"

"I don't know." I don't want to know. My stomach heaves. "You're the horror movie expert, Nate. What do you think?"

Does the blood-soaked snow look too red to be real? Do the bits of flesh and bone and fur (Is that brown fur?) look like something a person could pick up in a store?

"It has to be fake." But he doesn't sound so sure.

"Why?" I swivel my chair and turn my back on the screen.

"Because it's the only thing that makes sense. The whole point of creating these kinds of sites is to cash in. Start small. Build a big network and then sell advertising and harvested data you collect from all the users who are posting cat pictures and relationship crap."

Nate would know. He spends way more time than I do on social networking sites. For me, they're tools. A method for me to try to track down my father and a way to remind people that DJ needs help. Not that either has really worked. But it's better than doing nothing. Nate, however, loves watching how the people we know behave online. He says it's the only way to see someone's true nature. It's a fairly simple choice to be nice to someone who's right in front of you. After all, as Nate says, why risk a punch in the face if you don't have to? But online there's an invisible shield that Nate claims allows people to feel protected from the consequences of their actions. Because of that, they stop behaving like they are supposed to and instead do what they want. No matter who they upset or hurt.

"What's your point?" I ask as Nate's eyes remain latched on the grisly photograph with a strange intensity.

"My point is that no one would put that much time and energy into a potentially hot new social networking site if they weren't interested in a big payoff. And the only way someone rakes in the cash is if they rack up the number of users and keep the users coming back for more. Making users do things like that . . . It just doesn't make sense."

"Unless this network isn't about making money. I mean, really, think about the money the site has to be losing." I navigate to the screen with the NEED fulfillment counter.

```
NETWORK MEMBERS—688
NEEDS PENDING—685
NEEDS FULFILLED—214
```

"Someone has already spent a lot of money. If the site grew bigger, they'd have to spend a whole lot more." Certainly more money than they could make back any time soon. Maybe they could change the rules about what kinds of . . .

Wait. I look at the numbers on the screen again and suddenly I can't breathe. "Nate." My voice is thin. "Didn't you say the whole purpose of a social networking site is to get as many users as it can?"

"Yeah."

"And we've learned that once you create an account you can't delete it."

"Which isn't unlike a lot of the other sites out there. They claim you can erase your profile, but it never really goes away. Which is disturbing, but I don't understand why you're talking about it now."

"Because if no one can delete their profile, then the number of users should always stay the same or go up. Right?"

"Yeah. So?"

Blood pounds loudly in my ears as I think back to this morning, before I called the police. Before NEED shut down and updated its site. "So, Nate, the number of users has gone down."

Gina

"I DON'T KNOW how it happened, Jim. The car was fine this morning."

Gina slowly creeps down the hall outside the kitchen and rolls her eyes at the familiar argument. Her father loves to scream about every dent and ding in the car, and her mother automatically protests that it wasn't her fault. Then, after several minutes, Mom apologizes profusely and Dad goes off to watch football. Her mother always ends up being the one who says "Sorry." Mom says that being right isn't everything and you can get more bees with honey than with vinegar or some crap like that. Well, from the sound of it, Mom is going to need to dump a hell of a lot of honey on Dad. And it better happen soon because Gina has somewhere to be, and standing around bundled up like a mummy in this coat and scarf is starting to make her sweat.

"Well, it's not fine now," Gina's dad yells. "How the hell can something like that happen and you not know about it?"

"The car was fine when I got home from the store. I would have noticed if it hadn't been when I took the groceries out of the trunk. Did you leave the garage door open after you got home?"

"You think this is my fault?"

Gina shakes her head as she inches toward the side door.

"I don't know whose fault it is, Jim. Gina's been grounded from driving, but maybe she snuck the keys again."

Hey, that's not fair. It wasn't her. She's pissed as her father yells her name and orders her to come to the kitchen.

Now what? Stay and deny that she had anything to do with the car? Or leave? The choice is easy. She opens the back door and slips outside. The minute the door closes behind her she runs, feeling angrier with every step. How could her parents automatically think that she had anything to do with whatever happened to her mother's ugly car? Parents are supposed to be on your side. Hers missed that memo.

Gina ignores the ringing that comes from her cell deep in her coat pocket next to the bottle she found tucked into a small box on her windowsill. Shivering, she slows her pace and turns up the driveway of a brown house decked out in blue and white twinkly lights. When the front door opens, she smiles.

"Hey, I hope you don't mind that I'm early. Ever since I learned about Amanda I haven't been able to even watch TV without crying. I thought I could help you set up for the memorial thing. At least then I'd be doing something useful."

Lynn is happy to let her in. Lynn is one of the younger cheerleaders. She looks up to Gina and she probably wasn't sure who would come when she sent out an email about hosting a gathering to deal with Amanda's death. She asks Gina for her coat but Gina begs off. "I'll just keep it for a little while until I warm up. My parents didn't have time to drive me over, so I walked. It's really cold outside."

Lynn's parents are happy to see Gina too. They don't suspect a thing when she helps them put out bottles of soda and large plastic cups and then asks to use the bathroom. Her fingers are unsteady as she opens the door of the medicine cabinet and sees the Tylenol bottle on the middle shelf. Just where NEED told her it would be.

Hannah

HANNAH FROWNS at her reflection. The makeup has helped re-move most of the evidence of her tears. But no matter how much eyeliner and waterproof mascara she uses, her eyes still look tired and her face, washed-out. Maybe she should change her sweater. Amanda would have been able to tell her what color would be best. Amanda always knew.

Tears that Hannah has been working to keep at bay spill over.

"This sucks." She swipes at her cheek and ignores the ache at the base of her skull. Amanda would have been upset that Hannah has been crying all day. She didn't like tears or sad things. Every time they watched a movie, Amanda insisted on a romantic comedy. Something with a happily ever after. Amanda would have approved of what Hannah is doing to-night, though, including not telling her parents more than they need to know. They already said Hannah could go out. There's no reason to tell them that her destination has changed.

Crap. Whoever said this makeup is waterproof is dead wrong. Grabbing a tissue, Hannah dabs at the smears under her eyes and walks to her closet.

She puts on a fitted, deep green top with a V-neck that always elicits a raised eyebrow from her father. But it isn't as low as the tops he sees a lot of girls wear at school, so he never says anything. Hannah knows he would break that silence if she told him she was meeting a guy instead of going to the Amanda memorial, but what he doesn't know won't hurt him.

She checks her phone and looks at the text she received an hour ago.

Hey. It's Nate. Jack gave me the message. Are you okay? Which is irrelevant to ask because I know you aren't. If you need to talk, I'm here for you. Maybe we can get together the two of us? I hate thinking of you going through this alone. Oh—and this is a new phone. My parents don't know about it, so text me. Don't call.

A couple of texts later and she had a date with the boy she's been crushing on all year.

"Hannah, honey?"

"I'll be down in five minutes, Mom," Hannah calls, snagging a hoodie off the end of her bed. No point in having her father see the green shirt and ask unnecessary questions.

She glosses her lips pink, looks in the mirror again. She still looks sad, but Nate will understand. She knows he will, because he already understands how much she needs to be with him—with someone who gets what she's going through. Now she just has to do one small thing so they can be alone.

Hannah takes a last look in the mirror and heads down the hall to her parents' bedroom. The shouts she hears from downstairs tell her a video game competition is under way. The keys are in the middle drawer of her father's nightstand. The code to the security system is written on a yellow sticky note affixed to the inside page of her father's journal. Her father has a terrible memory, which is why he always carries the journal with him when there's a chance he'll need to turn the alarm on or off at school.

After sliding the yellow note and the keys into her purse, Hannah hurries downstairs. She doesn't want to keep Nate waiting.

Her mother volunteers to drive her to Lynn's. "The snow is really starting to come down," she says.

"Thanks, but if it's okay, I kind of want to walk. I think the air will help me feel better." Lynn's house is in the opposite direction from where Hannah has to go. But if her mother insists on driving, she'll just take the ride and let Nate know she'll be late.

The sympathy in her mom's face makes Hannah want to cry again. "Are you sure?"

Hannah nods and swallows back the tears that are fighting to escape.

"Okay. But text me the minute you get there."

Before her mom can change her mind, Hannah pulls on her boots, bundles into her thick purple coat, and tugs on her mittens. She carefully puts on her hat so her hair won't totally stand on end when she takes the hat off, and she wraps a scarf around her face. Her mom gives her a big hug and tells her to call when she's ready to be picked up from Lynn's. "I love you, Hannah," she yells as Hannah opens the door.

Hannah looks back toward the foyer, where her mother stands in her sweatshirt and fuzzy red and white socks. The sound of laughter rings from the family room at the back of the house, along with someone shouting "You cheated!" And for a minute, Hannah wants nothing more than to stay here with her mom and her family. But she only has to think of Nate waiting for her and she is yelling a careless "Love you too" as she races outdoors into the snow.

When the school comes into sight, her teeth are chattering and she's covered with snow, which is falling more heavily than it was when she left the house. A car is headed down the road and her heart leaps as she peers through the white flurry, hoping to see Nate behind the wheel. But the car doesn't slow down.

Tired of the cold, she runs toward the door to the building nearest the gymnasium, where she told Nate she could get them inside. Nate is nowhere to be seen. Disappointment swirls hot and fast, but she tamps it down. *Nate will be here,* she thinks, and when she checks her phone she knows she's not just fooling herself.

Running late. Kaylee needed help. Go inside out of the cold. I'll be there soon. —Nate.

Ugh. Kaylee. For the last year, Hannah was sure Nate was hung up on Kaylee Dunham. Why? She had no idea. It's not like Kaylee's funny or especially smart or sexy. Although Hannah wishes she had the olive skin that makes Kaylee look tanned even in the winter. Whatever the reason, Nate always defends Kaylee and hangs out with her at lunch even though everyone else has written her off. And there's something about the way he talks to her . . .

But he has assured her that he and Kaylee are just friends, and now he's on his way to meet Hannah so they can have their first official date. Hannah uses a penlight to key in the security code and breathes a sigh of relief as the light on the code pad goes from red to green. Quickly she unlocks the door, steps inside, and sends her mother a message to say she arrived safe and sound. Now all Hannah needs is Nate.

She shakes off the snow and paces the dark hall, too scared of getting caught to turn on a light. The dark will be romantic when Nate gets here, but he's not here and the small penlight is barely enough to help her find the drinking fountain. Maybe she should freshen up just in case he brings a better light and will be able to see her face.

A metal click makes her smile. The door opens and she can see the outline of Nate as he walks through the door. He's here. Amanda would have told her to play hard to get and make him come to her. But she can't help it. She rushes toward him.

"I'm so glad you made it. It's kind of spooky in this place without the lights on. But I have this."

She shines the light on the floor to make sure she doesn't stumble, and she smiles as he unwraps the scarf that covers his face. Then she sees the knife and screams.

Kaylee

"DOGS," I SAY as Nate walks back into the room, bringing the smell of melted cheese and tomato sauce with him. While he's been waiting by the front door for the pizza he ordered that took forever due to the snow, I've been searching other social media sites for more information about the things NEED has asked people to do. I haven't eaten in hours, but after what I've seen I don't have much of an appetite.

"What?" he asks, setting the large box and stack of napkins on the floor.

"The photograph with all the blood. Mrs. Markham's three dogs are dead." They were beagles, although what was done to them makes it impossible to tell in the photograph. I try to picture Mrs. Markham, but as much as I know I must have met her or seen her walking her dogs, I can't. For some reason that bothers me just as much as the blood and gore. "Something or someone attacked them."

"Wow." Nate runs a hand through his hair. "I guess we can

rule out an animal attack. Unless, of course, the animal has learned to upload pictures to the Internet. I know it's terrible to say, but I'm glad it's dogs and not another person. After Amanda, it feels like anything is possible. You know?"

I know.

"There's more." I push the image of the mangled flesh out of my head. Which is easier than it should be because there are other pictures to take its place.

"More?" Nate blinks. "What kind of more?"

"A bunch of people online are talking about Mrs. Frey getting arrested. She got into a fistfight with Lisa Jackson."

"Pastor Frey's wife decked Ms. Jackson?"

Ms. Jackson teaches first grade. Her husband died last summer in a boating accident. I remember helping my mother make cookies to take to Ms. Jackson's house on the other side of town. Ms. Jackson is petite and fragile. The opposite of Mrs. Frey, with her big broad shoulders and accusing eyes that pass judgment on everything they see—especially me. She enjoys thinking she's better than everyone else. Better manners. Better family. Better everything. The look in her eyes might tell someone she wants to hit them, but the Bible in her hands says she would never stoop to the devil's level. Which is why everyone online is abuzz with her actions.

"Mrs. Frey screamed at Ms. Jackson, slapped her, and pulled her hair all in the middle of a prayer meeting. From the sounds of it, Ms. Jackson didn't just sit back and wait to get rescued either. She fought back."

"Good for her. I can't say I'm sorry Mrs. Frey is hanging out in jail."

Neither can I. But I can't feel good about it either. Or about all the relationship status changes that I've noticed since Nate's last visit. Mostly, I roll my eyes when I see one of my classmates publicize his or her her dating issues on social media, if I look at all. Unless I'm searching for my father, I typically avoid all of the social media sites. But today I was looking for anything out of the ordinary, which is why I noticed the twelve who made the change from *In a Relationship* to *Single*. I can't help but wonder what circumstances prompted those posts or the other disgruntled updates.

"That's not all," I say as Nate grabs a slice of pizza and offers it to me. I shake my head, and start telling him about the break-ups and the other posts that could be connected to NEED. A missing cat. Shredded holiday decorations. Garbage strewn across the snow. A broken lock on someone's back door. All things that could be blamed on wild animals or a prank gone wrong. But the photos of the broken farmhouse mailbox, the tipped garbage cans, and official-looking papers filled with numbers posted on NEED tell me that there are other forces at work. Thankfully, I haven't found a picture of a dead cat. There's still hope the animal is huddled under a porch, waiting out the snow. I cling to that idea, wanting desperately to think that something is normal.

"Wow." Nate shoves the last of his pizza slice into his mouth and pulls his phone out of his pocket. He looks at the screen, shakes his head, and puts the phone back in his pocket.

"What's wrong?" I ask. As if everything isn't wrong.

He swallows and shrugs. "Jack keeps asking where I am, which is just strange. I mean, he normally couldn't care less what I'm doing. But I've gotten six texts in the last two hours. He's asked if I'm with you or at Lynn's for the Amanda memorial or whether I want to catch a movie. This last one says Mom is looking for me."

"Maybe she is."

Nate grabs another piece of pizza. "Mom has her own phone. Trust me. If she wanted me home, she wouldn't be counting on Jack to get the job done. Whatever Jack is up to, I'm sure Mom doesn't know about it. And if everything you've seen online is true, I'm going to guess the bug up Jack's butt has to do with NEED. The question is how to get Jack to expose what he's up to so we can call the cops on him and bust everything wide open without NEED knowing you had anything to do with it."

"Don't worry about me."

"You can't stop me from worrying." He puts down the pizza and leans toward me. "And now that I really think about it, maybe we have to just let the cops figure this out on their own and stay on the sidelines. You got a warning. NEED wants you to back off. You know me, I'd normally take that kind of message as a challenge, but after seeing what's going on . . ." He reaches out for my hand and wraps his fingers tightly around mine. "I don't want anything to happen to you."

I can't breathe as his hand tightens its grip. The sarcastic humor is gone. The self-deprecation. I don't know what to say. I didn't yesterday. I don't today. But instead of the haze of confusion, this time his words make me feel safe. I still don't know if I'm ready for us to be more than friends, but Nate isn't giving me space to decide as he kisses me.

I wait for whatever I should be feeling. Excitement. Attraction. Whatever a kiss between us should bring. But all I feel is wooden and inept, wishing I knew how to respond to this, because I'm certain that in this moment something has changed that can never be changed back.

He presses me close. Then suddenly he leans back to look into my face. More than anything I want to look anywhere but at him. But there is no point in trying to pretend Nate didn't kiss me. So before he can crack a joke or something, I say, "I don't understand."

"What's to understand? I kissed you." Nate rolls his eyes and shrugs as if amused. But I can see the hurt under his composure.

"I figured out that part. What I don't understand is why."

Nate shoves his hands into his pockets. "You're not all that bright. You know that, right?" His smile takes the sting out of his words. "You think I should be interested in Hannah or Lynn?"

That would make more sense than this.

"Hannah and Lynn only like me because they think they know me. They don't. No one does, except you." The smile fades. "You know what my house is like. Jack comes first. Even when he's screwing up he's king. It's always been that way. I'm popular because Jack's popular. People just assume I'm like him. They don't bother to look beneath the surface and see that I couldn't care less about the things they do. You're the only one who sees me for who I am. And maybe I should have left it at that. I told myself I would. Now I'm worried I totally screwed things up. Did I?"

Yes. Maybe. I don't know. Excitement mixes with the confusion and worry, making it hard to know what I feel. Aren't the best relationships grounded in friendship? And yet, there's something off. Because Nate's right. I know him. And he's not telling the entire truth. So I don't either. "No."

"Are you sure?" When I don't answer immediately, he pulls a crumpled flyer out of his back pocket. "Don't answer that yet. Not until I give you this."

Relieved to be thinking about something other than our kiss, I smooth out the paper and look back at Nate. "You don't want me to miss the drugstore's New Year's blowout sale on Christmas decorations?"

Nate laughs. "Look at the other side."

I flip the page and see Nate's handwriting scrawled across the back. His penmanship is doctor worthy. But this writing is unmistakable despite the hurried scribble. A phone number.

"I'm pretty sure it's your father's."

My father.

I stare at the number and feel my breath catch. Suddenly NEED and the kiss and everything else disappears. All that matters is the hope I hold. "Are you sure? How?"

"I'm just that good." Nate plops down on the bed. "Actually, I can't be one hundred percent sure the number will reach your dad. When I did a reverse search online, it came up as restricted. And no one answered when I called. But I can't imagine Richard Ward would have the number in his phone under your dad's name if it didn't belong to him. Do you agree?"

"You stole Richard Ward's phone?"

"No." Nate grins. "But I'm flattered you think I could. The real story is more luck than anything else." There's a ding and Nate's grin disappears as he fishes his phone out of his pocket. "Jack again. You'd think he could take a hint. Back to my amazing story. Where was I? Oh yeah—I dropped by the drugstore this afternoon and flirted with the airhead Jayleen, who was working the counter." He gives me a questioning look.

"What?"

"Just hoping you might be jealous. Anyway, when I saw someone go into the restroom, I asked her if I could use the one in the office. She said yes. Mr. Ward's phone was on his desk, and the rest is history."

I try not to get too excited. This is what I've been searching for. Months of my life, and here it is. But there's something not quite right about this whole scenario. Or maybe I'm just too used to bad things happening to believe in anything good.

"Mr. Ward just left his phone sitting out on his desk?" The man I've dealt with doesn't strike me as the type to trust his employees.

Nate stares at me for a moment, then says, "The phone was charging. I told you I got lucky."

"And the phone wasn't password protected?"

"What's with all the questions?" Nate slides off the bed and stands. "The number belongs to your father. I thought you might be happy that I got it and you'd want to call him. Do whatever the hell you want with it. I'm out of here."

"Wait." The word bursts out of me and Nate stops in the doorway. "Don't go. I'm grateful. I am. It's just . . ."

"It's just what?"

I look down at the pizza box on the floor and give voice to my deepest fear. "What if he won't talk to me?"

Nate's expression softens. He crosses to me and pulls me close. I lean my head on his shoulder as he says, "Your dad will be happy you found him, Kaylee. The minute he sees your number come up, he'll know how much you've missed him. He was foolish to walk away from you, but he isn't brainless. You know what I mean?" A ding tells me Nate has another message, but he doesn't reach for his phone. He kisses me lightly on the cheek. "Call your father. He'll answer. I promise."

I clutch the flyer in my hand and search Nate's face, wishing I could see the messages he's been getting. Because deep inside Nate's eyes I see conviction and something else. Something tense and guarded. Something that scares me. "Dad hasn't made contact in all these months. How can you be so sure he'll talk now?"

Nate gives me another one of his grins as he takes my phone off the desk and places it in my hand. "Trust me."

I always have. I want to now. But as I plug in the number and wonder what to do next, I see Nate check his own phone and frown. And I realize that while I have trusted him in the past, I no longer do.

Gina

"GINA, HONEY? Are you okay in there?"

Mrs. Head's voice makes Gina jump. How long has she been in the bathroom? "I'm fine. I'll be out in a minute."

There's a pause before Mrs. Head says, "Well, if you need anything else, let me know. We'll be in the kitchen when you're done."

She hears footsteps as Lynn's mom disappears down the hall, and she looks down at the bottle in her hand. Just a simple switch. The pills in her jacket pocket for the ones in the Tylenol bottle in the cabinet. And she has to do it now before Mrs. Head comes back.

Her hand is unsteady as she dumps the Tylenol pills into a small plastic bag she brought with her. Because while there's a chance the pills are harmless, she knows they most likely aren't. But it's not her fault. It isn't. She isn't the one who decided the pills should be placed here. She isn't the one who refused to give her concert tickets the first time around. Lynn or someone in her family must have ticked someone off good to have them screw with her like this. That isn't Gina's fault either.

She jumps as her phone rings, and one of NEED's pills falls to the floor. She gets down on her knees to find it. Damn. There. Behind the toilet.

Yuck.

She grabs the pill, pushes to her feet, and catches her reflection in the mirror—flushed cheeks, sweaty forehead, guilty eyes. No. Her eyes are the same. Everything is the same. This isn't a big deal. She doesn't know what the pills will do. Maybe nothing. Maybe give Lynn a buzz, which she could probably use after Amanda's death. Or maybe Lynn's dad will end up high. He seems nice but stuffy, so seeing him lose some of his perfect soldier posture could be fun. But if they do more . . . or worse . . .

The phone rings again. Her father is calling. He's left several messages and she's sure she knows what they all say. He'll scream that he wants her home this minute to face what she's done.

Anger and indignation burn away the nauseating fear. She knows her father will not believe that she had nothing to do with the car. He won't care that someone else is to blame. She'll be punished, which sucks big. Well, if she's going to be punished, she might as well earn it and the concert tickets, too.

She picks up the Tylenol bottle, drops the last replacement pill into the container, and places it back where she found it in the medicine cabinet. Nothing to it. Then, making sure the bag of the old pills is deep in her coat pocket, she flushes the toilet and splashes some cold water on her forehead.

The concert tickets will be worth it. It's all worth it, she tells herself as she walks out the bathroom door.

"Hi, honey, are you sure you're okay?" Mrs. Head asks as Gina walks into the kitchen. Mrs. H. grabs a tissue out of a box, walks over to Gina, and wipes a tear from her cheek. Gina hadn't realized she was crying. She never cries. But for some reason having Lynn's mother act so nice makes her cry harder.

"Your mom called looking for you. She said your father will be here any minute to pick you up."

"What?" Gina shakes her head. "I don't want to go home." Not now. Not yet. Wait.

A horn honks.

She can't breathe as Mrs. Head calls for Lynn to say goodbye and ushers Gina toward the foyer.

Lynn gives Gina a hug and tells her to come back tonight if she can. Mrs. Head gives her a hug too, presses the tissue into her hand, and opens the front door. But . . . The door closes behind Gina. She's changed her mind. She wants to go back to the bathroom and fix this. The horn honks again.

She thinks about telling the truth. She could confess and give the pills back. But then she'd be punished twice—for the pills and the car—and maybe by NEED for saying too much. NEED might do something to hurt her. What's to stop them?

"Gina, get in the car now."

As she climbs into the front seat, she catches sight of Mrs. Head and Lynn in the living room. They wave at the window as Gina's father puts the car in gear. Another car pulls up. Two people get out as Gina's dad says, "I don't know what the hell is going on with you, but you are going to explain yourself."

The snow is gaining intensity as her father drives down the street.

"Did you hear me, Gina? What the hell is going on with you? You damaged the car. You ran out of the house. What is wrong with you?"

Everything. "Wait. We have to go back." She can't do this.

"You're not going anywhere except home for a very long time."

"But I did something terrible." She grabs his arm and holds on to it. "Please. I have to fix it." She doesn't need the tickets. Not like this. Who needs concert tickets?

"You're damn right you have to fix it." He yanks his arm free and the car swerves and skids as it picks up speed.

"I don't know what the hell you think you're doing, young lady, but wait until we get home—" He turns to look at her and doesn't see the lights. But Gina does. A car. There's another car.

"Stop!" she screams. Her dad screams too as the cars collide. Everything screams. Metal. Her. Her father. Then everything goes quiet.

NETWORK MEMBERS—686
NEEDS PENDING—683
NEEDS FULFILLED—218

Bryan

BRYAN GLANCES at his watch, then back at the house he's been staking out for the past half-hour. NEED's requirement is clear. For Bryan to get what he asked for, this task has to be completed tonight. But it's cold and windy and the snow is getting heavier with each passing minute.

This sucks. It all sucks.

Everyone Bryan talked to, including Jack, gave him the same information about tonight's gathering. Technically, Bryan was on the invitation list. He's supposed to be inside talking about Amanda. Exchanging stories and sharing tears. Remembering her. As if forgetting who she was, what she meant, and what he did is even a possibility. The only way to forget is to get the gun that NEED will provide.

So Bryan stays crouched in the bushes, shivering against the wind, waiting, watching, hoping. For what, he doesn't really know. Doing this seems wrong. But doing nothing seems equally wrong. He wants to talk to someone, but the only person who knows what Bryan is up to is Jack Weakley, and Jack isn't exactly the type to have insightful conversations. Bryan hadn't thought Jack was really capable of holding a conversation at all until he called.

Thinking about Jack, Bryan pulls out his phone and types: *Where is he?*

A few seconds later, the return message reads: *I'm working on it. Hold your ass and wait there.*

Hold your ass? Yeah, Jack's a mental giant. "Wait there." Easy for Jack to say. He isn't the one in danger of getting frostbite. Although maybe his part is worse. After all, Nate is his brother. Betraying family has to be worse. And for what? What does Jack want that he's willing to go so far to get it? An iPad? A computer? Some sort of sports junk that he's always showing pictures of online?

A gust of wind makes Bryan shiver, or maybe it's his disgust. Not for Jack, but for himself. Because as pointless as Bryan thinks the stuff Jack probably asked for is, what Bryan has requested is no better. Sports equipment isn't a need. Neither is a gun. Suicide isn't noble. Bryan knows that. Killing himself won't bring back Amanda. Dying is easy. It means he no longer has to face what he's done. And using a gun is the easiest method of leaving his guilt behind. He's always believed suicide is for wimps who don't care about anyone but themselves. He's talked to his parents about it. His friends. The annoying school counselor when his mother was worried that he was depressed and stressed.

He was offended by the concern then. But somehow, in a matter of days, Bryan has become the thing he most despised. A coward. It's why he's out here in the freezing cold instead of inside where he used to belong.

One thing. He did one careless thing and now he no longer belongs anywhere.

His phone vibrates and he struggles to remove his glove so he can swipe the screen. Even with his glove off, it takes three tries.

Nate has already been there and gone. He must be at Kaylee's house. Am having my mother call him. Hang tight.

Gone before he got there. Maybe it's a freakin' sign. He should bail before he really does get frostbite.

The snow falls harder. His phone tells him five minutes are up. Jack hasn't contacted him again. Time to get out of here.

Bryan grabs a branch to help him stand upright. The cold has made his muscles stiff. If Nate had shown, Bryan doubts he could have moved fast enough to go through with the plan. So much for thinking he is smart. For someone his teachers say is a smart guy, how could he be so completely dumb?

Without a backward glance at the house, Bryan heads down the street to where he parked his car. If someone he knew saw and recognized it, he could just say he came, sat there for a while, and couldn't bring himself to go in the house and talk about Amanda. At least he's thought that much out. It was Jack who said it was best to wait outside. Bryan agreed it was the smartest plan because he didn't want to think too hard about what he was doing. Well, he's thinking now, and for the first time he's wondering why NEED exists. What's the purpose?

For what reason did it put a murder weapon in his hands? Why is it making Jack turn against his brother?

Bryan rolls his eyes as he brushes the snow off his car and thinks about Jack. He's popular, but not one of Jack's friends would call him smart, and unless he's on a football field he's barely aware of anything or anyone but himself. He wouldn't bother to read other people's posts on NEED. And if he didn't see the photographs, Jack might not understand that NEED is planning something unpleasant for Nate. In Jack's unquestioning brain, NEED is giving him a chance to score a cool gift and haze his brother all in one fell swoop. Talk about a great way to start the New Year.

Will Jack believe Bryan if he tells him that NEED means to do more than scare Nate? Probably not. Bryan knows that to convince Jack, he'll have to confess what he did to Amanda. And if he does that, he might as well turn himself in to the cops, because there isn't a chance in hell Jack will keep it a secret.

Bryan climbs into his car, reaches into his pocket for the syringe that he found in Mrs. Orlovsky's mailbox, and places it on the passenger seat. He should go home. He should text Jack and say he's done. He should call the police, turn the syringe over, and confess to delivering the cookies.

A simple mistake in judgment.

A mistake that turned him into a killer.

A murderer.

Which is why he can't confess and why he isn't going home. He can't stand the thought of disappointing his family. He doesn't want to live with the knowledge that everyone thinks he's a bad guy. NEED will tell them the truth if he doesn't go through with this. NEED holds all the cards. It knows what he's done. It can turn him in at any time. It can send one of its members after his family. Maybe it already has. And even worse, he knows from the posts he saw online that if he doesn't do what NEED has asked, someone else will.

Kaylee

No answer. Voicemail. I want him to answer. I need him to. I lean my head against the wall next to my bedroom door and listen to the automated recording. When I hear the beep, I hang up.

"What's wrong?" Nate asks, looking up from his sixth slice of pizza.

"He didn't answer." A weight settles deep in my chest. The automated voice means I still don't know if this is my father's phone number.

"Call back."

"Why?" Inside I flinch. "If he didn't answer before then it's not like he's going to answer now."

"He might." Nate throws his pizza back in the box. "Let's reverse the situation for a minute. What would you do if you were hiding for months and then suddenly you saw your father's number show up on a phone that you're certain he doesn't know about?"

"I'd answer the phone."

He laughs. "Really?"

"Maybe." Or I'd be too stunned or scared to answer.

"So call again. He's going to answer this time. I know it."
Nate smiles.

There it is again. The certainty and something more. Something that tells me Nate isn't telling the whole truth about this number or how he got it. Did NEED give it to him? Is that why he's certain my father will answer? It seems too coincidental that Nate just happened to come up with a method of contacting my father now. NEED has to be involved. Still, Nate's first NEED request hasn't been fulfilled. He can't ask for anything else yet. Even he said that. Unless something has changed. *Please don't let anything have changed.*

"What are you waiting for?" His phone buzzes and he looks down at the screen. "Save my place in this conversation," he says. I shift to my left and watch as his finger taps his password on the keypad. Upper right corner. Down, in the middle. Down again right corner. Left middle or upper? I can't tell. When he calls up his message, I walk over to my bed, take a seat, and grab one of my pillows so it looks like I'm lost in thought. Something is going on with Nate. Something that he doesn't want me to know about. Something . . .

"Well, that was pointless. Again." Nate sets his phone down on the carpet next to him. "I'm not going to answer him anymore. I promise."

"Jack?"

"I don't know what his deal is or why he cares if I'm going over to Lynn's house for the "Remembering Amanda" thing or why he needs me to go back there so he can show up and pay his respects without feeling awkward. He barely even knew she existed."

"Maybe that's why he needs you there," I say. "So no one wonders why he's suddenly showing signs of being human."

"Well, if that's the case, he's wasting his time. No one is going to be fooled by the caring Jack act. Everyone in this town knows him too well." Nate's phone dings again. This time he ignores it and says, "Back to our regularly scheduled program. You should call your father again and you should do it now."

"I will," I say, because while I am desperate to find my father, I have to find out if Nate has crossed a line. Making the call seems like the best way to find out. "Just give me a minute. Okay?"

"Sure." He grins. "So what should we do in the meantime? Watch TV? Eat more pizza? Flirt relentlessly?"

I glance up at the ceiling and then down at the floor. Anywhere but at Nate while trying not to look as awkward as I feel. Because . . . Well, because.

"I was kidding, Kaylee." Nate climbs to his feet. "Okay, not entirely, but mostly. Things are really intense with NEED and you may finally have the chance to talk to your dad and maybe convince him to help DJ. I'm not going to choose this time to push you into any deep, meaningful discussions about us."

Us.

Everything in me tenses as he walks toward me. Is he the same boy I have always counted on?

"You haven't eaten anything in forever," he says. "Since the pizza isn't cutting it, why don't I make you a grilled cheese while I'm giving you space?"

Out of the corner of my eye, I see Nate's phone sitting on the floor where he left it. Now I just need him to leave it there. "A grilled cheese sounds great." I reach out and take his hand and hold it tight. I want to believe in him. In what we have been. In what he says we could become. I want to have faith that this one thing in my life is still genuine and dependable. That one person still thinks I'm worthwhile. But I need to be sure.

"Nate," I say, wanting to ask him about the horrible feeling I have that he is hiding something. But the only word that comes out is, "Thanks."

"Don't thank me until you taste the grilled cheese," he jokes. Then his expression turns serious, and we stand there staring at each other. My heart pounds. I wonder if he will kiss me again. Despite everything that I don't understand, I want us to have another chance at that moment.

But Nate doesn't lean forward, and I'm too scared to initiate the contact. So I let go of his hand and walk him toward the door.

"I'll cook slow. That way you'll have plenty of time to call your dad." With that, he leaves the room.

I hear him go down the stairs. Still, I do not move. Only when I hear the clanging of pans do I stand up and walk slowly across the carpet. Nate's phone is lying face-down on the floor, so all I can see is the dark blue case.

All the reasons why breaking into Nate's phone is wrong run through my head as I pick up the phone. Our lifelong friendship. His willingness to stand by me. The worry that I will break if one more person betrays me. Still, I touch my finger to the screen.

An unread message alert appears on the display. The message is from Jack. *Where the hell is your lying ass? Mom is going to . . .* The rest is hidden. To see all of it, I need to enter Nate's password. Taking a deep breath, I think back to Nate punching in his password and I start to type.

One number.

Then the second.

On the third the phone vibrates. I jump and almost drop the thing as the screen resets. The number I pushed was incorrect. So I try again. The first number. Second. I type in a different third number and the phone vibrates and resets again.

Now what? How many wrong entries do I get before the screen locks? Three? Four? If I punch in the password wrong again, the phone might not let anyone else operate it. Nate will know what I'm doing. He'll ask me why. I can stop now and avoid that. I can accept Nate as the friend he's always been. Pretend there are no secrets hiding in his eyes.

But I'm tired of secrets. I want to try once more.

My finger touches the first two numbers. I wait for the buzz on the third, but it never comes and when I punch the fourth the screen changes. I'm in. Now I need to find what I'm looking for without knowing what that is. I can't read Nate's unread message or open his text message inbox without him knowing. So I open up his phone log.

Wow. Nate must have spent half his day on the phone with people from our class. Lynn called him twice. Probably about the meeting at her house tonight. Cassandra Clarke is on the list. Rachel Briggs. Emily Yorgen. Josh Martinez. Nick Wright. All kids we've grown up with. All friends of Amanda's. Nothing suspicious about any of them as far as I can tell.

Two other numbers have no names attached. By their area codes I can tell they are local, but I have no time to sit at my desk and look them up on my laptop. I move on to Nate's email.

The screen is loading as I hear more banging of pans in the kitchen, followed by the sound of running water. Nate must be cleaning up. He'll be back in minutes. I look at the door and then back at the screen. Come on. Load. Load.

Nate's inbox appears. For a second I just stare at it, wanting to see everything and knowing I only get to look at one or two messages. I quickly read the From column. The sender and time stamp of one email look familiar. I received the same message from NEED, saying the website was up and active. But it's the message above it that catches my attention. The sender is *administrator@nhsproject.gov.* The subject line reads: "Request fulfillment." The same terminology NEED uses.

"I hope you're ready for the best grilled cheese you've ever eaten in your life," Nate yells from downstairs.

I glance again at the doorway and back at Nate's cell. My hand is unsteady as I select the email and wait for it to load. Hurry. Hurry. I hold my breath and listen for Nate. I don't hear him. Then suddenly I do. As Nate reaches the bottom steps, there's a creak from the board that Dad always said he was going to fix.

The email appears.

"Room service," Nate calls. He has reached the top of the stairway and is coming down the hall.

No, I'm not ready. I reread the message and struggle to understand.

THANK YOU FOR YOUR TIMELY WARNING ABOUT
KAYLEE DUNHAM CONTACTING THE NOTTAWA POLICE
DEPARTMENT. WITH YOUR ASSISTANCE, OUR
PROJECT HAS BEEN ABLE TO REMAIN UNDETECTED
AND OPERATIONAL. AS PROMISED, WE HAVE
OBTAINED THE PHONE NUMBER YOU REQUESTED.
IT IS LISTED BELOW. WE CONSIDER THIS
TRANSACTION NOW CLOSED.

"Are you ready to eat?"

I turn toward the door. Nate's smile dissolves as he spots the phone in my hand.

"Kaylee, what do you think you're doing?"

"That's what I want to know," I say. There is a pounding at the base of my skull as I shift the phone so he can see the screen.

I doubt he can read the words from that distance, but his face goes pale. "I can explain."

"Fine. Explain to me," I say. "Explain why you're helping NEED."

Ethan

THE CHARACTERS IN Mercenary of War always wear gloves when they're on a mission. Criminals in TV shows wear gloves to make sure they don't leave fingerprints behind. Hell, even the cops in movies and on television wear gloves to avoid corrupting a crime scene. So why in all the movies or video games or or TV shows don't they say that while gloves keep fingerprints off things, they totally suck to work in.

He checks the time. A little behind schedule but not too bad. He'll still be home by curfew if he hurries. The last thing Ethan wants is for his mother to call Miguel's house looking for him. That would lead to all sorts of questions that Ethan isn't about to answer. NEED requires secrecy. It's his job to adhere to that rule.

Ethan grabs the duffle bag he brought with him and kneels next to the lamp so he can see better. He fishes out the plastic bags and the rubber bands. It takes him several tries, but after a few minutes he's satisfied with the coverings he's created over his boots. He takes a couple of steps. The bags crinkle but they hold and the rubber bands are just about cutting off circulation in his legs, which is perfect. Nothing in. Nothing out.

"Ethan?"

He stops and turns toward the faint sound of his name. Hannah must have gotten some of the tape off her mouth. Well, she can call for help all she wants. No one else is around to hear her. And really, he isn't going to be here all that much longer.

"Ethan, are you there? Please. Someone? Please. Help."

He picks up a metal jug and walks toward the office. The plastic coverings on his feet crackle with every step and his footsteps echo in the empty halls. He swallows hard and straightens his shoulders because there is nothing to be afraid of. At least not for him.

"Ethan." The sound is colored by tears. "Please. Please, Ethan." Desperate, hopeless crying that he doesn't want to listen to. So he starts to hum, which does wonders to block out the sound. *Whistle while you work,* he thinks as he picks up a can of gasoline and gets down to business.

Kaylee

"I'm not working with NEED."

Nate's face and voice are filled with such conviction that I might believe him had I not read the email. Had I not seen the secrets lurking in his eyes.

"If you aren't helping them, why are they sending you emails thanking you for your assistance?"

He puts the plate on my bed, runs a hand through his shaggy blond hair, and shoots a nervous look at the phone. "I don't know how much you read, but it's not how it seems, Kaylee."

How much I read? Oh God. How much more is there?

I blink back tears because I won't cry. Not again. Never again. I'm done being everyone's victim, including Nate's. "It looks like you betrayed a friend and made things even worse for her family in order to screw with this town. It looks like you aren't the person I thought you were. Get out of my house. Now."

"Let me explain." Nate holds out his hand and I step back. No way I'm going to let him touch me. Or maybe he is just reaching for the phone that I still have in my grasp. Well, he isn't getting it.

"Kaylee," he says, before I can order him out again. "Just listen. A few months ago, I got an email from someone claiming to be the director of some sort of government grant program that was looking to get information about Nottawa High School directly from the students. It asked if I'd be willing to take a detailed survey about the students and the town. I figured what the hell. Sounded interesting. So I did."

"Just like that? No questions asked? Without telling anyone?" Without telling me?

Nate sighs. "No. Not just like that. I looked up the grant program online and found the website. There were links to each school that had been nominated for grants. Nottawa was on the list."

I turn toward my laptop and he says, "The site isn't there anymore. I've checked."

"That's convenient." On the other hand, it sounds familiar.

"It's true. I saw the website, was feeling bored, and decided what the hell."

No. He's lying. The website disappearing is probably true. But there's more here. I can see it in Nate's expression. "There's a reason you didn't tell me about the survey. There's a reason you decided to participate. What's the reason?"

"It's not that important."

"Tell the truth or get out. I'm done." The phone in my hand dings, but Nate never glances at it. His eyes stay firmly on my face. Considering. Weighing.

"Okay." Nate closes his eyes and takes a deep breath. "I got the email like I told you and I deleted it. I figured it was some kind of phishing scam. The next day I got another email strongly encouraging me to reconsider my hasty dismissal of their request. They wanted information and they wanted me to give it to them. In exchange, they offered to help me get something I wanted."

"What did you ask for? A perfect score on a math test?"

"No. I wanted them to find a kidney donor for DJ. I asked them to help you."

"Help?" I stare at him, trying to understand what could possibly be helpful about a grave being dug in our front yard and DJ's pretend coffin thrown in it.

"Kaylee, you have to understand." Nate takes a step toward me. "I saw how sick DJ gets when he relapses and how hard you were working to keep him alive and to find your father. Hell, I was trying to track your dad down too. They knew that. The people behind that email knew we were friends before I ever told them. When I deleted that first survey, they threatened me by saying they'd hurt you. They knew how desperate I was to help your family, and they offered me a way. I thought I could help you fix things."

"You thought you were making things better?" The pressure in my chest grows stronger. "By lying to me? By making my brother a target?"

"I didn't know that was going to happen!" Nate yells. "I didn't know any of this was going to happen. They said they wanted information in exchange for their assistance. They said they had contacts who could find your father or, if that failed, could hook DJ up with a new kidney. I took them up on their offer because I love you."

The phone drops from my hand. Everything inside me squeezes until it feels like it's going to burst.

"Did you hear what I said, Kaylee?" Nate asks, shifting his weight from foot to foot. He's off balance. Scared. So am I. "I love you."

I step back.

"I've loved you for forever. Since that day at the party with the cupcake when you didn't care about who my brother was or how good he is at sports or how much my parents worship him."

I can barely breathe.

And Nate's words don't stop. "Loving you is the only really good thing about me. I hated what was happening to you. First DJ, then your dad, and then your mom and all of her issues. None of it was fair. You deserve to be happy."

"Love?" I yell, ignoring the small, vulnerable ache in my chest. "You don't know anything about love. All you care about is getting attention and being important because you're jealous of your brother. You're selfish. You always have been. If you aren't in the center, you—" I stop the flood of words as I hear what I'm saying. All the nasty insults that have been hurled at me, the accusations that created wounds that still haven't healed, I'm now throwing at Nate. The shield of anger cracks and shame floods through. "I'm sorry, Nate. No matter what you've done, you don't deserve me saying those things."

"You're wrong." He thrusts his hands into his front pockets. "I deserve worse. And you're right about me being selfish. I win in that department. I even have Gina Ferguson beat, which takes effort. Gotta give me points for doing something all the way, right?"

"You're not selfish." Guilt smears across my rage. "You're the only one who stood by me through everything. You were there when my dad left. You got yourself tested as a donor without me ever asking. And—"

"Don't." Nate shakes his head, walks to my bedroom window, and stares into the distance. "Don't give me credit. You always do that. You see the best in me and I let you, because it would suck large if you saw the real me. I suspected that there was something really off with NEED after we looked at it, but you said you weren't going to ask for anything. And I'm such a nice guy that I didn't really care if someone at NEED started blackmailing other people we knew as long as the people behind it would follow through on their guarantee to help me track down your father. So when I found a hyperlink buried in the Terms and Conditions that had the same email address that the survey used, I decided to send an email reminding them that they hadn't yet fulfilled their promise and since they hadn't, I'd like them to consider using NEED to help DJ."

He shrugs. "I figured, what was the harm? After all, they were going to start raising the stakes for need request fulfillments. Why not have them make one of the requirements be that users take a simple medical test? When they said they found my suggestion worthy of consideration, I knew I couldn't let you shut them down. Not without seeing if they would really follow through. I didn't know they were going to threaten you. Turns out, they decided against having students volunteer to be tested and gave me your father's phone number to thank me for my help. And yeah—I got myself tested to be a donor. Do you know why?" He turns to face me.

"Because you want DJ to live."

"That's the brave answer. That's the one I wanted you to believe because I needed you to." Nate squares his shoulders and sets his jaw. "I got tested because I didn't believe there was a chance in hell that I'd turn up as a match. No risk, all reward. How heroic is that?"

"It doesn't matter," I say, trying to decide if I believe my own words. "You got tested. You did what most people in this town never considered doing. It doesn't matter why or that you're not a match."

"That's what you think." He takes another step forward and searches my face. After several long seconds he says, "Whoever sent me the survey knew I wanted to help you, but they also found out that I had a secret. A secret I'd do almost anything to keep. That's why they picked me. If I gave them the information they requested, I'd be rewarded. They'd work to find a donor for DJ. But if I refused, they threatened to send the information they found to you."

I don't understand. "Me? Why me?"

"Because they found out what a coward I really am. My test to be a donor for DJ came back different than I said." He takes a deep breath as his eyes lock with mine. "I'm a match."

Bryan

BRYAN'S FINGERS DIG INTO the steering wheel as he drives past the house for a second time. He's glad the snow is coming down this hard. No one will question why he's going so slow. They'll think he's being careful, not trying to see in through the front window. The lights are on. There aren't any cars in the driveway, but someone must be home.

The street is quiet. He looks for signs of someone like his father. Someone who doesn't wait for several inches of snow to pile up before shoveling. Someone who could jeopardize his anonymity and give him a good excuse to steer the car toward home.

But all the garage doors remain down.

Nothing is going to happen, he tells himself as he fingers the syringe. He's going to waste a night sitting in this damn car, and that's totally okay. He's almost convinced himself of this when his phone buzzes.

He's inside with Kaylee. I know it. Just wait until he comes out, and offer him a ride. Couldn't be easier.

Damn. Maybe it will still be okay. Maybe Jack's wrong or Nate will stay inside. Bryan tightens his hold on the syringe and hopes.

Sydney

So far, so good.

Sydney finishes typing, hits Enter, then does a quick scroll through the NEED message board. So smart. The whole system is so freakin' smart. Too bad he wasn't the one to come up with it. Of course, even if he had dreamed up the idea, he would never have thought it would fly. It's amazing to him how many people haven't figured it out. How many still think it's a game. Maybe he's the only one who bothers to look at the number of network users. Maybe he's the only one who's seen it plateau and then go down.

Amanda.

The first drop had to be due to her. He feels bad for her and her family. Who wouldn't? But despite that, he can't help admiring the system that led to her death and whoever conceived it. Dribble out rewards for almost no price. Because, really, sending out invites to a new website and convincing your friends to play ain't worth jack. At least you wouldn't think so. And just by sending a few emails you get a reward. Something real. Something that makes you want more. Why wouldn't you, since you just got something for free? Or so you think. That's what they want you to think. Only those who are totally brain-dead could believe something so naive. Nothing is free. Not one thing in this life. Sydney's known that forever. How everyone else missed it is beyond him. And clearly they did miss it, because the ticker for need requests and fulfillments continues to rise.

Smart. Whoever created NEED is crazy smart. And probably flat-out crazy. The two aren't mutually exclusive.

But Sydney's smart too, and his crazy only goes so far. He can watch and learn and game the system while pretending to be stupid like the rest of them. He'll skim what he can from it before it implodes. So far he's racked up decent cash for his part. Almost enough to get out of this town.

His inbox dings. It's the message he's been waiting for. He reads the instructions and nods as he clicks back on to NEED's main screen.

```
NETWORK MEMBERS—686
NEEDS PENDING—684
NEEDS FULFILLED—220
```

Another member has bit the dust.

Sydney unlocks his desk drawer and grabs his grandfather's hunting knife. Just in case. He slides the knife into his backpack and slings it over his shoulder. With one last glance at the numbers on the screen, Sydney heads out to follow instructions and vaguely wonders if anyone will notice the drop in members. If not, he's pretty certain they'll notice the next one.

Kaylee

"YOU'RE A MATCH?" The words are a whisper as I reach out and take Nate's hand. Part of me needs to make sure he's real. That this conversation is real.

"I'm not a perfect match. Only five points out of six on the antigen scale," Nate explains, although the difference doesn't matter. Six-point matches outside of a family relationship are rare. Five points is as good as DJ is going to get unless Dad turns up, and even then it still might be the best. This is great news.

But it's not. At least, not to Nate. Suddenly, I get what he's saying. "You don't want to save DJ."

He shakes his head. "That's not true, Kaylee. You know I do."

"You'd let DJ die?" I yank my hand to free it from Nate's grasp, but his fingers bite into my wrist, not letting go.

"No. Kaylee, why do you think I've been working so hard to help you find your father? I want DJ to live. I'm just too scared to go through with the operation." He shakes his head. "When my parents and I read up on the surgery and the risks . . ."

"The risks are minimal," I say. I've studied just about everything that's been written about the physical effects of donating a kidney. I even talked to last year's school counselor, Dr. Mc-Goran, because they said there were psychological considerations as well. "You're healthy and you don't need both kidneys to live a full life. I can talk to your parents if you want or have DJ's doctor talk to your parents—they'll realize you'll be okay. They might give their consent and—"

"It's not just them, Kaylee. Although it's a miracle they care about it at all." Nate drops my hand and stalks toward the window. "It's me. I know all the statistics and have read all the research too. But the more I read, the less I wanted to go through with it. I'm not like you. I can't hear about surgery and pain and possible infections and future complications and say sign me up."

"Yes, but—"

"It's not that dangerous," he says, cutting me off. "It's done every day. It's safe and I'd be giving a great gift to your brother. I've told myself all of it, and even if my parents gave their okay, I still couldn't do it." Nate lets out a bitter laugh. "When you get to the bottom of it, as I told you, I'm a coward. And I hate that I know that about myself and I'm not willing to do what it would take to change it. So, when this government program email promised me something in return for my help, I took them up on it. Instead of asking for money or cars or a trip around the world, I asked them to find a donor for DJ. Is that so wrong?"

Yes.

No.

Yes.

I can't think. Anger. Sympathy. Hate. Confusion. I try to process it all. But Nate stands there staring at me, as if he's waiting for the worst. "There's something else you aren't telling me, isn't there?"

"Like what?" The lie is obvious.

"The number you gave me. NEED gave it to you. They gave it to you today." On the NEED website when a request is made, the site gives you a requirement to fulfill. Once that happens, the site member gets what they asked for and they get it quick. "What did you do for NEED, Nate? What did you do to get them to give you my father's phone number?"

"I told them you were calling the police to report the site. I'm the reason they shut it down." I gasp and Nate explains, "I told myself that I needed to do something for them so they'd give me your father's phone number, but really I was scared."

"Of what?"

"I was scared you were right." He walks back to the window. "That they knew about Amanda's allergy and orchestrated her death. I was worried they might do the same to me or someone I care about because you were calling the cops. And I told myself that if you were wrong, I didn't want to lose the chance to track down your father. If I wasn't willing to save DJ myself, I had to find the person who could."

All reasons I hate because I can understand them. I can see the rationalization for some of the things Nate did, but I'm angry. Angry at his lack of trust. At how foolish I looked this morning talking to Officer Shepens. At the way everyone, including my mother and Dr. Jain, thinks I'm crazy, again. At how his betrayal of me to NEED made my mother doubt me all over again. She's threatening to authorize a new treatment plan because she thinks I'm mentally unbalanced. All because of him.

"So now what?" Nate demands. "Tell me what I have to do to fix this and I will. I'll do whatever you want."

No. He won't save my brother. He doesn't love me no matter what he believes. He loves that I need him. But I don't. Not really. Because despite what I thought, what I counted on, he has never been there for me. There is no safety with him. I've always been alone. I just didn't know how isolated I was until now.

"Get out."

"Don't tell me to leave." Nate moves toward me but stops when I shift out of his reach. "Not with NEED out there doing who knows what. I'll go downstairs and stay out of your way, or work with you to help shut it down, or maybe we could—"

"Get out!" I throw his phone at him. "Take your promises and your lies and go find someone else to tell them to. How about you call your brother so the two of you can do NEED's work together? You deserve each other."

His shoulders hunch and I know I've scored a direct hit when he back away.

He reaches the door, stops, and says, "Be careful, Kaylee. Whoever is behind NEED has to be here in Nottawa. And they're watching us."

And then he's gone. I start to tremble as my understanding of Nate's betrayal deepens. Sinking to the floor, I wrap my arms around my legs. Nate's gone, and so is everything I believed about our friendship. He lied about being a match and lied to me about the website and lied to cover everything up until he had no choice but to tell the truth.

Love.

Tears fall as that word echoes in my head. Nate said it was all for love. Maybe I don't understand love because no one who has said they loved me has ever put me first. I've always wanted to be loved, but if that's love I don't want any part of it. Because it isn't real. For a while the illusion is enough, but once you see beyond it, the only thing that's left is pain.

NEED knows this. It gets that under all the smiles and high-fives and laughter in the hallways, when push comes to shove, most people put themselves first. Their wants. Their needs — or what they think they need, anyway. Especially if they think they can hide it.

Good. Let NEED use that. Let NEED punish them all. Turn brother against brother and friend against friend. My brother and mother are gone for now. I'm safe in this house. NEED can do its worst. I don't care anymore.

Anger burns away the tears. But then, shame slides through me.

Because I do care. No matter how much I think I want payback for everything the people in this town have done to me, I don't. Not really. If I did, I would be like them. Like all the people who have made me a joke and called me an attention whore. Being like them would be worse than being alone.

I rub my hands over my face and wipe away the tears. Crying is useless. Other people could be dying because NEED is using their fears and their selfishness and their egos against them. Well, two can play that game.

Pushing to my feet, I walk to my desk and take a seat. NEED

showed up and infiltrated our lives in a matter of days without almost anyone noticing it was happening. We're all so used to new things appearing on the Internet every day that we don't question what's behind them before welcoming them into our lives. Because they don't feel real. NEED knows that. It feeds on the belief that what's on the public forum of the Internet can't be all that bad. All sorts of things people wouldn't have the nerve or the heart to do face-to-face show up online, and most of the time people shrug them off because it's just the Internet. You can ignore them or convince yourself they aren't real. And since NEED insists on secrecy for both the network and the users, it's easier for members to pretend nothing bad is happening. Well, they aren't going to be able to pretend anymore.

I log on to NEED and start taking pictures of the message board with my phone. NEED thrives on anonymity, and members use it to hide from what they have done. Well, I'm going to make it impossible for them to hide. I'm fighting back. Let NEED come after me. I don't care. Because I'm not going to just break their rules this time. I'm going to shatter them.

Ethan

ETHAN COUGHS and wipes his forehead. The fumes are making his chest burn, but he has to finish. His hands shake as he takes the box out of his bag and opens it. He looks inside at the timer device and the New Year's Celebration Fireworks Fountain. The faster he gets this celebration ready, the sooner he can leave.

Sweat pours down his face. He tries not to breathe too deeply as he clears a spot on the desk for the big, colorfully wrapped fountain. His dad likes fireworks. Every year their mother freaks and yells and hides behind her hands as they blow off dozens of fountains, rockets, and mortars. None of the fountains they use are this heavy. This thing must burn for at least four minutes, maybe more. Plenty of time to get the party started.

Juggling the flashlight and the timer is tough with his gloves on. He can't make a mistake. His head pounds. He leans on the desk to keep his balance and knocks something to the ground. Crap. He shines the flashlight to see what it is. A metal and plastic desk nameplate. He's lucky the metal part didn't hit anything and strike a spark. Thinking about what could have happened makes his head swim. He can't stay in here much longer.

Suddenly he doesn't care about doing things exactly right. Not as long as he stays alive.

Ethan pulls off his gloves and stuffs them in his bag. He picks up the nameplate, then puts the flashlight on the desk next to the timer. Without the bulk of the gloves it's easier to make sure the timer is set and working. He barely breathes when he places the wick for the fountain on the ignition wire.

He did it. It's set. Now he has to get out of here.

Ethan grabs his bag and feels his knees buckle as he heads for the office door. It's not far, he tells himself. Just down the hall. His feet slide on the slick tile. Just a few more steps now until his mission is accomplished. He took too much time on this one. Next time. He'll do better next time.

"Ethan."

He turns and shines his beam into the hallway behind him. The floor glistens with gasoline just waiting for the spark that will ignite it.

"Ethan. Please don't leave me here."

Hannah's voice is groggy. It's hard to tell one word from another the way she slurs them. The gas fumes must be getting to her, too.

Good, he thinks as he pushes the bar on the exit door and walks into the fresh air. He hopes for her sake she's unconscious when the alarm goes off and the fireworks start. If she hadn't seen his face he might be able to help her out, since NEED didn't say she had to die. Actually, the instructions spelled out a way to get this done and let her go. But he can't, because she brought a flashlight and she saw, which means it's a choice between Hannah and him. And that's no choice at all.

Kaylee

I WORK FOR FIFTEEN MINUTES pulling the pictures I think are the most telling about NEED. The only time I stop and let myself feel anything other than anger is when my mother texts to make sure everything is okay at home. I say yes, then lie again and say that Nate sends his best to DJ before turning back to my project. It takes some editing to make sure the photographs are positioned so that people can recognize the image while understanding that it came from the website. Those who aren't on the website will probably think I'm up to my old attention-seeking tricks. There's nothing I can do about that.

My fingers hover over the keyboard as I try to decide what to say to accompany the photos. I'm scared of typing the wrong thing. Scared people will ignore me. Scared they won't. Annoyed that I still worry about what people think. If it weren't for their belief that they can get something for nothing, NEED would be harmless. It would just sit out there on the World

Wide Web—powerless to cause harm. As much as I blame NEED for Amanda's death and any other disasters it has caused, I blame us. All of us. Because I was gullible and asked for something too. Something I never believed would be delivered, but still I asked. No one gets something for nothing. We all should know better.

And that's when I realize I know what I want to say.

Is what you thought you needed worth this?

I hit Post and wait for the photo and caption to appear before loading another photo. This one of a Santa sleigh that's been beaten to a pulp and what I think used to be light-up reindeer. A broken baseball bat is also in the photo.

What did you think you needed enough to do this?

Another photo—this time of the grave that was dug in my yard.

And this.

Finally, I post the photo of the bloodstained snow.

Red streaked on white.

Bits of fur.

Pieces of flesh that belonged to pets someone loved.

And what could you possibly need enough to do this? Stop doing what NEED asks. Nothing is worth the price we will pay. Nothing is free.

I hit Post. For better or worse I have broken the Terms and Conditions NEED threatened me with. Now what? Waiting to see what people say would be torture, so I click back on the NEED shortcut and start looking for other things that I should document. Some people will ignore or attack what I've done, but others will be less selfish. Even if it's only one or two, I can ask them to talk to Officer Shepens with me. He will have to believe me if there are others who say the same thing. Won't he?

```
NETWORK MEMBERS—683
NEEDS PENDING—685
NEEDS FULFILLED—228
```

Oh God. The network is down more members. Who else is dead? And who killed them? The numbers swirl before me. I blink my vision clear and notice a red exclamation point in the top right corner of my screen. That's new. I move my cursor so it hovers over the symbol. The message *One notification* appears. I click on it and feel a scream build inside me.

```
A KIDNEY HAS BEEN LOCATED AND IS IN
THE PROCESS OF BEING PROCURED. YOU CAN
REST ASSURED YOUR NEED REQUEST WILL BE
FULFILLED.
```

Beneath the message is a picture of a cell phone with a blue case sitting atop an ugly purple knitted hat.
Nate.
Then my screen goes black.

Yvonne

"YVONNE."

She flips the page, hoping her mother will stop calling her. At least until she gets to the end of the chapter. She has to know if—

"Yvonne, did you hear me?" Her mother stands in the doorway of the living room. Her dark bushy hair falls over one eye, but Yvonne can see her mom's annoyance in the way she stands with the phone in one hand. "Mrs. L. is on the phone for you. It would be nice if you actually paid attention to what's going on in this house instead of what's in those books. Those books aren't the real world, you know."

"I know, Mama," Yvonne says. She gets off the couch, walks over to her mother, and takes the phone. She hopes Mrs. L. isn't going to ask her to work extra hours this week. With break ending and finals less than two weeks away, she needs the time to study.

"Hi, Mrs. L." Her sister yells that Javier is hitting her, and someone cranks the volume on the music, so Yvonne leaves the room to ask, "Are we going to have a snow day at the bakery tomorrow?"

"I hope not." Mrs. L. laughs. "The weatherman swears the snow will stop around two a.m. That should give the plows plenty of time to clear the streets before the store opens. But if you have any trouble getting there, just give us a holler and I'll send Jed and his truck to pick you up. Sound good?"

"Sounds great, Mrs. L."

"Lovely. Now, on to other business. Do you remember taking an order for a box of seventeen cookies? The police contacted me and asked, but I'm at home and don't have the paperwork in front of me. With the snow, I'd rather not go out so I've been calling everyone who might have manned the front the last couple days. Seventeen is an unusual number, so I thought it might stand out in your mind."

The police. Damn.

Yvonne thinks of the form she filled out. She'd forgotten about it, with the store being so busy in the afternoon and her brothers and sisters screaming and racing around all night. She hasn't even logged on to the computer since she got home because her dad's been on it. He promised he'd finish soon so she could check her email and message some of her friends. The fake order was supposed to be no big deal. Who cares about a box of cookies? It's just something she did because of a website. It doesn't really matter, unless Mrs. L. finds out she faked it and basically lied.

"You know, I do remember that order." Putting her hand over the receiver she yells. "Would you all hold it down in there so I can talk? Please?" The screams subside to loud giggles. So she says, "It came in yesterday or the day before." She can't think of exactly what date she put on the form.

"Oh, good," Mrs. L. says. "Do you happen to know if it was one of our regulars? If you don't remember, that's okay too. Now that I know it's real I'll go over to the store and check the forms."

"No. I remember." And because Mrs. L. is going to see the order Yvonne wrote anyway she says, "It was placed by a girl I go to school with. Her name is Kaylee Dunham."

Kaylee

No.

I hit Enter again and again and again.

No. No. No. No. Why won't the screen load?

Then I realize the computer hasn't stopped working. It's only the Internet page that has gone black. I shut down the browser and fumble with my mouse as I click on the NEED shortcut. A black screen appears with red lettering.

ACCESS DENIED

"Denied." I click on it again. The same message appears. This has to be a mistake. The message I saw before the screen went dark is a mistake. Nate was here. He was fine. A total jerk, but a jerk who was fine.

Until I made him leave.

I won't feel guilty for that. I won't. After what he did, I had no choice. He isn't my friend anymore. He never was. But . . .

NEED could just be screwing with me. They must have seen or heard about the pictures I posted. They sent the message about Nate and then locked me out because they're angry.

But as much as I want to believe that's true, I don't. I pull out my phone and dial Nate's cell phone, praying that he's okay. I don't want to talk to him, but as angry as I am, I want him to at least be okay.

Straight to voicemail.

Now what? Think. Think.

NEED has Nate, and even though he's scared and doesn't want to be operated on, they've chosen him to be a donor for DJ. They'll force him. I want to feel satisfaction at that. I want to believe it's okay, since he should have made that decision on his own. But while removing a kidney isn't usually a life-or-death operation for the donor, if NEED takes Nate's kidney without his approval there is no way they'll let him live. They can't. Not without being exposed. DJ would live, but for that to happen Nate would die. NEED has already killed Amanda and possibly others. They will have no problem killing him, too.

Oh God. No. He deserves a lot of things for what he's done. I want him to feel the abandonment and pain I'm feeling. But I don't want him dead.

There has to be a way out of this. This was my request. NEED's doing this for me. And I do want what I asked for, but not like this. There has to be a way to tell the website. And then I remember that there is. I open up my email, hit Reply to NEED's message for me to stay silent, and type.

Cancel my need request. I no longer want it.

I shift in my seat, staring at my email, waiting for a reply.

Hoping that the message reaches someone in time to stop whatever they are doing to Nate. I try to think of something else I can do. I have no idea who is running NEED. There must be a way to find out. Everyone says that nothing on the Internet is truly anonymous. Right? Isn't that why our counselors and teachers tell us not to post anything online that we don't want colleges or future employers to find if they do a search? Nate figured out that the site is tied to the people who sent him the survey. But he understands how the Internet works better than I do. I've only had to log on to sites or search for information. I've never thought about where the information is really stored or how to go about finding something that someone has worked to keep hidden. It might as well be on a real cloud for all the chance I have of reaching it.

I wish I could rewind the clock. Make this all go away. But I can't do that. I can't track down Nate because I don't know who took him. I can't call my mother and ask her to help — she already thinks I'm just trying to grab attention. I can't do anything.

"Stop it." I shake my head and shove back the hopelessness that threatens to choke me. I can't let it or I really will be useless. Feeling sorry for myself won't do any good. If I flip out I won't be able to think. Nate hurt me by lying. He's screwed up the only relationship I thought I could count on. I don't know if I can ever forgive him for his actions, but I deserve the chance to find out. And he deserves to live with what he has done. Right now he's probably scared and alone and thinking that no one is looking for him. His parents think he's with me, and I kicked him out. No one else will be wondering where he is because he never shows up for them when he says he will.

He's just as isolated as I am. If he's going to survive this, I'm his only hope. I have to focus.

If I were NEED and I wanted to force someone to donate a kidney, how would I do it? A hospital would be required. So would a recipient. Heart racing, I text my mother asking if DJ knows where the TV remote is. My heart stops pounding when she texts back that DJ put it next to the TV and Aunt Susan says hello.

They're safe and DJ is still in Milwaukee. That's what I wanted to know. As long as they are away from Nottawa I have time to find Nate. I turn back to my laptop when I hear a ding. I have mail and it's from NEED.

DEAR KAYLEE,
   DUE TO SECTION 7 OF THE TERMS AND
CONDITIONS, WE REGRET TO INFORM YOU THAT
THE UPDATE TO YOUR NEED REQUEST CANNOT BE
GRANTED. NEED REQUESTS ONCE ACCEPTED CANNOT
BE TAKEN BACK. IT IS ALWAYS IMPORTANT TO
CONSIDER THE IMPLICATIONS OF WHAT YOU THINK
YOU NEED. WE HOPE YOU WILL TAKE MORE CARE
IN THE FUTURE.
   ALSO, WE REGRET TO INFORM YOU THAT
YOU ARE ONCE AGAIN IN VIOLATION OF THE
THIRD SECTION OF THE TERMS AND CONDITIONS.
PUBLICLY POSTING INFORMATION ABOUT THE
NEED NETWORK IS PROHIBITED. AS A RESULT,
YOUR NEED ACCOUNT HAS BEEN SUSPENDED AND
DISCIPLINARY ACTION HAS BEEN INSTITUTED.
   THE NEED TEAM

Oh God. What do I do now? Any chance of learning more about Nate's abduction through photos or posts on the network has just been eliminated. I can't wait for whatever disciplinary action NEED is sending to me while Nate is out there . . . somewhere. I stare at the screen unable to move. Unable to think.

Well, I can't just sit here and do nothing. Dr. Jain says most of my troubles stem from reacting out of emotion first and thinking things through later, or something like that. I roll my eyes every time she spouts that kind of psychological garbage, but that doesn't mean she isn't right. Tears and anger and flipping out won't help me now. I need a plan.

I can't get to NEED without knowing who's behind it, but I can try to get to the person who took Nate. After all the text messages Jack sent, I have to believe he knows something.

I dial his house. When Mrs. Weakley answers and starts chatting about my mother and asks if I'm excited for the start of a new year, I cut her off and ask to speak to Jack. "I know he's busy and he probably won't want to talk to me, but I'd appreciate it if you'd ask him. It's about Nate. Just tell him it'll only take a minute, please."

She puts down the phone to go in search of Jack, maybe thinking I'm trying to broker a peace treaty between her sons. If I save Nate and find a way to forgive him, maybe I'll actually try.

"Jack's in the bathroom. I can have him call you back in a minute if that's okay."

Like I have a choice.

While I wait, I grab a piece of paper and write down what I

know about NEED. Maybe I'll spot a pattern that can help me. Doing anything is better than sitting around, waiting.

NEED appeared less than a week ago.

NEED is an invitation-only website for students of Nottawa High.

NEED sent a survey to Nate. Others must have gotten it, but who?

NEED directed people to deliver cookies to Amanda, photograph documents, and kill dogs, as well as orchestrate fights, flat tires, and Nate's kidnapping.

NEED knew Nate is a match for DJ before it launched, and used that information to blackmail Nate into giving it assistance.

How?

I stop writing. How did NEED know? And who knew enough about Nate to understand how much he would risk to keep that secret? Nate said the people who contacted him were members of a government grant program looking for information about the people here in order to approve or deny the grant. But that can't be right. Whoever is behind NEED had to know enough not only to dig for Nate's medical records, but also to know why he was being tested, who the recipient would be, and why it would mean so much for Nate to refuse.

And now that I think about it, how did they know which people would be acceptable to invite to the site? Did they check every email address individually, which seems unlikely given how fast membership acceptance happened, or did they already know what our email addresses are? Somehow, the people operating the site seem to know everything about us. When Nate first talked about NEED, he said whoever is behind it is incredibly smart. They understand how to entice and capture users quickly. In no time nearly everyone in our high school belonged.

What are the odds that the site randomly picked the exact right people to send the initial email to? Had they chosen me, I would have most likely deleted the email without much thought. Lots of other kids I know would have done the same thing, if they even bothered to log on to their email at all. But Nate's brother, Jack, likes checking his email. He does it all the time, as if to prove how popular he is. And Jack isn't the type to delete anything that promises a shot at getting something for nothing. Between his influence and his greed, Jack was a perfect choice to help get NEED up and running. And since he was among of the first members, he was one of the first to get his request granted. Jack isn't the type to keep a secret, especially if he can use whatever he knows to brag. He bragged to his friends about his new phone. He bragged about getting the slide board. He was a walking, talking advertisement. Just like NEED knew he would be.

The surveys would have given NEED some information, but they seem to know everything. Our emails. Our likes and dislikes—otherwise how could they have gotten requests fulfilled so quickly? And it had to be quick, or the whole thing would have lost momentum.

Who could know those things?

As I look at the list, the last thing Nate said to me makes sense. The power behind NEED has to be from Nottawa. It has to be people who know us. Really know us and not just by sight. I think about the first time Nate showed me NEED and the opening screen. It pointed out that there's a difference between a want and a need. If the creators of the site actually knows all of us, they would know if what we asked for is necessary or simply something we desire. If that's true, then they would know DJ needs a new kidney. They could know Nate didn't *need* an A to pass his class. Originally, I'd assumed I wasn't asked to perform a task because NEED couldn't fulfill my request. But they're working on it now. Maybe I wasn't asked to do anything because they knew it was a genuine need.

Almost everyone here in Nottawa knows about DJ and my search to help him find a donor. So that alone doesn't narrow anything down. But I doubt many know about Nate's test results, which say he is a match, or that those who do would also be dialed into Jack. If Jack's parents were computer whizzes, I'd wonder if they were involved, but as absorbed as they are in Jack, they would never threaten to hurt Nate. So, who? And thinking of Jack, I realize too much time has passed. I need to call back.

Mrs. Weakley answers the phone again and is filled with apologies about Jack not getting back to me. "I'm sure he was going to call any minute."

I'm sure he wasn't, but I thank her again and wait.

The murmuring on the other end suggests that Jack isn't in the mood to talk. But whatever his mother says must do the trick because, after a few minutes, Jack comes on the line. "Yeah, what do you want?"

"Where's Nate?"

"Why should I know or care?" he sneers. This is why Nate avoids him. Belligerent. Arrogant. Incredibly annoying.

"You must care," I snap back. "You texted him almost a dozen times tonight asking that same question."

"Well, I guess having my texts ignored changed my mind. If Nate doesn't want to talk to me, he doesn't have to. And I don't have to talk to you either."

"You do unless you want me to call the cops and tell them you helped kidnap Nate because NEED told you to. Who did you work with? You told someone Nate would be at my house. What do you need so badly that you're willing to hurt your brother to get it?"

"Calm the hell down," Jack says quietly. Someone must be close enough to overhear him. Or me, because I realize now that I was shouting. My breathing is shallow and rapid. Fear is gaining control.

"Look," he says. "Nate might be pissed off when he finally comes home, but this is no big deal. Nothing bad is going to happen."

"You can't be that clueless." He starts to protest but I talk over him. "Log on to NEED. Look at the pictures of the dogs it asked someone to kill and tell me nothing bad is going to happen. I don't care what you want enough to convince yourself that betraying your brother is no big deal, but I'm betting your parents will. Tell me exactly what NEED asked you to do and who you're working with or I'm going to make sure your dad knows what you've done."

"It's just a dumb joke." But he no longer sounds certain. "I asked for a home gym, since the stuff I have here is junk. I was told Nate was unwilling to help someone fulfill a NEED request and that they wanted to haze him a little for his attitude." Oh God. "I just had to deliver him to the person who was going to do the hazing. We haze the new guys on the football and basketball teams all the time. No big deal."

"Who?" I ask, since there is no point in discussing what this hazing might consist of. "Who did you deliver Nate to?"

"Bryan VanMeter. Only Nate wouldn't answer his text messages to hook up with me, so I changed the plan. I told Bryan where he could find Nate and let him deal with the rest. To be honest, I'm amazed someone that's such a wuss pulled it off."

"What's his cell phone number?"

Jack lets out a frustrated grunt. "I have to look at my phone to tell you. One minute while I put you on speaker."

I've known Bryan VanMeter forever, but clearly I don't really know him. Not that we hang out or anything, but still I would never have guessed he would want something badly enough to lie in wait and hurt Nate.

Jack gives me the number. I write it down and am about to hang up when Jack says, "Nate's going to be fine. I'm sorry you were scared when he disappeared, but he's going to be fine. Honest. Bryan doesn't have the balls to do anything really bad."

It's hard to tell if Jack's trying to convince me or himself.

Bryan

THE SNOW is coming down harder. Or maybe he only thinks the storm is getting worse because of how cold and ill he feels as he huddles in his car, watching the building across the way. Where Nate is. Where Bryan left him cuffed with his hands behind his back, lying on the dusty floor. The back entrance of the old post office was open when he got there. The lock hadn't been broken. No splinters of wood lay on the floor near the door. Someone must have gotten hold of a key. From the realtor maybe? It's the last place anyone would look for Nate. The post office was closed last year despite the petition his dad and his dad's friends circulated. Not enough business, the government said. So it was shut down and has been empty since. Until now.

He jumps as his phone buzzes.

"Hi, Mom."

"Are you okay?"

"I'm fine," he lies, trying to make his voice sound upbeat even though everything inside him wants to scream.

"Are you sure? We just heard about Lynn's mom."

Lynn's mom? "What about Lynn's mom?" he says before he remembers that his mother thinks he's at Lynn's house for the Amanda memorial.

"Where are you?"

He can't tell her he's sitting in a parking lot next to a Dumpster across from the abandoned post office. Instead, he says, "The snow was starting to fall so hard I decided I should drive home before it got any worse. Most of the streets haven't been plowed so I've been taking it really slow. I had to pull over to answer your call. What's going on? Did something happen after I left?"

"Lynn's mother collapsed. The paramedics are having a hard time getting anywhere due to the snow. Dan Gallimi called your dad. He heard it on some kind of scanner he listens to."

NEED.

He hopes there's another explanation for Lynn's mother getting ill, but he doubts it.

"Maybe I should go back and see if I can help." But Bryan isn't going anywhere, because he can't help Lynn's mom. As much as he'd like to, only the doctors can do that. But maybe he might be able to help Nate.

"Come home. Just please come home." Worry coats his mother's voice. "Your father and I are concerned, with everything that seems to be happening out there . . ." Her voice catches and Bryan's throat tightens. "We just don't want to be among the parents who are calling everyone trying to find their kid. Okay?"

Parents are trying to find their kids? Like who? Have Nate's parents figured out he's missing? Are others out there who have been taken or who have fled?

"Bryan. Are you there? Are you sure you don't want Dad to come get you? You can leave that car where it is and go back and get it when the snow lets up."

"No. It's okay. I think I see a plow turning onto this street." What's one more lie? "I'll let it do its thing and then drive home. And tell Dad he's right. Second gear means you have to go slow, but it's really good for driving in the snow. I'll let you know when the plow passes and I'm on my way. And Mom?" He hits the windshield wipers to get a clearer view of the building. "I love you."

He hears her sniffle. "I love you too, Bryan. Drive safe."

"I will, Mom." Bryan looks at the phone for several minutes after the call is over, trying to decide what to do. Stay and see who comes to get Nate? Or go home? Maybe no one will come. Maybe this is just supposed to scare Nate. Maybe Jack is onto something and this is just an intense hazing thing.

Lights. He sees a pair of lights at the end of the street, coming through the snow. Slowly. Not that anyone can travel fast in this weather. But more slowly than the fictitious plow he told his mother about would travel. He turns off the engine in case they can hear it running, and finds himself holding his breath as the lights come nearer. Damn. He wishes he had cleared the windshield again before he shut off the car. The snow is coming too fast to see out. But if he had, that might have given him away too, because why would a car with a clean windshield be parked without anyone inside in this weather?

He forces himself to breathe in and out and clutches his phone as he waits. The lights are still getting closer. By the time the movement of the lights slows down, the snow is too thick on his windshield to see any details about the approaching car. Then he can't even see the lights.

Did the other car park? Should he get out? If he does and the driver hasn't entered the post office yet he'll be screwed. Bryan doesn't know what to do. If he gets caught he could make everything so much worse for himself and his family. He promised his mother he'd come home. He doesn't want to disappoint her. He has to get home.

Still, he wraps his fingers around the door handle and pulls. The door comes unlatched and he eases it open as his phone starts to ring.

Damn. Oh damn. He closes the door, puts his phone on vibrate, and sits still. Like that's going to help. Whoever is out there must have spotted him opening the door. Or if they didn't and haven't gone inside the building, they probably heard the ringer. He thinks of the dogs. The blood.

He doesn't know the number on the display. Should he ignore it? If it is them, they know he's here. It would be better to answer and pretend to think he's done nothing wrong. His instructions were to bring Nate drugged through the back door, restrain him, and go home to wait for his NEED request fulfillment. But he can say because of the snow he was worried about Nate. That the building was cold and the floor was colder and he wasn't sure anyone would be able to make it through the storm to get to him.

They'll know it's a lie. NEED will know.

The phone lights up on vibrate. Bryan forces himself to breathe and does the only thing he really can do. He answers the phone.

Kaylee

"BRYAN? IS THAT YOU?" When no one responds, I say, "Hello. Bryan?"

"Who is this?"

I blow a sigh of relief when I hear his voice. It's him. Jack didn't give me a bogus number. "It's Kaylee Dunham."

I expect him to say something. Anything. After all, he kidnapped Nate outside my house. He has to know why I'm calling. "Jack gave me your phone number, Bryan. Where's Nate? What have you done with him?"

"I don't know what Jack told you—"

"He told me he helped you kidnap Nate so you could deliver him to NEED. All so he could get a home gym. It's not a surprise that Jack is shallow. But you?" Bryan, who planned the winter coat drive at our school for lower-income families and always had a book in his hand—I thought he was smarter. Kinder. He's never once picked on me, and while he never told me, I know he got tested as a potential donor because his mother mentioned it to mine. I don't know him well . . . probably my fault . . . but I've always thought of him as one of the good guys. Someone who would do something important and wonderful with his life. Someone who was better than most of us. "What did you get for kidnapping Nate and giving him to NEED? Is it worth sacrificing his life for? Because if you don't let him go he's going to die."

"You don't know that." But I can tell Bryan believes my words might be true. "And I can't talk about it now."

"Why?" I don't want him to hang up. He might block my calls or not pick up again. "Just tell me where Nate is and I'll go find him."

"Give me ten minutes," he whispers. "There's something going on here that could help me learn who's behind this whole thing. I'll call you back. I promise."

"Wait!" Crap. He's gone. I try to call again, but he doesn't pick up. If Bryan had asked me yesterday to trust him to call me back in ten minutes, I would not have questioned him. I would have waited for his call. This Bryan I don't trust. Not with so much riding on this. They can't have done anything to Nate yet. Right? I hope that's true. But NEED has been moving so fast. Ten minutes is too long to wait. I have to find someone else to help me.

I dig into the left pocket of my jeans and pull out the two cards I received this morning. The one from Dr. Jain I shove back. Then I dial the number on the card from Officer Shepens. I didn't have proof to show him before. Now, even though I've been banned from the NEED site, I do. The emails and my photos of the NEED posts should be enough to convince him that I'm not making this stuff up. And maybe there will be others who will back me up. There have to be. Still, I squirm at the idea of being called a liar again.

I steel myself against the nausea that churns inside me and dial. One ring. Two. He picks up. "Officer Shepens."

"Hi. It's Kaylee. Kaylee Dunham." Maybe not the best opening, but now that he's on the phone, I'm scared to say the wrong thing. If I screw this up, he won't help Nate and it will be my fault. "The website is back up. I took pictures to prove it. There are lots of bad things going on and you have to help."

"Kaylee—"

"Someone has to help or who knows what will happen next. Nate is missing. Someone took him and I know NEED is behind it and—"

"Kaylee."

I stop. I know I'm rambling. This isn't going to make him listen. To make him believe. I have to pull it together.

"Sorry, Officer Shepens. I'm worried about Nate and I don't know who else I can tell, but I made a request on the website that I told you about this morning." Was it only this morning? "The site asks what you need and I said I need a kidney for DJ. I didn't know that Nate was a match, but the website did and—"

"Kaylee, is your mother there?"

"What?" I blink. "No. She and DJ are out of town. That's why—"

"Where out of town? I'd like to come talk to you, but it might be better if you had your mother there. Would you mind if I call her?"

"Her cell phone's been having problems, but you can try," I lie, because even if Mom could be convinced to return to be with me, she can't come home. She and DJ have to stay away for their own safety and for Nate's. If DJ is around there's a better chance Nate will be forced into whatever NEED wants to do with him. Which is why when Officer Shepens asks for the number, I change the last digit from a 9 to a 1. Most of the kids I go to school with don't know their parents' or even their best friends' phone numbers because they're on speed dial. So it won't be too great a stretch for Officer Shepens to believe I simply got one of the numbers wrong. I hope.

"I'm going to give her a call. As soon as I'm done I'll come talk to you. Are you home?"

"Yes, but you should be out looking for Nate. I think I know—"

"Sit tight. I'll be there in about thirty minutes. And Kaylee, if you talk to your mom before I do, let her know I think she should come home tonight."

I hang up more anxious than before, but hopeful. Officer Shepens is coming. He didn't dismiss me out of hand.

Eight minutes have passed since Bryan hung up on me. Not the ten he asked for, but I don't care. I call his number anyway.

No answer. I try to focus on the hope that Officer Shepens will start searching for Nate the minute he's done hearing my story and seeing the proof I have.

With that in mind, I decide to organize all my information. I log back on to my laptop and in one window I call up the last email NEED sent. Then, in another browser window, I pull up my home page, where I posted the NEED photographs that got me in trouble. Maybe some of the people who saw the posts will agree to step forward and talk to Officer Shepens.

On the first photograph I find two responses:

You're not supposed to be posting this.

Get a grip. Get a life.

On the next two, I get the same kind of messages.

Don't ruin it for everyone else.

I bite my lip and force myself to read the comments on the last photograph:

I didn't know. I swear I didn't know. I'm sorry. Please tell her I'm sorry. Tell everyone I'm sorry.

Sameena Jahn.

I don't think I even remembered that the two of us are "friends" online, but friends or not, the guilt in the post and the implication that she will not be able to apologize to anyone herself make me gasp, and I start to send her a private message. That's when I notice I have a message waiting for me. A message from another "friend": Yvonne Gutierrez.

Hey—I'm not sure if this is important, but I saw your posts. I don't think it's a big deal or anything, but there's a receipt with your name on it at the bakery. According to the receipt, you ordered seventeen cookies for Amanda Highland. The police know about the receipt. I'm not sure why they care, but I figured you deserved to know.

A receipt with my name. Seventeen cookies that I never ordered. But the police think I did. Suddenly I know why Officer Shepens is coming over. Why he cares if my mother is home when he talks to me. He thinks I ordered and delivered the cookies that killed Amanda Highland. He's not coming to help me stop NEED. He's on his way to arrest me.

NETWORK MEMBERS—683
NEEDS PENDING—681
NEEDS FULFILLED—223

Ethan

THE HOT SHOWER felt great. Everything is so much better now that he no longer smells like gasoline. One more mission for the record books. Or it will be when the timer goes off and school lets out—for good. The whole Hannah thing still makes him feel a little guilty. He doesn't really want her to die. He had never once in his life considered hurting anyone intentionally until NEED came around. He isn't a serial killer or anything. It's not like he picks targets and goes after them for his own sick reasons. Like any military or mercenary operative, he's just a tool. Is it his fault NEED pointed him at Hannah in order to reach a goal? Hannah is a pawn, plain and simple. He'll just have to compartmentalize his guilt and move on. CIA guys must be able to do that, so he'll do it too.

"Ethan." His mother's voice comes from the other side of his bedroom door. "Is everything okay? I think I smell gasoline. Do you?"

He kicks the wadded-up ball of clothes under the bed and walks over to unlock the door. "The gas smell is me." He stays calm. Thinks on his feet. Keeps as much to the truth as he can so it doesn't sound like a lie. "I spilled gas on my jeans and boots when I was at Miguel's earlier. He needed help refilling the snow blower. Turns out I'm not much help. At least not with stuff like that."

"You have other gifts," his mother says with a smile. But the smile doesn't look real. Or is he just reading something into it? After a few moments, she asks, "Are you okay . . . you know . . . otherwise?"

His mother stares at him and he fights to keep his expression unruffled. "I'm fine, Mom. I mean, as okay as I can be, considering." He shrugs and looks down at his hands. People always do that in the movies when they want to look sad. And he's supposed to be upset about Amanda Highland's death. "It was good to hang out with Miguel. It made things less freaky."

"Well, I'm here if you need anything. And if you don't want to talk to me, Dr. Jain called us a little while ago. She's available for any students who are upset. I promised her I'd pass that information along."

"Thanks, Mom. See you in the morning."

She hovers in the doorway for a minute before wishing him good night. He counts to ten, locks the door, and walks over to the desk to turn on the computer. The red letters of NEED glow bright. He gets a buzz just seeing them. And the buzz grows more exciting when he clicks on his home page and sees a new assignment. Unusual, since technically he hasn't finished his last one, but he's not about to complain. After all, if he wants to become a professional operative, he needs to practice. Practice makes perfect.

He grabs his coat out of the closet, pulls his work bag out from under the bed, and unlatches the window. NEED doesn't want people to break its rules. She opened her mouth. Said too much. Now he has to make her pay.

Kaylee

I SLIDE MY CHAIR BACK and stand up so fast that I almost lose my balance.

I didn't do it. I didn't order the cookies and kill Amanda. I can show Officer Shepens the message Yvonne sent, but when I read it again I realize she has chosen her words carefully. Nothing in the message suggests that the receipt for the cookies is a fake. Yvonne is warning me about the oncoming danger, but she isn't willing to risk incriminating herself in the process. The evidence against NEED is stacked in my favor, but how long will it take to convince Officer Shepens of that? Too long. Because every minute spent proving my innocence is time taken away from saving Nate. My mother warned me to stay home. But I have to get out of here before Officer Shepens arrives.

I slam the lid of my laptop shut, then grab my backpack from beneath my bed and stash the laptop inside. I don't know where I'm going or what I'm doing, but I know that I have to move—fast.

I have nowhere to run to that is indoors and safe. The snow is still falling hard. I don't have my license yet. I don't have a car to drive and I don't know if I could actually drive without crashing in this weather, so it doesn't really matter. What matters is that I get out of here quick.

I pull off my jeans and sweater, race to my dresser, and yank out the top left drawer. Where are they? There. Under the pantyhose and slip my mother insists I need but I never wear is the two-piece long underwear set I wore the last time I went skiing with my dad. Ugh. They're tight and too short and rip in the crotch when I squat in an effort to stretch them. But the tear makes them feel more comfortable, so I leave them on and pull my jeans back over them. Not the best fit, but most of my sweatpants are ratty and have tears in them. It's better in this weather to have something be tight and warm than roomy and drafty.

I go downstairs, grab a box of granola bars I spot sitting on the counter, and shove it in my bag as I run to the front closet for my coat, scarf, hat, and boots. Time to go. I sling the backpack over my right shoulder, grab a flashlight from the garage, then hurry to the front door.

No. If Officer Shepens is close by, he'll spot me when he turns down the street. I have to go another way.

The back door is in the family room. It opens onto the patio, which is directly in the middle of the house and can't be seen from the street. I take off my glasses and tuck them in my pocket next to my cell phone so I can find them quickly if I need them. The blurred vision adds to the fear tightening in my gut, but I grit my teeth, open the door, and head out into the cold.

The snow is deep. At least a foot of snow has fallen in the last couple of weeks and several more inches have fallen today. The faster I try to go, the more I lose my balance. I turn toward the wooden fence that separates our yard from the Jeffersons'. A fence with a loose board that I've snuck through hundreds of times. Although not when carrying a backpack on my shoulder and wearing heavy winter clothes.

I wiggle slowly through the tight opening and then I start to run.

I veer to the left of the Jeffersons' property, where the snow isn't as deep, and race toward the street. A car door slams somewhere. In the quiet of the snowy surroundings, the sound makes me jump as if it were a gunshot, and I run to Jeffersons' house. Is Officer Shepens at my door? Is he ringing the bell? Does he know I've run?

I reach the road and wrap my arms around myself as I look in both directions. Which way should I go? A pair of tire tracks makes the choice simple. Running on packed-down snow will be easier than making my own path. And there won't be as many footprints to follow. It's as good a plan as any.

As I reach the end of the street, I hear my phone ringing in my pocket. I pull it out and glance at the display. Officer Shepens. He has to be outside my house, wondering why I'm not answering the bell. Sweat trickles down my neck as I consider what to do next. I had only thought as far as getting away to keep from being arrested. But I have no idea what to do now that I'm out here. Alone. Where do I go? How do I find Nate? And gnawing at my nerves is the terror of whatever NEED is planning next.

I follow the tire tracks toward downtown Nottawa and push

myself to move faster. When I reach a stop sign, I glance behind me. No one is there. Yet. I'm not far from Nate's house. I can make it, but I'm betting that's where Officer Shepens will go next—although I'm less scared of that than of Jack telling NEED that I'm there.

A church? They have to give sanctuary, right? Somewhere in the distance I hear a siren and I start running again.

I have to find Nate. Who can help me do that?

Bryan? I could look up his address and wait for him there. But if his parents or anyone else spots me hanging around, they could call my mother or the police.

The cold makes it harder to breathe. My jeans are caked with snow. I have to get out of the cold, but I have no friends to turn to. I used to have friends. Before Dad left. Before DJ got sick. Before I felt so guilty and unhappy and angry. I told myself I needed only Nate. Suddenly I realize how much better this would all be if I had allowed my other friends to help me. If I hadn't pushed them away because they didn't fall in line with what I thought I needed. I have no one I can ask to help me. For the last year my life has revolved around our house, Nate's home, the hospital that's been treating DJ, and school.

School.

I stop to get my bearings. Nate lives another block away. The school is just a couple blocks from there and the houses nearest to that building are far enough away that I won't be noticed—especially not in this snowstorm. I can't go inside, but the high school has all sorts of alcoves and overhangs where kids without cars wait for their rides after classes. And if those are too exposed, I can duck under the bleachers on the football field or see if I can break the lock on the Newt Café that's used to serve soft drinks and hotdogs during games. The place has looked like it's going to fall down ever since I can remember, but it would be shelter.

Even if I can't get in the café, I now have a plan and a direction to run in. I avoid Nate's street on my way to the school. The tracks I was walking in have disappeared. Here and there I find new ones to use, but mostly I keep to the side of the road. The two cars that pass me go slow. One looks like it might stop to ask if I need help or a lift, but I keep my head down and veer toward a driveway so it looks like I've reached my destination.

I rewrap my scarf around my nose, mouth, and chin and pull my hat down so it almost covers my eyes. Finally, in the distance I see the blurry shape of a long brick building and pick up my pace. I doubt I've ever been so happy to see Nottawa High School before.

I force myself to run toward the front entrance, which is covered by a large overhang. When I reach the alcove, I stand in the corner next to the wall that is out of the wind to rest a minute. I slide down the brick to the cold, snowy cement and huddle against the wall, wishing I were somewhere warm.

My phone rings. I reach into my pocket and pull it out, expecting that it's Officer Shepens. Instead, it's Bryan.

Oh thank God. He must have changed his mind about Nate—otherwise, why else would he be calling?

I fumble to take my gloves off so I can answer the phone and say, "Hello?"

"Kaylee?" Bryan's voice is strained and he sounds out of breath. "I'm so sorry. It's Nate. He's gone."

Sydney

DRIVING IN THE SNOW SUCKS. Driving in the snow with a guy screaming his head off in the back seat of the truck sucks way worse. Sydney is just glad his dad didn't need the truck. Otherwise, he'd probably have driven his mom's Civic into a ditch. Someone in this hick town should think about plowing at some point. It's not like the snow is just going to remove itself.

Suddenly, everything gets quiet. Thank all that's holy. The screaming has been getting on his last nerve. Who can drive in this weather and deal with something like that? Of course, Sydney really can't blame Nate. After all, who wants to be trussed up like a duck and thrown into a truck to be taken God only knows where? Sydney's glad he's the driver instead of the duck. Still, guilt tugs at him and he's sorry it isn't Nate's brother, Jack, that NEED has plans for. Jack is a first-class jerk. Nate never did all the bull the popular kids do. He wasn't the type to pick on the freshmen or laugh at someone when they tripped in the hall. Hell, he didn't even care if someone laughed at him.

Jack and Sydney, however, don't get along. In fact, they went a couple of rounds last year when Jack mouthed off about Sydney's dad not having a real job. But Nate. Nate had been okay.

Had been. Has been, he corrects himself. Nate is still alive, and will be after Sydney drops him off. For how long . . . well, there's no way for Sydney to tell. Not without asking questions. And Sydney knows that if you ask a question, you have to be willing to hear the answer. For this, Sydney already knows the answer will be bad.

The documents he was told to forge Nate's signature on gave him an idea of what is coming. Turns out, the two of them have a similar writing style. And even if they didn't, Sydney doubts anyone will look that closely at the signature. After all, the facts are right there.

Of course that's only *if* Sydney decides to follow his instructions. While he's racked up a bunch of cash from the work so far, there might be a bigger payoff. A bird in the hand is good, but at this point he might risk that for the flock sitting in the bush. His dad likes to say that life is filled with opportunities. For once, his dad might be onto something. And Sydney isn't about to let this opportunity pass him by. One stop will tell him which path to take. If things work out, Nate won't have to worry about that forged piece of paper. If not . . . well, sacrifices have to be made. And Sydney isn't about to sacrifice himself.

Kaylee

GONE.

"What do you mean Nate is gone?" I yell. "Where did you take him?"

"I'm sorry. NEED told me to put Nate in the back room of the old post office." Bryan sounds tired. Lost. Confused. As angry and scared as I am. He takes a deep breath and keeps talking. "I like Nate. I didn't want anything to happen to him, but I figured I had to do what I was told. If I didn't, someone else who might not like Nate would have, and they know what I— That doesn't matter. What matters is that I parked across the street and waited to see who would come for Nate. But the snow made it hard to see, and by the time I checked the post office again, he was gone. Someone took him and I don't know who or where."

Gone. I lean my forehead against the icy bricks and shiver. Nate.

I want to scream, but I have to think. Think.

"Where are you now?" I ask.

"I'm driving home. I promised my parents I'd come home."

"Come to the school. That's where I'm at." Getting Nate back is the only thing that matters. Bryan has to know more than he's saying even if he doesn't think he knows it. Just one detail that he doesn't think is important could make a difference.

"Why are you at the school? Is it open?"

"NEED set me up. The police are looking for me. They think I caused Amanda's death."

"What? How is that possible?"

"The cops were told . . ." I remember the way everyone doubts everything I say and change course. "Look, it's complicated. I'll explain when you get here."

"I have to go home or my parents will flip and start looking for me. They might even call the police."

Having the cops looking for Bryan won't help me.

"Okay. Go home. Check in with your parents, and when they go to bed, come to the school and find me." My phone says it's 10:36 p.m. His parents won't stay up all that much longer, probably. I guess I can stay warm enough until he gets here. When Bryan doesn't say anything, I add, "Please, Bryan. Nate's out there somewhere, scared to death, and you're the reason why."

Not entirely fair, since Bryan wouldn't have taken Nate on his own or without the help of Jack, but I don't care.

"Fine." He sounds unhappy. Too bad. "But it might be a while. My mom likes to stay up and watch reruns on the weekends."

"Just promise you'll come as soon as you can," I insist, shivering as the wind whips again. The alcove shields me from the worst of it, but my teeth have started to chatter. "And check NEED before you come. See if anything else has happened. Maybe someone will post a picture that will help locate Nate. Promise?"

"I promise. I'll call or text as soon as I'm on the way. Try to stay warm."

"Sure." Then Bryan is gone and only the cold remains.

The roads are bad, and it will take Bryan a while to get home. Then his parents will have to make sure he's okay, and probably finish watching a show before they go to bed. That means it will be close to midnight at the earliest before Bryan shows up and I can climb into the warmth of his car. And if his mother decides to watch a rerun marathon, it could be a whole lot longer.

I wrap my arms around me and rock back and forth. After several moments, I realize the snow is easing up. The wind just makes it seem like more. Soon the plows will be out clearing the roads. If someone drives by the school and glances this way they'll see me sitting here and wonder why. I'm going to have to move.

My phone dings. DJ is texting to say good night. I type my response, then gather up my things and head toward the faculty parking lot that's on the side of the school nearest the field house. Newt's Café is not far from there. It has to have an oven or something with a heat source. At this point anything warm would be good.

I wonder if Nate is warm wherever he is. Is he scared and thinking of me the way I am of him? Or is he hurt and bleeding and thinking that no one is looking for him and the worst is coming? It isn't, though. At least not yet. My mother will text me if she gets contacted about a kidney for DJ. The longest that kidneys can last outside the body before transplant is about thirty hours, and less than a day is better. Mom and DJ would have to be contacted if the transplant were going to happen any time soon. And there would have to be a medical team and a hospital ready to perform the procedure. Nate's parents would also have to approve, and surely they would contact me if they heard something terrible had happened to Nate.

My phone rings and I shield the screen to look at the display. Officer Shepens. Nope. Not answering. On TV shows, cops trace cell phone signals. I'm not sure how accurate that is, but I'm not about to find out the hard way. If he has something important to say—like he knows I didn't hurt Amanda and he wants to help me take down NEED—he can leave a message. I need to think.

I trudge through the snow as I consider who at this school could be behind NEED. Most of my teachers are about as good with computers as I am. I guess Mr. York might be good enough to create a website like NEED. I've never taken a computer science class with him, but a lot of the gaming guys think he's a genius when it comes to all things programming. But what reason would he have? And really, unless his faded sports coats and out-of-style shirts are a deliberate fashion statement, I doubt the guy has the cash to pull this whole thing off.

Some of the students might have the skills to create and manage the website. Sydney . . . What the hell is his last name? Doesn't matter. Sydney designed his father's real estate website last year. Everyone was talking about it, probably because they were also talking about how bad his father is at selling houses.

But unless Sydney's father got a heck of a lot better at his job or they won the lottery, Sydney and his family don't have the cash to fund all the NEED requests.

So, who does? Principal Dean? I doubt it. And she's about to retire anyway. Who else? Everyone says Mrs. Hennessey married a guy with money, but it's hard to imagine our nutrition and health teacher doing anything more evil than adding butter to a recipe.

As far as I can tell, no one is wealthy enough to give away phones and workout gear and hundreds of other "needs" that have been fulfilled. If this is about a personal grudge, that's a lot of money to spend. And who carries a grudge against an entire school? So it has to be something else. Who would be involved in something more? And what could that something be?

People suck, but I can't believe it's someone who has lived and taught here forever. It has to be an outsider. Or at least someone who is newer to the area. Someone chose this town because they wanted to cause problems. Someone . . .

I stop not far from the side entrance of the school as I notice something different about the ground. Footprints. Covered with fresh snow, but not enough to conceal them. They lead from the faculty parking lot to the side entrance. And they're not that old. They're filled with only an inch of snow. So are the car tracks in the parking spot where the footprints originate from. There are also another set of prints near where I'm standing. They, too, lead to the side door.

Part of me wants to run so I don't get caught. The other part wonders if whoever is behind NEED is associated with the school. Did they go inside? Could Nate be in there? School doesn't start for several days. It would be the perfect hiding spot.

I should wait for Bryan. I should go hide in the Newt Café, but I know there's something wrong here. The footprints. The car tracks. Something is off.

I walk to the door. The smell hits me.

Gasoline.

My heart hammers as I pull the flashlight out of my backpack. I expect the door to be locked, but still I pull.

It opens and I stumble back. My eyes water as fumes swirl around me. Waves of an oily, noxious smell that I can taste as I breathe. One step inside and I feel suffocated by the odor. The floor glistens where the light touches it. Not just here at the door, but as far as the beam will reach. The entire hallway is coated with gasoline.

One spark. That's probably all it would take to engulf this place in flames. I have to get out of here—now.

I'm turning back when I hear it.

The wind. I want to believe it's the wind. Then the sound comes again.

Scraping. A clank of metal. And a whisper that sounds like a voice calling for help.

Bryan

FINALLY.

His mother looks back at him with a tense smile before going up the stairs. She's worried that he's upset about Amanda and Lynn's mother and has hovered since he got home, telling him how proud she is to have a son who is so concerned about others. Mom and Dad are so pleased that they don't have one of those kids who cause trouble. They'll blame themselves if they learn what he has done. They'll say it was heartless to not understand how much he needed the acne cream and shoulder the responsibility that is his alone. Because it wasn't really the cream that started this. It was his anger and his desire to hurt someone the way he had been hurt.

Bryan figures it will be at least ten or fifteen minutes before his parents fall asleep and he can slip out of the house. Maybe more. Time enough to check online to see if anything else has happened.

He goes upstairs and logs on to his laptop. What he sees on the first site makes him let out a sigh of relief. Post after post of New Year's resolutions and chat about what everyone is wearing to the big party tomorrow night. Post after post of normal stuff. Then he stops scrolling.

Lynn's mom is dead. Some kind of severe reaction to medication. Because of the snow and the number of other accidents tonight, the ambulance couldn't get to her in time.

There are a bunch of sympathetic responses. But under that are several more posts about clothes and shoes and dates. Buried in the middle of self-portraits and inane quizzes is another post that kicks him in the gut.

Sameena Jahn is dead. Suicide. There is shock. Outrage. Questions as to whether the announcement is real. Links to statistics on how suicide happens most during the holidays, along with assurances that the family will let everyone know about funeral details when they're available.

Quiet. Sameena was quiet and tried so hard. He tutored her once until her father found out and assured Bryan that his daughter no longer required assistance.

Bryan fights the urge to hurl and clicks on the link for the NEED network to see if his request has been fulfilled. No.

DUE TO THE STORM, YOUR NEED REQUEST DELIVERY HAS BEEN DELAYED. ONCE THE STORM HAS PASSED, DELIVERIES WILL RESUME. WE APOLOGIZE FOR ANY INCONVENIENCE AND WELCOME YOU TO SUBMIT A NEW NEED REQUEST WHILE YOU WAIT.

Make another request? No way in hell. But even as he is repelled by the message, he's also relieved. The gun he has been promised isn't here. The decision about how or if he should use it has been taken out of his hands. Because he no longer wants to kill himself. He wants to track down and kill whoever is behind NEED.

But there is no gun. For now.

Bryan checks to see if his mother is asleep yet. Nope. A faint light glows under the door at the end of the hall. He's stuck, which gives him time to check on the NEED message board like Kaylee asked. He doubts he'll find anything that will help them track down Nate, but it couldn't hurt. After all . . .

He stops and scrolls back up to see the image that he just passed. The photo is dim. But something familiar about it catches his eye. The desk with a large calendar pad on it with lots of dates x'ed off. The nameplate next to a coffee cup that says Nottawa Newts. Next to that a clock that has wires coming out of it and a large fountain firework. He squints at the photograph but can't make out the name on the desk, so he copies the image and pastes it into a program that allows him to change the contrast and zoom in.

Dr. Amelia Jain

School. The photograph is of an office at school. Bryan clicks back to the message board, this time scrolling down far enough to see the caption above the photograph. One word that has him reaching for his phone and running for the door.

Boom.

Kaylee

CRAP. MY PHONE RINGS as I stand with my hand on the door, trying to decide what to do. I silence it and listen again to the sounds of the empty school. No. Not empty. Because the whisper comes again and this time I can make out what the word is.

"Please."

I jump as my phone vibrates, and I pull it out of my pocket. "Bryan?"

"Thank God. Kaylee, are you still outside the school? If you are, run. There's some kind of bomb in one of the offices. It's on a timer. You have to go."

"I can't." The plea comes again and, no matter how much I want to, I can't turn away. "Someone is trapped inside."

Bryan yells my name, but I hit End and shove the phone back into my coat pocket. Bryan told me to get out. My eyes and throat already burn from the fumes. Somewhere a fuse is ready to be lit. This place is going to explode. God, I'm scared. I don't want to die.

Scraping. I hear it again. The sound of something being dragged. And the voice cries again. A girl's voice. It's not Nate. And since no one else except DJ cares what the hell happens to me, it shouldn't matter who might be somewhere inside this building waiting to die.

But it does.

Bryan's warning screams in my head. My phone vibrates again in my pocket as if duplicating the plea. But as much as I don't want to die and I don't want to care about whoever is somewhere down the hallway, I have to help.

The floor is slippery. Each step makes me sick with fear that I will do something to ignite the gas and engulf myself in flames. Coughing, I pull my scarf over my nose and mouth and grip the flashlight tighter. Don't drop it. Don't send up a spark. No sparks.

I don't call out. If the person who set the bomb is still around, I don't want them to find me. I doubt they are, but I don't know for sure. So I stay silent. Which is good because the dry, burning ache in my throat is getting worse the longer I'm in here.

Go toward the offices or turn toward the gym? I don't know when the timer will go off. Any minute? My phone says it's eleven forty-five. If I were the one setting the timer, I would set it for midnight. That means I have ten minutes at most to find whoever is trapped if I want to have time to get out.

Oh God. I don't want to be here. I want to go home.

Propelled by the fear that the timer will go off any second, I come to the next hallway and stop as I hear the sound again. To my right. Away from the offices. Toward the English classrooms.

The floor has a line of shiny wetness running along it, but the entire surface isn't as slick and the smell isn't as strong. Or maybe that's just wishful thinking. I don't care. I cling to the idea that this part of the school isn't as coated in gasoline and listen for the person to call out again.

"Hello? Ethan? Please."

The last word, spoken as almost a whisper, makes me run. The girl's voice comes again. To the left. An open doorway and a trail of gasoline into the room beckon me forward and when I turn the corner and flash my beam I see her. Tied to the chair of the school desk is Hannah Mazur. Her eyes are wide. There's blood on her terrified face. The smell of gas is stronger in here and I see the pool of liquid that surrounds her chair.

"Help me."

The words hit me like a slap and I realize I've just been standing there looking at her, doing nothing.

As she struggles against her restraints, the desk she's tied to scrapes against the tiled floor. "Help me. Whoever the hell you are."

"It's Kaylee Dunham." I pull away my scarf and point the flashlight upward so she can see my face. I cross the few feet between us and squat down behind the chair to get a better look. Tape. Lots and lots of duct tape that's become bunched and twisted so it's almost impossible to see where to pull it free. It would be easier if I could turn on an overhead light. But can I? Could something that simple cause the fumes to ignite? I don't know.

What should I do? Cutting her free would be easiest. But I don't have a knife. What else would work?

"Keys." I left mine at home. "Do you have keys somewhere?"

She coughs. "Please don't leave me here."

"I won't," I agree. "But if you don't help, we both might die." Time is slipping away. "Where are your keys?" I yell.

"In the left front pocket of my coat."

She shifts so I can reach the deep coat pocket and I realize she's wet. Gas. Hannah is soaked with gas. I pull out the keys and almost drop them as I flip through looking for the one that will give me the best grip.

"Okay." I put my bag down on a dry section of the floor and lay the flashlight on top of it so it shines toward Hannah's hands.

I attack the restraints with the key. The tape is thick. Wrapped at least several times to strengthen the hold. How much time is left? How long will it take for the gas here in this room, on Hannah and now covering my hands and who knows what else, to ignite? I keep sawing at the tape, all the while I can't help remembering mean comments I've heard Hannah make. Comments directed at me. I wonder for a second if she remembers those moments.

My eyes sting and I try to stay focused. My phone vibrates again in my pocket and I ignore it. No time to answer. The key rips through part of the restraints. It's a start. I saw harder. Hannah yelps that I've hurt her, but who the hell cares. She's going to hurt a heck of a lot worse if this place goes up in flames. I tune out her hoarse babbling and keep working.

More bits of tape break free. Getting there. "Hannah, pull your hands apart as much as you can. Harder." She grunts as I saw. Another rip in the tape gives me hope and makes me attack it more furiously. We're going to get out of here. We are.

"Got it." One down. Two to go. Only now Hannah can help. "Here," I say, handing her the flashlight. "Shine this while I work on getting your feet free."

The light helps. The tape isn't as thick on her legs, but still it takes time. How much time? I don't look at my phone because that would take precious seconds. My phone vibrates again as I get the top part of the tape around Hannah's left foot to rip. "You do the other," I say, shoving the keys into her free hand. Then I grab the ripped sides of the tape and pull. It gives a bit and I pull again. The rip widens until finally the tape is off one foot.

"Hurry," I say, coughing, and I blink as the world spins out of focus. The fumes are making me dizzy. Hannah can barely function. So I grab the keys back and attack the tape around her other foot.

This restraint takes longer to cut through. Or maybe it doesn't. Maybe it's just knowing there are minutes—or seconds—until midnight that makes me feel as if the sawing is endless. I shove the keys back in Hannah's coat pocket and pull at the tape with my hands. Finally she's free.

"Thank you, Kaylee. Thank you." I hear the tears. The panic. The fear as she tries to get to her feet and falls back down. Crap. We don't have time for this now.

"I know you don't feel good, but you have to get up. This place could explode any minute." Hannah pushes to her feet. I grab my backpack, shrug the strap onto my shoulder, and grab Hannah's arm as she sways. Her legs start to buckle. She grabs on to me and almost takes us both down to the floor. It's a miracle I stay on my feet, but I refuse to bite it in this school. No way. No how.

"We're going to die if you don't move. Don't make me leave you behind," I threaten. I don't mean it, but she doesn't have to know that. "You have to hurry. Okay?" I pull Hannah upright and don't wait for her to agree before I start to move.

I want to run, but Hannah isn't capable of running. She jerks and stumbles, but leaning on me she stays on her feet and we reach the hallway.

"Hannah, do you know if the side door you came in through is the only door open?" I hope she says no. I don't want to go back that way. Maybe she knows another way out since her father works here. When she doesn't answer, I yell, "Hannah? Is there another unlocked door?"

"I don't know," she says, crying. "I don't know. I don't know."

Perfect.

"Stop it," I snap. I can't help it. I'm scared too. "We'll just go back the way I came." Following the path of gasoline that is waiting to catch fire. The rest of the doors in the school are probably locked up tight. They might even be chained shut as they sometimes are for security reasons. It will only be worse if we waste time heading for an exit and end up trapped.

Hannah isn't big, but she's taller than me, which makes our progress awkward. So do her tears and the way she starts to ramble about stuff I don't understand. Nate. Ethan. Her father. A date. The end of the hallway is just a few feet away. Then one more length of hallway to go. We can make it.

"Kaylee!" Oh God. That sounds like Bryan's voice and it's coming from inside the building.

"Bryan?"

Hannah jolts against me, loses her footing, and lets go of her hold on me as she trips and goes down in a heap onto the gas-slicked floor.

"Kaylee!"

I stumble toward the wall and use it to keep from landing on the ground as Bryan races around the corner. Hannah shrieks and cries harder.

"You shouldn't have come in here!" I yell, but I'm glad to see him. Glad to have someone who isn't sobbing to help get us the hell out.

Bryan kneels next to Hannah. "I think I can carry her if you help me get her up."

Between the two of us we pull the wet, hysterical Hannah to her feet. Bryan grunts as he picks her up and tells me to run. And I do. Around the corner. Down the hallway. I don't need to glance over my shoulder to know Bryan is back there or that he is falling farther and father behind. His footsteps and Hannah's crying are enough to tell me that. I pull out my phone and look at the time. Eleven fifty-nine. I want to be wrong about the timer. Please let me be wrong. I have to be wrong.

I reach the door well before Bryan and push it open. The fresh air whips in my face as I hold the door. Bryan is still at least thirty or forty feet away from the exit.

"Hurry!" I yell, even though I know he's doing his best. I look at the door, tamp down my instinct to flee, and run back down the hallway to help. Bryan shakes his head as I try to take on some of Hannah's weight.

"Hold the door open for us." He coughs and struggles to speak. "I've got her."

Okay. I race back toward the door, making sure not to get too far ahead just in case Bryan needs me. The clock on my phone hits midnight. I hold my breath as I reach the door and fling it open again. Bryan's head lifts and I know he feels the fresh air. Less than ten feet away. Almost there. Come on. Come on. Bryan stumbles across the threshold and I follow, letting the door slam shut behind me. Hannah must be heavy as hell, but it isn't until we reach the parking lot that he puts her down in the snow.

Bryan doubles over to catch his breath. Hannah is crying and I'm coughing like I've got pneumonia. We're a mess, but we're alive. And I was wrong about the timer.

Or not. As soon as that thought crosses my mind I hear a rumble, then the echo of shattering glass. A moment later the school goes up in flames.

Ethan

NOT AT HOME. Not at Nate Weakley's house. Ethan frowns as he thinks about where to look next. Someone has clearly been at Kaylee's house recently. The tire tracks in the driveway were dusted with fresh snow. Whoever was there couldn't have left very long ago. Ethan could have assumed Kaylee drove off with whoever paid her a visit, but a professional can't rely on assumptions. Which is why he knows Kaylee left on foot. Her footprints were partially covered, but not enough. He was able to track them to the fence and when he drove to the next street he was easily able to spot where she'd come out on the other side.

The boy has skills.

The streets are icy. Not many cars are out. Too bad a plow already came by. Otherwise Kaylee's footprints would lead him all the way to her. Of course, that wouldn't be nearly as challenging. The bigger the challenge, the better the reward.

Come out, come out, wherever you are, he thinks.

Although, as much as Ethan likes the idea of stalking his quarry, he's not sure he'll be able to find her. The town isn't that big, but it's dark and snowy and Kaylee could be anywhere and he hasn't a clue where to start looking. More information is required.

In Mercenary of War, players earn power-ups, which provide clues to the best method of locating and eliminating their targets. It's too bad there isn't a way to earn clues in this game. Then again, NEED wants Kaylee. If it wants her bad enough, NEED will help him track her down.

Ethan steers the car to the side of the road and pulls up the email he received after the website came back online. Since he can't access the site from his phone, this is the next best thing.

Quickly, he types his message and hits Send. Now what? It's not like he's going to go home. Not with his mother starting to question him. He has time to kill until NEED gets back to him. So why not drive by his last project and see how it turned out? What better way to wait for instructions on his next assignment than to see that school and everything in it go up in flames?

Putting the car in gear, he realizes it's too bad he didn't think to bring hotdogs or marshmallows. He could roast some snacks while cheering *Burn, baby, burn.*

Kaylee

ALARMS SOUND. Smoke billows into the night sky. Fire crackles and the smell of gasoline hangs thick in the air. The sight of the school in flames is mesmerizing against a backdrop of snowy white. I jump at the sound of more glass shattering from somewhere inside. I was in there. I could have died. We all could have died.

Hannah is curled up in the snow, sobbing. Bryan is crouched beside her, consoling her while watching smoke spiral up from the building. I don't say anything. I can't.

Alarms continue to scream.

Alarms. I try to shake off the horror and think. Help will be coming soon. Firefighters. Police. They'll come to put out the fire and if I don't get out of here they'll find me. Question me.

Nate. The shock of finding Hannah and the explosion made me forget for a moment that I was looking for him. Nate doesn't have time for me to stand around talking about how I got here and why. He needs me to find him. I have to get away.

I shift the backpack on my shoulder and look down at Bryan and Hannah. Her sobs have changed to whimpers and that should make me feel sorry for her, but instead it irritates me. Probably because I wish I had time to cry. I wish I could wait around for help to arrive. Later. I can cry and freak out later. When Nate is safe and NEED is taken down. Because seeing the school engulfed in flames makes me realize again the lengths to which NEED will go.

"I can't stay here," I say loud enough to carry over the crackle of the fire and Hannah's moaning. "Can I borrow your car, Bryan? I have to find Nate."

Bryan coughs, shakes his head, and stands. "I'm going with you. Let's just get Hannah further from the school first so she's not breathing in the smoke."

Easier said than done.

The minute Bryan tries to help her stand, Hannah starts to scream her head off and kicks and claws to get free. I can't blame her for flipping out, but this isn't helping. I try to pull her to her feet, but she's dead weight and the adrenaline that kept me moving up until now is wearing off. We're about to try one more time when I hear sirens.

"If she doesn't want to move, I vote to leave her," I say. "Five more minutes of sitting here won't hurt."

Bryan shakes his head. "Here." He reaches into his pocket. "Take my keys. Get the car started."

He tries to reason with Hannah. I run to the car, unlock it, and put the key in the ignition. The radio and the heater come on full blast. Crap. How do I turn the radio off? I hit the button to silence it and realize the sirens are louder still.

"Bryan!" I yell. "We have to go!"

Bryan gives up on Hannah and hurries toward the car as I climb over the middle console to the other side. Bryan gets in, puts the car in gear, and asks, "Where are we going?"

"Just drive." We can figure out the rest when the cops aren't closing in.

The tires spin before they catch hold. Hannah screams and I see Bryan flinch as he turns off the car's headlights. His hands tighten on the steering wheel while he drives the car out of the parking lot and onto the road.

"Can you go faster?" I ask.

"No." The car fishtails as if to confirm. Knowing I can run faster than we are moving makes me want to jump out and sprint. In the distance I can see red and white lights flash as they approach. I hope if they spot our car they'll be too worried about the blazing building to give chase.

I hold my breath until I see the first emergency vehicle turn into the school lot. The rest follow. Bryan and I remain silent until he turns the car onto the next street beyond the reach of the flashing lights.

After driving another block he turns the car into a parking lot, flips the headlights back on, and asks, "Now what?"

I don't know. I look behind us to make sure no one is following. No one is there. For now. The digital clock on the dashboard reads 12:10 a.m. So much has happened in so little time. That more than anything terrifies me. How fast things can change. One minute the school is fine. The next minute it's burning to the ground. Had Bryan not shown up when he did and helped me get Hannah out, we could have died.

"How did you know?" I ask.

"What?"

I turn toward him. "How did you know about the bomb at the school? When you called me, you told me to get away from the school because of a bomb. How did you know? Did someone tell you?"

"I saw a picture." He shifts in his seat to face me. "Someone posted a photo of the timer sitting on Dr. Jain's desk."

Wait a minute. "The bomb went off in Dr. Jain's office?"

"Yeah. Why?"

"I don't know. That has to be significant." I have to think it through, but waiting for us to be discovered is making that impossible. "Can you just drive?"

"Where to?"

"Anywhere that isn't here."

As Bryan pulls the car back onto the road, I close my eyes and focus. Dr. Jain's office is in a far corner of the building. Near the administration offices and the rest of the counselors, but away from most things students deal with every day. The students who are all on NEED. If someone wanted to damage the school in order to shut it down for a long time, hitting another area—like the cafeteria in the center of the building or the science rooms where chemicals are stored—would make the most sense. At least, that's what I would do.

"Did NEED tell you how to kidnap Nate and what to do with him once you got him?" When Bryan squirms I say, "Look, I'm not trying to upset you. I'm trying to figure out if NEED let the person who set fire to the school decide where to set the bomb or if they gave explicit instructions."

"I don't know about the bomb, but for Nate's kidnapping they gave me pretty detailed instructions." Bryan looks up and stares out the window as he speaks. "The whole plan was spelled out. Working with Jack. The drug to knock Nate unconscious. Even what I should use to tie him up in the back room of the old post office. I found the drug, a pair of handcuffs, and a bunch of tension ties in a box in our neighbor's mailbox. Just like they said I would."

Specific instructions for a specific purpose. If the same applies to the school, NEED wanted the fire set in Dr. Jain's office. No matter how quickly the fire department responded to the alarms, if the timer went off and the fire was set the way it was supposed to be, the damage in that room would be the worst. Someone wanted everything of Dr. Jain's destroyed. Who?

Who knows us well enough to predict how we would act when we were invited into NEED?

Who knew that Nate could be a donor?

Who has access to students' medical files and knows almost everything happening with our family and friends because it's her job to know?

There's only one answer: Dr. Jain.

She's new this year, but not new to the area. She lived here or somewhere near here years before. Did she say that to my mother or to me? I don't recall. But I know she said it. Where did she come from? Somewhere on the East Coast. I think she said she moved from here to Maryland before returning. She also said that people can make choices that take them somewhere they didn't intend to go, and continue to make it worse by not admitting their mistakes. I thought she was referring to me. How no one trusts me because of the things I did. But what if she wasn't talking about me at all? What if she was referring to NEED?

As much as I've disliked being forced to talk to Dr. Jain, I believed her interest in me was sincere. She said she was invested in me. In my family. That she understood what it's like to be abandoned by someone you love. Lies? Truth? I don't know. But my gut tells me the fire was set in her office to eliminate evidence. And she's the one who's counseling my mother. Telling her that I need new treatments. That I'm a danger to my brother.

"I think Dr. Jain is behind NEED."

Bryan hits the brakes and the car skids wildly to the left before stopping. I fling my arms straight in front of me to keep from flying into the dashboard. "What? That doesn't make any sense."

"I think it does." It's the only explanation that makes sense. "Faculty are always told when a student has medical issues. Every teacher and administrator at DJ's school has all sorts of information on what to do if he falls ill. We didn't know about Amanda's allergy, but it wouldn't be a secret to Dr. Jain. And the school shrink has a good shot at knowing who has grudges against whom and which students are more susceptible to rewards than others. All the things NEED knows."

Bryan stares out the window then quietly says, "She knew about me."

"What did she know?"

"Dr. Jain knew . . ." Bryan takes a deep breath. "She knew I was upset about something that had happened with Amanda. She stopped me in the hall just before break started and offered to give me a pass to come talk to her. She said some of my teachers were concerned and thought I might be depressed. I told her I was okay, but she said she was around if I needed to talk. Or if I didn't want to talk with her that I might feel better if I discussed whatever was bothering me with the person who caused the problem. She said people often regret not discussing their problems until it's too late." He turns and looks at me. It's dark, but the shadows don't hide the tears in his eyes. "I didn't talk to Amanda. I was too angry. So when NEED told me to deliver a box to her doorstep, I was pretty sure there was something wrong with it, but I didn't care."

I gasp. "Oh God. You delivered the cookies." Bryan killed Amanda. No. NEED did. Bryan didn't know Amanda was allergic. He didn't want her to die. "But Amanda's death isn't your fault."

"Yes, it is," Bryan says softly. "You know it is."

Maybe it is. Maybe not. I don't know. All I know is that the empty look on Bryan's face scares the hell out of me.

"It doesn't matter what I think."

"I guess not." But his tone tells me it does. In a flat voice he says, "When Amanda died, I didn't want to tell anyone what I had done. I should have told my parents or the police or left it alone. Instead, I asked NEED for something else. I knew it was wrong, but I talked myself into thinking it wasn't. And I can't take it back. I can't make it right."

"You weren't the one who planned to kill her." This much I'm certain of. "You didn't set her up to die or call the bakery and have a receipt created with my name on it to make it look like I planned to murder her."

"What?" The emptiness is replaced by confusion.

"You made a bad choice. Lots of our friends made bad choices. Decisions they would never have thought of making on their own had someone not suggested these sick ideas and dangled a big, honking carrot in front of their faces." Stupid. We are all stupid for not talking to each other. For believing anything our friends did was okay for us to do too. But NEED is worse because it used that. It used us. For what? Why?

"So now what?" Bryan asks. "Do we call the cops and tell them we think Dr. Jain is behind NEED?"

"The police think I'm the one who ordered those cookies for Amanda. They'll arrest me first and ask questions later." If I'm lucky. And boy do I not feel lucky.

"Which means we're never going to find Nate."

"Yes, we are," I say as I reach into my jeans pocket and come up with two crumpled business cards. I put one card back and hold the other, from Dr. Jain, in my hand. The one with her personal cell phone number that she encouraged me to call anytime—day or night.

Is Dr. Jain sleeping? If she's behind all this, *can* she sleep, knowing the harm she's caused? Or does she sleep soundly, knowing her plans have gone so well? I guess I'm going to find out. I dial the number and wait while it rings.

"Hello. This is Dr. Amelia Jain."

No confusion. No worry at being contacted in the middle of the night by a phone number she doesn't know. Just the same calm, controlled voice that has always irritated me.

"It's Kaylee Dunham. I'm sorry to call so late." I'm not, but it's the polite thing to say, and I don't want to arouse her suspicions before I get to the point.

"Kaylee. Thank goodness. Are you okay? The police contacted me a while ago after they went to your house and you weren't home. Where are you?"

Crap. It didn't occur to me that the cops would contact

her. "I'm okay. But I'll be better if you can answer a question for me."

"Anything. I've been so concerned."

Yeah, right. I take a deep breath because after this moment there is no going back. "Where's Nate? What have you done with him?"

I wait for her to act confused or shocked or something. Instead there is silence. I look at the phone to make sure the call is still connected. Yes.

"Dr. Jain, are you there?"

"I'm here, Kaylee," she says softly. "And if you ever want to see Nate again, you'll have to come here too."

NETWORK MEMBERS—682
NEEDS PENDING—673
NEEDS FULFILLED—225

Sydney

SYDNEY SLIDES BACK into his car, tosses his backpack and a brief-case he snagged from inside onto the passenger seat, and revs the engine. His luck is holding. When the house goes up in flames, eliminating any evidence of his involvement, his lucky streak will continue. So far, so good. The question is, how much does he want to push it?

He turns to look in the back of the cab at Nate, who is drooling on the seat. The second dose of tranquilizers hasn't worn off yet. Sydney didn't want to put Nate under again, but he didn't really have a choice. When involved in breaking and entering, it's a bad idea to have someone screaming his head off outside. It's probably more humane that Nate's unconscious, and chances are he'll wake up soon anyway. Although Sydney's dad would have a fit if he could see the mess on the leather seat: the pool of drool in the center, the puke from when Nate woke up the first time, and the footprints where Nate was kick-ing before Sydney felt forced to give him the next round of drugs. Well, chances are good Dad isn't going to have to see any of that. It all depends on which step Sydney takes next. Both paths have challenges. Both have rewards.

Despite the late hour, he can still deliver Nate to the designated location. So far, the bad-weather excuse seems to be holding pretty well. But not for long. The plows are out clearing the streets.

He looks at the last message he received, then at the bags on the passenger seat. Files. Contact information. Next steps. This trip has been worthwhile. He needs to spend a few minutes going over the new files. When he combines that information with what he already knows, it will be enough to make the choice about which path to take. Knowledge is power. He now has knowledge. The question is, will he have the courage to use it?

Kaylee

HERE.

"Where is 'here'? Your house?" I ask. I don't know where Dr. Jain lives, but in a town this size it can't be very far.

"No," she says. "I learned the hard way that it's best not to bring work home. Besides, there are many things about this project that require larger facilities. But I'm sure you'll be able to find us if you're sufficiently motivated. Are you motivated, Kaylee?"

"Yes." Fear swirls at the detachment in her voice. Like this is all just a case study. A test for some poor rats in a maze. As if real people—real lives—aren't involved. "Tell me where I have to go."

She gives me the address and the town. Not Nottawa, but one that's ten minutes away in good weather. Repeating the address back, I wave my arms at Bryan, hoping he understands that I need him to write it down or memorize it or something. Just in case I forget. And I wonder if this is a trap. Because nothing about NEED is done without purpose or comes without a price.

"It's too far to come on foot, but I trust you'll be able to find transportation," Dr. Jain says. "I promise to take good care of your mom and brother if they arrive before you."

My heart stutters. "They're in Milwaukee." They're safe. Please. Let them still be safe.

"They were in Milwaukee. Officer Shepens called me when the number you gave him to reach your mother didn't work, and I volunteered to call her for him. She then called him to listen to his concerns, and is very disappointed to be returning home to deal with your issues. You do seem to have a lot of them, which means you'll have plenty to discuss when you both get here. I'll be curious to see what treatment plan your mother chooses for you. Until then, I have work to do."

"No. Wait." But she doesn't wait and the display changes to "Call ended."

She has to be wrong. My mother's last text said they were going to bed. She would have called me if she were coming home now, especially if she thought I had screwed up again. She wouldn't drag DJ back here simply on Dr. Jain's say-so. Or would she? I stare at my phone, trying to think. If Dr. Jain is telling the truth about Mom talking to Officer Shepens, she now knows I'm under suspicion in Amanda's murder. Given those circumstances, she'd have to come home, wouldn't she? If she didn't, what would people think?

But Dr. Jain could be lying about everything, and my mother could be asleep at Aunt Susan's right now, unaware that any of this is happening. If that's the case, a call from me would alert her that something is very wrong. But if Dr. Jain is telling the truth, Mom and DJ might at this very moment be en route. A call from me could prevent whatever Dr. Jain has planned. Or just make it happen faster, because my mother won't believe me. I don't know what to do.

"What's going on?" Bryan asks.

Instinctively I start to say nothing, but then I realize that Bryan is in this with me. He might see something I don't, so I tell him what Dr. Jain said. "What do I do?"

"Don't call," he insists. "Dr. Jain has to be lying. She's probably hoping you'll call your mom and set things in motion so that your mother comes back. I doubt Dr. Jain would make that call on her own. Your mom might tell your aunt and draw attention Dr. Jain doesn't want. NEED is all about making other people do the dirty work while it stays anonymous. Dr. Jain is NEED, which means she'll operate the same way."

"It sucks not to know for sure," I say, putting down my phone.

"Yeah. Yeah, it does. But think of it this way—even if Dr. Jain is telling the truth and your mother is coming back to Nottawa, she's got a lot farther to travel than we do. No matter what happens, we'll get there long before her."

What Bryan says makes sense. Dr. Jain is probably lying, but if not, we have time to stop her before my mother and DJ return. That has to be enough.

"Okay then," I say with a nod. "I guess we go find Dr. Jain and finish this."

"Works for me. Although, it's weird that she gave you the address like that." Bryan frowns as he punches the location into his GPS. "There are lots of ways she could get rid of you or make things worse in your life. Instead, she wants you to come find her. Why?"

"I don't know." There must be a reason, but damned if I know what it is. That gives her a big advantage. But I have one too. "She doesn't know you're with me. With two of us, there's a chance we can surprise her."

"How?"

"Just drive. We'll figure it out on the way." We have to.

Bryan drives while I consider what I know about Dr. Jain. Her husband left her. She used to live around here. Why is she back? Nate said it takes hundreds, maybe thousands of hours to create a site that works the way NEED does. This project must have been started before Dr. Jain came to work at Nottawa High School.

"Why did Dr. Jain start NEED?" I ask Bryan. "And why here?" There has to be a reason beyond causing students to kill their friends.

"I don't know." Bryan glances at me. "It seems strange that she'd pick Nottawa of all places."

Yes, it does. But I don't know how to find the answer. If Nate were here . . .

I bite my lip, take a deep breath, and push away thoughts of Nate and what could be happening to him.

"We need more information," I say.

"Yeah, but how do we get it? If you haven't noticed, we're on our own and don't exactly have a lot of time."

He's right. But so am I. Right now, Dr. Jain holds all the cards. She has the anonymity of the Internet on her side, not to mention all the chaos she's caused. There might be a few students who want to stand up and tell their parents or the police about NEED, but if they've performed a fulfillment requirement the worry that they'll be held responsible for whatever terrible thing they did will keep them silent. And even if someone does report it, they won't know everything. The website could vanish again at any moment and then what? Dr. Jain has to be shut down. She cannot be allowed to lie in wait for the right time to relaunch NEED again. We have to find some way to stop her.

"I have my computer with me," I say. "If we find somewhere for me to get online, I can do a search on her."

"Why not use your phone?"

"Reception out here sucks. The laptop would be easier." Besides, I haven't a clue what I'm looking for. I need a bigger screen and a lot of luck if I'm going to come up with something useful fast.

"It's the middle of the night." Bryan is exasperated and tense. "We can't go to my house without my parents flipping out. You can't go back to your house without risking arrest, and nothing is open at this time of night."

"No." But Bryan has given me an idea. "You know, locking the doors and flipping off the lights doesn't turn off the Internet signal. A lot of places just leave the signal up and running at night. If we can find a business with public Wi-Fi, we can park next to the building and I can log on."

While Bryan steers the car down the snowy streets, I try doing a few searches on my phone. All it yields is a link to the school's website, with her credentials as a psychiatrist— an undergraduate degree in psychology from the University of Wisconsin at Madison. A graduate degree in public policy and a Ph.D. in behavioral science from Johns Hopkins. Well, there's no denying the woman is smart. The psychology degree I sort of understand, and behavioral science seems self-explanatory. But what does public policy have to do with either one of them? I'll have to wait until I get a better signal to find out because the Johns Hopkins website won't load on my phone.

But wait. There is one other interesting piece of information on the high school's site. Dr. Jain is quoted as saying, "Wisconsin has held many fond memories for me. It broke my heart eleven years ago when I moved away. I hope I can help ease the hearts of many Nottawa High School students and make my mark on the community now that I am back."

Eleven years. Dr. Jain moved out of the area more than a decade ago. That had to have been when her husband left her. Unless she wasn't telling the truth about that. Maybe it's a stretch to think why she's here now is related to why she left then, but what other reason could she have to return and bring something so terrible with her?

I look at my phone. Twelve fifty a.m. Nate has been missing for only a couple hours, but there's no telling what has happened. My brother and mother might be on their way to Dr. Jain's place. Part of me thinks we should skip trying to hook up to the Web and just go to the address Dr. Jain gave me. I wish I knew what the right thing to do was. Will talking to Dr. Jain help? Or am I rushing headlong into danger and dragging Bryan along with me?

There's only one way to find out.

Ethan

ETHAN SMILES at the message on his phone. Asking for more information is always a good idea.

An ambulance cruises out of the school parking lot. Lights flashing. Siren blaring. Both give Ethan a rush. But beneath the rush nags worry. From his spot down the street he can't see what's happening, but the speeding ambulance makes him think that perhaps Hannah survived the explosion and fire. He should have moved her closer to the explosion, but he figured she'd be dead no matter what.

Maybe she is dead and someone else is injured. He has to hope for that outcome, because if Hannah is alive and she recovers she'll be able to point her finger at him. He can't allow that to happen.

He looks back at the message on the phone. Does he follow instructions and remove the assigned target or head after the ambulance? Or maybe he should just blow town.

No. He can't leave. He has no money and nowhere to go.

So really, he has two choices in front of him. Which to choose? He pulls a quarter out of the cup holder. Heads he goes for the target. Tails he covers his own tail and makes sure that Hannah is eliminated for good.

Ethan gives the coin a flip, catches it, and slaps it onto the back of his hand. He glances at the quarter and dumps it back into the center console. *Fate has decided,* he thinks as he puts the car in gear. He takes one last look at the smoking building and the lights flashing in the school parking lot. Fate decides everything. Too bad Fate is a total bitch.

Kaylee

OUR SLOW PACE on the slick roads and the lack of reception on my phone make me want to scream. But I have to hold it together. Dr. Jain expects me to lead with my emotions. To charge into the situation without thinking it through. She thinks she knows who I am. But she doesn't. How could she when I'm not sure I really know who I am yet myself?

"I think Jammin' Joe might have free Wi-Fi and I doubt the staff is tech savvy enough to turn it off when they leave," Bryan says. "You want to stop or keep going?"

All sorts of terrible scenarios have been playing in my head while Bryan has been driving. Most I know are unrealistic and worthy of the horror films Nate is so fond of. But one of them won't let go. If Dr. Jain has figured out a way to orchestrate an accident for Nate that will put him on life support, then she doesn't need my brother here yet. The hospital can keep Nate alive with machines until his family decides what to do. Dr.

Jain could believe she can convince them to turn an apparently innocent tragedy into something positive.

As much as I want to tell Bryan to keep driving, I open my laptop and say, "Let's see if we can get a signal."

Bryan misjudges the size of the parking space and the car jumps the curb. I clutch my laptop and scream. So much for staying calm. But he misses slamming into the handicapped parking sign by a couple inches, so that's good.

When the car is stopped, we look at each other for a second. I take several deep breaths before typing my password into the laptop and let it search for a network to connect to.

Come on.

The cursor spins and spins.

"How long does the GPS say it will take to get to the address Dr. Jain gave us?" I ask.

"Seven minutes. But fifteen minutes ago it said it would only take that much time to get this far. And it took double that. The streets are plowed better here, but it will probably be worse outside of town."

I try to figure out how long Dr. Jain thinks it will take me to get to her location. A while, especially since she believes I'll have to find a car. Arriving faster than she plans would be a huge advantage. One I don't want to lose.

"Ten minutes," I say as the cursor stops spinning and *Accept the Terms and Conditions of the free Wi-Fi page* appears. Score. "I'll look for information for only ten minutes. Then, no matter what I say, I want you to put the car in gear and go."

Bryan nods and I open up my browser and get to work. The first thing I search for is the address we are going to. What is it? What's around it?

Not much. At least not from what I can tell. It looks as though it is out in the middle of nowhere. No surprise. But there is one entry for that address—a link to something called Everything Nature—Stone Pottery. Martin A. Boone is the owner, but when I click on the link a message tells me the site no longer exists. So I do a search on "Martin A. Boone" and find a new address for Everything Nature—Stone Pottery. I click on the link and watch the site load.

There's a picture of a blond man standing in front of shelves filled with bowls, plates, and vases. Something about him looks familiar. I click on the bio page and learn that he's a lifelong resident of Wisconsin who has embraced techniques used by Native American tribes from this area to create his art. He's newly remarried, has a studio-gallery in Burlington, Wisconsin, and travels to art festivals around the country, displaying and selling his work.

Remarried. And Dr. Jain is divorced. Is he her ex-husband? Burlington isn't far. Fifteen miles. Twenty, tops. And his business was once located at Dr. Jain's mystery address. He's connected to her in one way or another. As interesting as that is, I don't find anything that tells me why he looks familiar or if he is tied in to what's happening now.

I copy the link into a document and then glance at the time. Four minutes used up. I have to move on to the next search. This time I dig for information on Amelia Jain herself.

"I see headlights," Bryan says. I crane my neck and look toward the road, hoping they belong to a plow. A cop might stop to see what we're doing here.

The school website information that I had previously found appears, as do a couple of articles from local papers about her accepting the job at Nottawa High. The first article shows a photograph of Dr. Jain looking stern yet calm and includes a press release the school must have written for the occasion. An article on the *Racine County News* website starts off the same, and I'm about to click away when I notice it continues where the other stopped. This reporter must have actually talked to Dr. Jain because he writes that while she enjoyed the government research job she took after earning her Ph.D., she wanted a chance to get out of the lab and apply all she had learned to real communities.

Research.

Apply what she had learned.

"The headlights turned into a parking lot up ahead. I think it might be a police cruiser."

"Give me one more minute."

Typing as fast as I can, I search for the program Nate thought he was taking a survey for. Not there. I think about the email address I saw on his phone and do a search for information about .gov websites. Access to registering those sites is restricted to government entities and the domains are administered by the General Services Administration. An agency that is part of the federal government. Nate wasn't fooled into thinking the Nottawa Project was a government program. It *was* a government program.

"I think the other car is turning around."

"One more minute," I say as I open up my email. As fast as my fingers will go, I type out the things I think NEED is responsible for—Amanda's death, Nate's kidnapping, the dead dogs, fights, broken mailboxes. I then mention the Nottawa

Project survey that was sent to Nate. I stress it was a government website that came up when Nate looked for information. This isn't just about Dr. Jain. There is more at work here.

"The car is coming back this way."

I add the email address for the police department from Officer Shepens's card and then go back to the body of the email to add the URL for the NEED site and my belief that Dr. Jain, with her prior government connection, is involved in the administration of NEED. I even tell Officer Shepens that the motive for her launching this in Nottawa might somehow involve her ex-husband, who lives nearby. It's not a lot. But Bryan is starting the car and I don't have time to write more. Hoping it's enough to help Officer Shepens start looking for answers, I hit Send.

We are turning onto the road as the approaching car slows. Neither of us says a word as the distance increases between our car and the one behind us. If it is a cop, he must have decided we aren't in trouble.

Bryan glances at me. "So did you learn anything useful?"

"Maybe." I give him the rundown on everything I found on Martin Boone and his business, how I think he might be connected to Dr. Jain, and the government website that Nate saw when he got his survey.

"Why would the government be involved in creating a scary social media site for a bunch of high school kids? Call me crazy, but I can't imagine iPads and iPods would be approved as a line item in a departmental budget. Our government does some stupid things, but I have a hard time believing they'd be part of something like this."

"People are apparently capable of lots of things we'd have a hard time believing as long as the reward is high enough." NEED has hammered that lesson home.

"But we're kids." Bryan shakes his head. "If we were adults, I guess I might buy it. But the government isn't supposed to screw with kids."

"I don't think that's a law." It should be, but I'm pretty sure I'm right. Yes, it seems crazy, but it's the only thing that makes even a little bit of sense. "Dr. Jain did research for the government and helped develop government programs. It would make sense that they'd want to test programs on a control group to make sure things work before launching the program for a wider audience." Science isn't my best subject, but I'm pretty sure I understand the way test subjects work.

Bryan opens his mouth, then closes it and frowns. He drives in silence as I look out the window. The town is behind us. According to the GPS, we're a mile from our destination.

Minutes. I'm just minutes away from confronting Dr. Jain. From seeing if Nate is okay and maybe learning if my brother and mother are all right. I wish I could call Mom and hear her voice. But I can't. I just hope if things go bad for me she'll eventually understand what I did. That she'll know I was telling the truth. I can't bear the thought that she'd never understand what I'm doing now or why. I'd like to believe that she'd be proud.

"Stop!" I say louder than I mean to. Bryan jams on the brakes and the car skids.

"What's wrong?"

"You can't keep driving."

"Why not?"

"Dr. Jain doesn't know you're with me. If I drive in on my own, you can follow on foot and help me if I get into trouble. Here." I take the flashlight from my bag and hand it to him.

"I can't let you go in alone," Bryan says. "The whole reason I'm here is to help fix things."

"That's why you have to let me go by myself," I insist. "Dr. Jain knows all of us. She knows how we think, which is why she has been able to manage everything that has happened up until now. We have to surprise her. Doing something she doesn't expect might be the only way we survive this. We have to go in separately."

Bryan sighs and puts the flashlight in his lap. "Okay. Once we get to the right street, I'll get out and you can drive the rest of the way in. You have a license, right?"

"I haven't taken the test yet." And I suck at driving because my mother never bothers to take me out to practice. But Bryan doesn't need to know that. I'll just go slow. "Don't worry. I'll get the car there in one piece."

"I'll hold you to that." He drives to the nearest intersection, slows down, then stops. No one's on the road, which will make it easier for me to drive. At least, that's what I'm telling myself. The cold wind slaps me as I get out of the car and walk to the driver's side. Bryan is already standing next to the car.

"Keep it in second gear," he says as I slide behind the wheel. "I'll give you a few minutes' head start and then I'll follow. Be careful."

"You too."

Bryan closes the door, touches the window, then turns and

jogs off into the snow. For a moment I just sit there and watch him go, hoping that we're doing the right thing even as I know this is the only thing we can do. But before I put the car in gear I have one call to make. I can't talk to my mother, but maybe . . . just maybe I can speak to my father.

The phone on the other end rings. A late-night call might concern him enough to make him pick up. But he doesn't, and that's okay. Because there is nothing he can do to help me now. However, instead of a hang-up, this time when voicemail comes on, I close my eyes, picture his face, and say, "Dad, this is Kaylee. I wish you were here because there's a lot going on. You'll probably hear about it. I'm not sure what's going to happen tonight, but if . . ." I shake my head and swallow the knot that's lodged in my throat. "In case I don't get another chance, I just wanted to say that I love you. Tell Mom I love her, too." Then I slide the phone back in my pocket and start the car.

My fingers grip the steering wheel so tight they hurt. Bryan's car is bigger than ours. I feel as if I'm going to mow down the mailboxes on the side of the road. Thank God no one else is out driving and I can stick to the middle of the street. Bryan is probably watching me, wondering why I'm going this slow, but I don't look for him. I don't take my eyes off the road as I search for the street number Dr. Jain gave me. I can do this. I can face driving alone in the middle of the night on snowy roads and whatever comes next.

The heat blasts and makes me sweat, but I don't try to find the controls to turn it down. I think about my driving and Dr. Jain and NEED. Bryan is right. There has to be a reason for creating a network that targets teens. People get freaked when kids are involved. So why create something that could cause trouble if it ever got leaked to the press? What's so special about high school students?

There. I see a light on the side of the road illuminating a sign that reads ART STUDIO NOW CLOSED. PLEASE CHECK BACK LATER. The address is also visible. Someone came out and cleared off the snow.

My stomach clenches as I turn the wheel and follow a path that has been plowed up the long stone drive. I stop the car fifteen feet in and study what lies before me. There's a big white house with a snow-covered wraparound porch on the right side of the drive. A brownish gray barn sits to the left of it, along with a bunch of smaller outbuildings. A walkway has been cleared to the barn door, and light shines from one of the windows there. The house is totally dark. I guess Dr. Jain is indicating where she wants me to go.

There's no car, though. My mother's car isn't here.

I turn off the engine and put the keys in the center console for Bryan. I wouldn't blame him if he decided to get the hell out of here.

Taking a deep breath, I unfasten my seat belt and open the car door. I step outside and shiver as the cold air hits my sweaty skin. I wish I had thought to bring something I could use to defend myself, but there's nothing I can do about that now.

I slam the car door shut. There's no point in trying to be quiet. I'm pretty sure Dr. Jain knows I've arrived.

I force myself to move. One foot in front of the other. Every crack of a stick or rustle of a branch makes me jump and walk faster. I'm about ten feet from the door when I see it open.

"Hello, Kaylee." Dr. Jain stands there with a gun in her hand. "Won't you come in?"

She steps back and smiles at me. The smile makes me want to slap her. Instead, I meet her eyes and hold them as I move forward. A crack splits the air. I hear it a second before I cry out from the pain.

Oh God. Oh God. Oh God. I've been shot.

Bryan

Wow. Kaylee drives slower than anyone he's ever seen.

Her pace means he can almost keep up on foot, though. He should be afraid, but he's not. If Dr. Jain really is behind this, she's going to do whatever she has to protect herself and the project. She isn't going to let either of them out of here alive. Still, he isn't scared as he trudges toward the house. He knows what he's doing is finally right. Maybe after this he'll be able to live with the rest.

He reaches the side of the big white house and considers his options for getting to the driveway. He could go around the back of the house to avoid being seen from the street. Or he could climb up on the front porch and sneak around that way. The porch might be quicker, but the back is less noticeable.

A car door slams. That decides it for him. Kaylee is out of the car. Quicker is best.

He tucks the flashlight Kaylee gave him into his jacket,

grabs the rail of the porch, and pulls himself up and over. Ha. Take that, Mr. DeAngelos. Bryan might suck at pull-ups during gym class, but he can do it when it counts.

Crouching, he hurries across the porch to the driveway side of the house. He sees Kaylee walking toward a barn door. The door opens and he squats near the porch steps, hoping to blend into the shadows. Dr. Jain appears, and she has a gun.

He hears her invite Kaylee inside. The combination of her measured voice and the pointed gun triggers something. Resentment. Hunger for revenge. Rage at himself. At Dr. Jain. At everyone involved with NEED. Everything that changed his life forever.

Out of the corner of his eye he sees something move near the far edge of the barn. Before he can yell a warning there's a flash and a crack. He's halfway down the steps when he sees Kaylee go down.

"Kaylee!"

Let her be okay. Let her be okay.

He sees Dr. Jain swing her gun, but he doesn't stop running because the person who shot Kaylee is moving closer. He looks familiar, but it's too dark to see him clearly. When the guy with the gun stops and aims again, Bryan doesn't think. He doesn't feel fear. He embraces the anger, puts his head down, and sprints toward him.

Ethan

ETHAN SMILES. Time to finish what he started and bump up his character's kill ratio.

Ready. Set. Fire.

He pulls the trigger as something smacks into him. Hard. Pushing his arm upward.

What the hell?

The kick of the gun and the momentum of whoever just hit him send Ethan reeling backwards. He grabs a fistful of his attacker's coat to keep his balance but goes down into the snow anyway, pulling the coat with him.

His arms are pinned to the ground, so he bucks at the weight on top of him. The snow is deep and cold, making it hard to move, and having someone on his chest makes it hard to breathe. Kaylee is screaming and crying from where he shot her. She's supposed to be dead. *This isn't the way this is supposed to work,* Ethan thinks. *This is wrong.* This never happens in the game. But he's not going to stay on his back or go back a level. He's not going to be taken down. Not now. He's come too far.

The weight on his chest shifts and he takes advantage by shoving hard. His attacker rolls into the snow, and Ethan struggles to a sitting position. His gun. Where the hell is his gun? He pushes to his knees and scans the snow, one hand reaching toward his ankle for his backup piece. As good as the backup is, he wants his gun. It has to be here somewhere.

And when he hears a click, he knows exactly where it is. He holds his breath, slowly looks up, and almost laughs. Bryan VanMeter stands with his arms straight in front of him, gun pointed, looking as surprised to see Ethan as Ethan is to see him.

"Bryan?" He doesn't have to fake his confusion. Bryan isn't supposed to be here. Unless he has an assignment too. Well, only one of them can win. And when it comes to games, Ethan never loses.

"Ethan."

Bryan's arms release some of their tension. His finger doesn't grip the trigger quite as tight. He's soft. But Ethan isn't. His fingers wrap firmly around the handle of his hunting knife.

"What are you doing here?" Bryan asks.

Ethan smiles as he slowly slides the knife from his leg holster. "Winning."

He springs forward with the blade extended. His arm jolts as the knife slices through fabric and plunges into flesh and bone. Blood trickles onto his hand. Warm. Wet. He doesn't care. The blood doesn't matter. Neither does the fact that he's known Bryan for years. The only thing that matters is that he's won.

There's a muffled pop and his knees buckle as something punches hot into his chest. Pain. Blinding pain. He can't breathe. He can't stand. He hits the snow face first and tries to lift his head, but there's too much pain.

Help, he thinks as his chest explodes with heat and agony. He needs help. He needs . . .

Kaylee

"No!" I SCREAM as I grab my upper arm and I lurch to my feet. It hurts. God, my arm hurts, but hearing the shots and watching Bryan crumple hurts worse. "Bryan!"

The world swoops and spins as I struggle to stay upright. I stagger across the snow to where Bryan lies so still. Bile burns hot up my throat as I see a thick black handle sticking out from his deep blue coat and the blood that is seeping from his wound onto the snow. Streaks of his life against a cold white blanket. It should be me. He was helping me.

"Hang on, Bryan," I say, letting my legs collapse to the ground. "I'm going to call for help. You're going to get help."

"No, he's not." Dr. Jain wrenches the phone from my hand and shakes her head as she steps back, her gun aimed at me. "And before you try something heroic, I will tell you that a deep knife wound in that section of the abdomen tends to be fatal without immediate assistance. There's nothing anyone can do."

I want to believe she's lying. Bryan is alive. I know he is, because I can see the way the air frosts when he lets out a breath. But there's so much blood and he's not moving. I put my right hand on his shoulder and say his name again so he knows I'm here. He deserves to have someone who cares near. For the last year, I thought I didn't care about anything other than saving DJ's life, but I do. God, I do.

I go still as I hear the whisper of my name.

"Bryan." I swallow hard. "I'm here with you. Right here. I'm sorry." I'm so, so sorry.

"No." His eyes open. There is pain in them, but something else. Acceptance. For some reason that makes this worse. "Do me a favor?"

"Anything." I lean closer, not caring about the pain that flares through me. His voice is so weak. So quiet. Oh God.

"Tell Amanda's parents that I'm sorry." He winces and closes his eyes. I can feel his struggle to breathe and I squeeze his shoulder, wishing I could do more. When he opens his eyes again they are filled with tears. "Tell them . . ." He stops and has to start again. "I loved her too."

"I will," I say as his breathing slows until I can't see it anymore. I want him to breathe. Please breathe.

But he doesn't. And when I skim my fingers over his face I know he's gone. "I'll tell them everything," I promise.

The wind flutters the hair next to Bryan's ear and I smooth it back, unable to say goodbye. Unable to walk away.

"Fascinating." Dr. Jain's voice cuts through the silence. "The most interesting thing about being a scientist is seeing how subjects deviate from projected behaviors. Bryan's profile doesn't skew toward heroic acts. That must have been your influence, Kaylee. You're not always the most thoughtful, and you have a compulsion toward self-destructive behavior, but the thread that runs through it all is a desire to make things right. That compulsion for some reason makes you brave and unique. Bravery among your peers is not as common as you might think. Truly, I find it so intriguing that people raised in the same community can be compelled by such different things. Look at you three. Bryan's concern about his physical appearance and desperate wish for acceptance. Your compulsion to fix what is broken. Even Ethan's actions, which most people would term sociopathic, can be tracked down to his desire to feel special, and to be in control."

Ethan?

I wipe my cheek on my uninjured shoulder and then turn to look at the body lying face-down in the snow. He's wearing a black coat and a yellow and green hat. Suddenly I get it. Ethan is the one who dug the grave in my yard. Ethan Paschal. That doesn't make sense. He's not one of the kids who loves hunting or eggs houses for fun. And yet he tried to kill me. He killed Bryan. And now he's dead too.

Because of her. As I turn toward Dr. Jain, I see the gun in the snow next to Bryan. If I can only . . .

"Don't make me shoot you, Kaylee." She smiles. "Leave the gun where it is and stand up. Now."

She steps forward and grabs my injured arm. The world swims around me and my stomach heaves as she pulls me to my feet. She must realize I'm going to throw up, because she turns me away from her as my stomach empties again and again.

Once the worst seems to pass, she says, "Walk." And I do.

I don't look back. There's no point. I can't help them. I only hope I can find a way to help Nate and my family and anyone else who has been a part of NEED.

"Where are my mother and brother?" I ask as we reach the door to the barn. "You said they were coming to meet you."

Dr. Jain shrugs. "I lied. Although if you called your mother, as I suspect you did, she and your brother are probably headed back this way now. For someone who rarely trusts, Kaylee, I'm surprised you assumed I was telling the truth. Then again, maybe you did think I was lying and it didn't matter, since you still had to come for your friend." She motions for me to go inside the barn, then follows and closes the door behind her.

I blink at the brightness, and look around for something that can help me escape Dr. Jain and her gun. The inside of the barn is nothing like the ones I've seen. No animals. No hay or farm equipment. The floor is cement. The walls are stained wood. Lining two walls are shelves filled with boxes of all sizes, along with colorful stone vases and other carvings. In the center is a large glass table equipped with enough desktop computers and printers and other machines to fill the lab at school. It's the other two walls that grab my attention. On them are whiteboards filled with numbers and names. The name at the top is Amanda Highland. It's followed by others:

VICKI BOCKNICK
LOUIS VAZQUEZ
MICHAEL DILLMAN
SAMEENA JAHN

GRADY OSTERMAN
AARON ZACHOWSKI
GINA FERGUSON

Dead. They must all be dead. Vicki, with her annoying laugh. Michael, who always wore brightly colored gym shoes. Aaron, the captain of the football team. Gina, with her mean smile and even meaner spirit. All dead. And the list isn't complete. Two more, lying in the snow outside, have yet to be added. I'm sure I'm going to be ill again when I realize Nate's name isn't there. I just hope he's not attached to machines that are the only thing keeping him off this list.

At the top of all the whiteboards is the same header: NOT-TAWA EXPERIMENTAL EXCHANGE DIFFERENTIAL

"Is your curiosity satisfied? I suppose you deserve some answers after everything. Take a seat." Dr. Jain points to a black leather computer chair near the whiteboard with the list of names. "Now, if you'd please snap those cuffs around your right wrist, I'll take care of the left one and do what I can to make that wound a little more comfortable. You're lucky. Ethan was a terrible shot in real life. He should have stuck to video games."

I look at the gun and at the chair, trying to ignore the pain in my shoulder and the way my body trembles. If I sit, I'm giving her permission to kill me. I don't want to die. My shoulders droop as I turn toward the chair. I let out a sigh in hopes Dr. Jain will think I've admitted defeat. I don't have to work too hard to stumble so it looks like I'm grabbing the chair arms for support. Pain shoots through me as I tighten my grip, pivot, and hurl the chair toward her. The gun goes off and I scream as fire sears through my injured arm. When I stumble this time there's no chair to catch my fall, and I slam against the concrete floor.

"I asked you to take a seat. And rest assured I am a much better shot than Ethan. If I had wanted to kill you, I would have."

The cement is cold against my cheek. I try to focus on that and Dr. Jain saying she chose not to kill me instead of the fire burning through my body. Everything hurts, but I won't give in to the pain. I want to, but I can't.

"Now, let's try this again." Dr. Jain stands the chair upright, places it back where it stood before, and comes to squat next to me. The gun is pointed directly at my head. "Can you stand on your own or do you need help? One way or another, you're going to get in this chair. The only thing you control is how many more holes I have to put in you before that happens."

"I don't need your help," I say, and grit my teeth as I struggle to my knees, then to my feet. "I never needed your help." Blood drips down my arm from the two gunshot wounds and I sway back and forth. I take a step forward, determined not to show how weak and nauseated I feel as I drop into the chair.

"You're right. You didn't." She smiles at me as she clicks a cheap metal handcuff that looks like a toy around my right wrist and around the arm of the chair. I decide I'm offended that she didn't bother to spring for stronger handcuffs. It's easier to focus on that than everything else — the way she restrains my other arm, how I'm starting to shiver, the sweat pouring down my back, the death of a friend who has been left outside in the snow, another who is missing, and whatever is going to happen next.

With a nod, Dr. Jain puts down her gun and takes out her

phone, taps the screen several times, then walks to a cabinet on the other side of the room. "In case you were wondering, I meant it when I said I don't plan on killing you."

Hope flares and then just as quickly fades. "I know you can't keep me alive. Not without jeopardizing your project."

"You're smart, Kaylee." She turns, holding a syringe, gauze, and other medical supplies. "Despite what some of your teachers think, I've always known you're smarter than you demonstrate in class. You've just put your attention in the wrong places. But you're correct. A decade of work has gone into this project and there's too much at stake. It has to be protected. So, yes. I won't be the one to end your life, but I know who will."

Sydney

DEAR NEED ASSOCIATE,
A SPECIAL ASSIGNMENT HAS ARISEN AND NETWORK
MEMBER D385 IS NO LONGER AVAILABLE TO
TARGET PROBLEM AREAS WITHIN THE SYSTEM.
WHEN YOU DELIVER THE SUBJECT, YOU WILL
FIND ANOTHER NETWORK MEMBER, KAYLEE
DUNHAM, ONSITE. RETURN HER TO HER HOME,
WHERE ANOTHER MEMBER WILL BE ASKED TO
PERMANENTLY REMOVE HER FROM THE NETWORK—
UNLESS YOU WISH TO ELIMINATE HER FIRST. IF
SO, COMPENSATION WILL BE DOUBLED TO REFLECT
THIS ADDITIONAL ACTION. THANK YOU FOR YOUR
ASSISTANCE IN THIS PROJECT.
THE NEED TEAM

Sydney reads the email on his phone and shakes his head. Email with this kind of information is sloppy. It can be traced. Sending messages through the website is a better policy. The whole thing is more contained and easier to control. Network messages can still be printed out, but paper can't be tracked back to the origin. This type of email can only lead to trouble.

From where he's parked down the street, Sydney eyes the house and barn. Unlike the person who sent him the email, he knows it pays to think through all potential problems before picking a course of action. Which is why he prepared for every contingency.

Leaning across the seat, he pulls the handgun out from under the passenger seat. Sydney prefers the shotgun for hunting, but his grandfather made sure he knew how to use both with equal accuracy. He always told Sydney that a person had to pick the right tool for the job. Grandpa might not approve of the job, but he'd approve of the weapon. He should. It was his.

Sydney checks to make sure the gun is loaded. He knows it is, but he checks anyway. He's just stalling and really, why? He's made his decision and has taken the first step. Unless he wants to bow out, he has to follow through.

He looks back at Nate. Sleeping peacefully, but he should be waking up at some point soon with a hell of a hangover from the drugs. Well, it could be worse. And really, Sydney thinks as he opens the car door, it probably will be.

Kaylee

"HERE . . ." She unzips my coat and frowns. "I've never treated a patient who's tied up in a winter coat before. This is going to be tricky. I don't want to cause you more pain than you're already in."

"Why does it matter? Since you've admitted you're going to kill me anyway." I resist the urge to kick her. I hope I get to later.

"Just because something has to be done doesn't mean it has to cause suffering," she says, stepping back. "As a rule, I dislike pain. I think I'm going to have to cut the sleeve of your coat." She takes a pair of scissors from the supplies she placed on a nearby table and begins to work. When she's done, she rolls up the sleeve of my sweatshirt and pulls out a syringe. "It's pain medication. I told you I won't be the one to facilitate your elimination. Not unless there's no other option. I'd rather not contaminate the project data if I don't have to. Now hold still."

I do, because I want the pain to end. Then maybe I'll be able to think clearly enough to find a way out of here.

Dr. Jain is efficient. In less than a minute, she has cleaned, poked, and put a bandage on the injection site. Compared to the pain in my shoulder when she cuts the fabric around the wound and bandages it, the jab with the needle is nothing.

As she puts the supplies back in the cabinet, I finally can't help but ask, "Where's Nate? What have you done with him?"

Dr. Jain stares at me, then shakes her head. "He doesn't deserve your concern or your loyalty. We often trust those who don't. It's human nature, really, to trust those we love. Your father trusted your mother. I trusted my husband. Then I realized my trust was unfounded. Your father took longer to see the truth, probably because your mother was better at concealing her emotions. Betrayals are hard, but I had it easier in many ways than he did."

"I thought we were talking about Nate."

"We are. And we're not." Her smile is humorless. "You're angry at your father for abandoning you, but you're more like him than you might imagine. As soon as your brother's illness progressed to the point where doctors felt a kidney donation would be needed, your father got tested. Like you, learning that he couldn't be a donor for your brother was difficult. But his test results showed something he didn't believe, so he had them run the test again and finally understood that he isn't DJ's biological father. The confirmation of that betrayal by your mother shattered everything. In many ways you could say that this all is her fault."

"What? No. I don't understand. What are you saying? My

mother loves my father." She flipped out when he left and has only spoken about him when I push her. *He's* the one who shattered *her*. She loves him. Right?

"Maybe she did. But that didn't stop her from sleeping with my husband and ruining my marriage. Didn't you ever wonder why she didn't want you to find your father? If you did, you'd know what she did. Everyone in town would know that she isn't the victim here. And your mother likes playing the victim. It's hard to get sympathy when you're exposed as an adulterer. I could tell you a lot about her personality type, but I think you can figure it out on your own if you really want to."

She's lying. She knows what buttons to push because she knows how I feel. I've spent months telling her how I feel. The world swoops around me and I blink back the lightheadedness and notice the pottery sitting on the far shelf and how it resembles the vase on our living room end table and the piece on my mother's nightstand. And then I think about the days before my father left. The silences. The way he stared at my mother and then at DJ, as if he couldn't bear to lose him. I thought my father couldn't handle the terror and unhappiness that come with having a sick child. I thought he was too scared to stay. Only, I was wrong. Dr. Jain is telling the truth, and it's worse than anything I thought I knew. My father couldn't handle knowing DJ isn't his child. That loss meant more to him than I did. I wasn't important enough for him to tell me the truth. Like my mother, he chose to leave me behind.

I don't know what to do with the rage I feel, but I can tell by the gleam in Dr. Jain's eyes that she wants me to be angry. She wants me to feel betrayed.

I do. But I won't cry. Dr. Jain has taken enough. If it kills me, I won't give her more. I swallow down the anger and do my best to sound calm when I ask, "My mother and your husband are the reasons you came back to Wisconsin?"

"No." She smiles in a way that says she understands what I am doing and approves, which makes me angrier. "NEED is the reason." She glances at her watch and frowns. "After years of research and development the program was finally ready for a controlled test. Since I know the area, it was easy for me to insert myself into the community in a manner that put me in a position to evaluate the accuracy of the data we received on our surveys. I could also monitor the reactions of the network members after the site went live. It's interesting, but out of all the subjects, circumstances made it so I knew you best, and yet you were the one who presented the biggest surprise. When your chance came to ask the network for something you needed, I thought you'd ask for a way to find your father. If you had, it would have changed everything."

"Why?"

"If you think about it, I'm sure you'll figure it out."

The pain has faded but my mind is fuzzy. Yet when I think about it I do know. "Because my father couldn't be a donor for DJ. Locating him wouldn't qualify as a need." And like the site states—there is a difference between a want and a need. "I would have been given a NEED fulfillment request." DJ could live without finding Dad. A kidney is necessary. I'd like to think I would have ignored the request, but I'm not so sure that I could have given up on the chance to help DJ. I wouldn't have cared about the consequences of fulfilling the request until it was too late. And then, like Bryan had, I would probably have done anything to prevent my mother or the people in this town from finding out what I had done. I would have been just as bad as everyone else. I might have been worse. It was all a trap. One that I escaped, because Dr. Jain played God and deemed my request a need.

Her smile is slow and satisfied. "See, I told you you're smarter than people give you credit for. Yes, you asked for something that your brother will not be able to live without, and that changed everything for you. It also changed everything for Nate Weakley, who thanks to your request will no longer need that physics grade he wanted. I'm told he's been delayed due to the snow, but he should be along soon. Weather is something we can't seem to anticipate with any consistent accuracy. Human reactions, thank goodness, are much easier to predict. Otherwise, I'd be out of a job. As it stands now, this accelerated test has been far more successful than any of us planned."

"The test is for the government?" I try to shake off the fog and I tug at my restraints. "This isn't just about revenge for what happened between my mother and your husband."

"Of course not." She walks over to the whiteboard and picks up one of the markers. "Although this project would never have existed had it not been for that betrayal. I wouldn't have taken a government job or been assigned to the design team that works to infiltrate and gain intelligence from foreign nations. I don't know if this will make it easier for you, but everything that has occurred over the last few days will help keep our country safe for years to come."

"How does Amanda dying or blowing up the school keep anyone safe?"

She shrugs. "Every culture has unique social structures that make it difficult to acquire data through typical channels, especially now that security measures are at an all-time high. Those who handle secure data have a heightened awareness of infiltration and are doing more to protect sensitive information. Information we need in order to keep our country and its citizens safe." She takes the cap off the marker, adds the names Bryan VanMeter and Ethan Paschal at the bottom of the list, then steps back and points to the board. "High-school-age citizens, however, aren't always on alert. Their parents aren't either, no matter how much they claim to be watching. No matter how many warnings are posted, no one actually believes that online behavior can hurt their lives or the lives of others. Especially if there is a cloak of anonymity. Everyone feels shielded, safe, and invincible. Add the anxieties that come with being a teenager—the things you want and feel you need in order to be successful or admired or happy—and it's easy to see how your demographic can be molded into a group that is willing and able to collect information for rewards. Especially if it is unaware of the importance of the data collected. After all, what's the harm in taking a photograph of a neighbor's house or printing off a file from a parent's computer? It's just a little thing. Correct? And what they need to make them happy is so much more important. Especially if all their friends are getting rewards. No one wants to be left out."

She puts the cap back on the marker and returns it to the holder on the board. "Obviously, this accelerated model was intended to demonstrate how far I could push my subjects before losing their willingness to cooperate. I am now also able to pinpoint which personality types are best suited to which types of tasks, and which ones will be the most likely to report the network to their parents or to the authorities. The real program will expand the timeline and avoid the termination of network members or government targets until the very end of the appointed cycle. There will, of course, have to be a few adjustments made for cultural differences and—" She stops and pulls a cell phone out of her pocket. Her eyes narrow as she reads the screen, and when she turns back to me, she no longer looks like the Dr. Jain who is always calm and in control. Her face is contorted with fury. "The police are on their way here."

Officer Shepens must have gotten my message. He believed me. "Good," I say as I struggle against the cuffs, hoping against hope that they might break.

"You should have just let things be." Dr. Jain strides to the table, sits down at the computer, and begins to type. She stands again in less than a minute and walks toward me. "The one good thing is that we now know that the most important thing we can do to perpetuate each network cell is to identify those who fit your personality type and eliminate them."

She pulls the gun back out of her pocket as I yank at my restraints. I know it's pointless, but I have to try to save myself. I pull to the left and feel the chair tilt. It starts to keel over and takes me with it. Pain explodes in my shoulder as I crash against the concrete. My glasses skitter somewhere and I fight to get to my knees, to crawl or hide or something. I have to do something because out of the corner of my eye I see the blur of what can only be a gun aimed at me as Dr. Jain says, "It's a shame, because I really didn't want to do this."

Oh God. My heart stalls and I jump at the crack of the gun.

But I'm not hit. I wait for the next shot to fire, but instead the gun tumbles out of Dr. Jain's hand and she falls to the ground. Without my glasses, everything is out of focus. But I can still make out the trickle of blood oozing from Dr. Jain's head, and I know. Dr. Jain is dead.

Sydney

"Kaylee, get up."

She blinks at him and then screams. Great. Although he figures if he were handcuffed to a chair, threatened at gunpoint, and then forced to watch as someone got shot in front of him he'd scream too.

"Hey, calm down. I'm here to help you. We have to get out of here, though. I think she hit something on the computer that's going to blow this place sky high." The wires that have no other reason to be snaking around the base of the room have to be attached to something. And he doubts that Dr. Jain or the United States government is interested in leaving evidence just lying around.

Hearing about the prospect of a bomb seems to get Kaylee moving. "I'm stuck to this chair," she says as she drags herself to her knees and lets him help her get the chair back into an upright position.

The handcuffs are the same type that were used to restrain

Nate. Good thing, because it means he has a key. "I'm going to get you free. As soon as I do, clear out of here. My truck is parked on the street. Nate's in the back seat."

"What are you going to do?" she asks as Sydney slides the key in the lock and turns it.

"I want to take a look at something. I won't do anything crazy. I promise. Go."

She does. She's unsteady, but she's out the door in a flash. He has to give her credit. The girl has guts. She'll be back to look for him if he doesn't get out of here soon.

Sydney walks over to where Kaylee's glasses lie on the floor, picks them up, and slides them into his pocket. Then he heads for the computer and gets to work.

The system is incredible. Pretty sad it's going to end up torched. Oh well, it's not like he can just walk away with the hardware. And maybe someday soon he'll have a setup like this of his own. After his stop at Dr. Jain's house in Nottawa, breaking into the system is easy. The government should have taught the woman to change her passwords. It takes him only a few minutes to find what he's looking for. He types her password again to verify his request. A confirmation message appears on the screen and he smiles as he hears a beep telling him the failsafe has been set.

He pushes back from the computer and heads for the door. Before he ducks out, he looks back at Dr. Jain's body and then at the wall filled with the names of people he's known almost all his life. He reads the words at the top of the board: NOTTAWA EXPERIMENTAL EXCHANGE DIFFERNTIAL. The true meaning behind NEED.

As he runs down the drive, he sees Kaylee waving at him

from inside the truck. He braces for the explosion he has set to go off. It's time to wipe the slate clean. Kaylee smiles with relief as he gets closer, probably because she doesn't realize how long he was hiding in the shadows. He heard everything Dr. Jain said, and he agrees. NEED is a pretty good idea. With some work, it can be better. The person he reached tonight at the Department of Defense was open to a discussion, which is good. Sydney knows he can either seize this opportunity or go down with the ship. He's done too much to hang around and wait to be used as a scapegoat. He'll stash some of the information in a secure place with some fail-safes just in case his new friends decide he knows too much, and then he'll get in touch with them again to set up a meeting. He's pretty sure that once he shares the ideas he has gleaned from his firsthand experience and explains to them that he can expose their super-secret plan if they aren't careful, well, he'll be able to help make NEED great.

Kaylee

TOWN TERRORIZED BY A STRING OF
TEENAGE HAZINGS GONE WRONG

FEDERAL GOVERNMENT DENIES ALL
CLAIMS OF SOCIAL NETWORKING SITE OR
INVOLVEMENT IN TWELVE DEATHS

MERCENARY COMPUTER GAME INSPIRED
TEENAGER WHO PLOTTED AGAINST TOWN

FIRST RESPONDER WRACKED BY GRIEF
GIVEN LEAVE OF ABSENCE

I slam my computer shut without bothering to read the articles
and try to shut out the beeps and chatter coming from the hospital hallway. How the news about what happened got screwed
up so fast is beyond me. It's only been three days since Officer
Shepens and several other policemen arrived at Dr. Jain's barn
in time to see it burn to the ground. No one has been able to

figure out who alerted her to their arrival. Her phone and mine went up in flames. Thankfully, the pictures I posted online still exist. Along with the damage to the school, those photos, the kids who are dead, and the fire that destroyed Dr. Jain's house all confirmed that what I was saying was true. As did Sydney's statements about why he came to the barn and how he got me out before I died. I thanked him then and have been hoping he'll come by the hospital so I can thank him again. But he hasn't. I plan to swing by his house when I get out later today. It'll give me something to do besides going home—a place I don't know if I'm ready to return to. And not just because of the reporters who my father says are camped out on our street.

My father.

When I woke up after the surgery to remove the bullets in my arm, I found him at my bedside, with my mother hovering behind him, and I smiled. Then I remembered. He's sorry. She's sorry. Everyone apologized for their mistakes and their secrets and all of the hurt they caused. I know I'm supposed to forgive them even though they say I'm entitled to be angry and they'll give me time to work through my feelings. They've even suggested we go to a family counselor. Yeah, right. Like that's ever going to happen. After Dr. Jain, I don't plan on talking to a shrink ever again. Not even for DJ.

Although I will lie for him. He still doesn't know about Mom's betrayal and his biological father and I don't plan on being the one to tell him. I refuse to break his heart. Mom can do that herself. For the last year I thought I knew what was right, and I turned out to be horribly wrong about almost everything. Things are messed up enough without me screwing them up even more. It's a step in the right direction, I hope. A step away from the person Dr. Jain thought I was and the things she was certain drive me. I'm angry at my mother for cheating and my father for lying and I've shut them out when DJ isn't around, even when they want to talk about his biological dad.

According to my mother, Dr. Jain's ex-husband was tested months ago—not long after my father walked out the door. I think about how things could have been different had I known that before. But I didn't. I'd like to think we're all sorry for that, but the way my mother asks me to be careful of what I say to others about our lives tells me some things haven't changed. Mom doesn't want everyone in town to gossip about her mistakes. I understand the feeling, but I can't be sorry that she's the one who's going to be talked about this time. If she had told me the truth, I would have done things differently. At least, I hope I would have. I'm so different now from the person I was only a week ago. It's hard to tell.

The worst part is that DJ's biological father isn't a match. But he's been quietly asking some of his family and friends to be tested, and now that my mother plans to break the news to DJ, he'll be able to ask even more. The test for his cousin came back with a four-point match. He's willing to donate. There are lots of steps between now and then, and maybe a better match will be found. If not, I'm glad to know there's one person who is willing to help my brother. Seeing someone step forward to do something good without the promise of an external reward gives me hope.

DJ will be told soon about our father and his biological dad. I'll help DJ when he learns the truth, and I'm going to try to forgive my mother for not telling me why she didn't look for my dad when he left or what DJ's biological father was doing to save my brother's life. I won't be able to forgive immediately and maybe I won't ever be able to forgive completely. But I have to see if there's more to me than the bitterness and distrust that Dr. Jain counted on. I don't want those things to define me. There are no more secrets. NEED is gone. I have to find a way to move on.

"Hey." Nate stands in the doorway, one foot in the room, one in the hallway.

"Hey." Not exactly the best response, but I don't know what else to say. I saw him once after he woke up from whatever drug he'd been given by NEED. But not since then. Between the questioning by police and the surgery and the revelations about my family, there wasn't time to talk. Then there was, but he didn't show up. Now he's here. Things have changed. There's no going back to what we thought we were or who I was. The old me would have shut Nate out. This me says, "Come on in."

Relief flickers across his face. "I drove by the school on the way here. They already have crews cleaning and rebuilding. The offices need a hell of a lot of work, but the rest isn't as bad as it could have been. My parents say that several churches in town are volunteering space for us to have classes until the school gets fixed. From what I've heard school will start again next week."

"I guess you'll have to study for that physics test," I say.

"Yeah." He looks down. "I guess, which kind of sucks. Personally, I think we should all be given straight A's until such time as we come to terms with the trauma inflicted upon us."

He jams his hands in his pockets, a familiar gesture. "I was going to bring flowers, but your mom said you're getting sprung today, so I figured I should probably wait."

"You don't have to get me flowers," I say, because I can tell by the way he looks at me that he's asking about more than carnations. And I don't have any answers right now.

"Then I guess I did something right this time." He walks to the foot of my bed. "I'm still figuring out what happened after I left your house. I was halfway down the block when Bryan drove up. He asked if I wanted a lift and I climbed in because it was Bryan and I figured there wasn't anything to worry about. Wow, was I wrong. I would have guessed if Jack had been behind the wheel, but Bryan . . ."

Bryan. I've thought about him a lot. His parents came to see me and I told them everything, including how he saved my life. He made a mistake when he got involved with NEED, but to me he'll always be a hero. Unlike Nate's brother, Jack.

"How is Jack?"

"Screwed. He lied about how he got the phone and the slide board, so my folks aren't buying the excuses he came up with about helping NEED kidnap me. They've taken away his new phone, are selling his car, and he's no longer allowed to have a computer in his room. Not like that'll stop him from being idiotic online, but it looks like that's the route a lot of parents are going around here. Almost no one from school is on social media right now. It feels like everyone dropped off the face of the earth or something."

Or something.

"With the Internet embargo and school still being out, I've

had a lot of time to think. I'm sorry. I know I said it the other night, but I was more sorry then that you found me out than about what I'd done. This whole thing with being a donor—"

"It's okay," I say, trying to mean it. "It has to be your choice."

"I saw your dad outside. You must be thrilled to have him back. But I guess I just want you to know that if DJ has another relapse and he needs someone to save him . . . Well, you saved my life. I'd like the chance to return the favor for someone who really deserves it. I don't know if my parents will agree, but they're suddenly listening to me, so maybe."

But probably not. Nate wants to do the right thing, but he's still scared and he's using his parents as an excuse. However, I realize that I meant what I said. It has to be his choice. He doesn't know about my mother's affair, or the potential donor from DJ's dad's side, and I'm not going to tell him. And I realize that while I forgive Nate, I no longer trust him. That will take more time.

"Have you brought flowers to Sydney?" I ask so we don't have to talk about my father or DJ anymore. "After all, he's technically the one who saved your life."

"I tried yesterday. Well, not flowers, because people will talk, but I went by his house with a cake my mother insisted on baking." He smiles. Nate's mom is legendary for her lack of cooking skills. She burns pans on a consistent basis.

"Did he like the cake?" I ask with a grin.

"He wasn't there. He left town."

"What? Why? Is he okay?" I remember the way he watched the barn before it exploded and the way he calmly took charge of calling 911.

"I guess he's fine." Nate sits down on the edge of the bed. "Sydney's parents said they woke up yesterday morning and found a note on the table. It said something about him taking a computer job out of town and how the events of the past few days had shown him that you have to seize an opportunity when it presents itself."

A computer job?

"But he's not out of high school yet."

"I guess that doesn't matter if you have skill," Nate says. "And Sydney has a lot of skill. Probably as much as the person who put NEED together in the first place."

I frown and remember the way Sydney said that he wasn't a hero. Even though he was. Sydney said he was supposed to deliver Nate to NEED but decided to find out what NEED intended to do with him before completing the job. When he heard Dr. Jain talking to me about NEED and how it was responsible for so many deaths, he realized he couldn't do it. I accepted that then, but suddenly none of that makes sense, and I feel ill as I think of something that does.

"Wait a minute." I flip open the lid on my laptop and type in my password.

"What's wrong?" Nate asks, coming over to the front of the bed so he can see what I'm doing.

"Dr. Jain was in charge of NEED," I say as I type. "But could she really have done it alone?"

"Well, she must have had people who helped her develop the program."

"Yeah, but they're in Washington, D.C., or somewhere out east." Officer Shepens has searched for anyone in hotels near here who knew her and interviewed her neighbors to see if she had visitors. So far he's come up empty. And with the government denying any responsibility, I doubt he'll be able to share any information even if he finds it. "Wouldn't she have needed help here to do some of the basic tech stuff like approving email addresses and verifying NEED fulfillment request completions? There were so many so fast. And what about all the things that had to be delivered to people's houses. Could she really have done it all herself?"

Dr. Jain said I was the only personality type who made choices that she couldn't predict. For days, I've felt lucky that Dr. Jain misjudged Sydney, too. That she thought he could sacrifice Nate and kill me when he wasn't able to do either. But what if she wasn't wrong? I never questioned why she would have given Sydney the address to the location where she ran NEED. After all, someone had to deliver Nate. But in accordance with her "rules," she didn't insert herself into the data. She wouldn't have killed Sydney herself to protect her secret. But there was no secret to protect if he already knew it. If he had been recruited to be part of the team. If he had already proven himself loyal. Until he saw an opportunity and seized it.

"What are you doing?" Nate asks.

"Checking on NEED." I've looked every day and have gotten the same error message, but I want to see if anything has changed. I assumed Dr. Jain nuked the website the same way she blew up the barn. But what if she didn't do either?

I click on the link and an error message appears.

THE SITE YOU ARE SEARCHING FOR IS NO LONGER AVAILABLE.

I stare at the message for a long time, hoping that Dr. Jain deleted the site. That I'm wrong. That NEED really is gone for good. But even as I explain my suspicions to Nate and he assures me that NEED won't come back, I can't help but wonder.

What if it does?

CONGRATULATIONS. YOU HAVE BEEN INVITED TO
NEED—THE NEWEST, INVITATION-ONLY SOCIAL
MEDIA SITE FOR NORWAY HIGH SCHOOL STUDENTS.
JOIN YOUR FRIENDS IN DISCOVERING HOW MUCH
BETTER LIFE CAN BE WHEN YOU ARE PRESENTED
WITH AN ANONYMOUS WAY TO EXPRESS YOUR
THOUGHTS AND ARE GIVEN THE TOOLS TO GET THE
THINGS YOU NEED.
WHAT DO YOU *NEED?*

Acknowledgments

NOTHING THAT I DO would be possible without the support of my family. Topping the list are my husband, Andy, and my son, Max, who put up with me every day, and my awesome mother (and champion assistant), who reminds me that I need to sleep at some point. Thank you to the rest of my family and friends, who always cheer me on and make me believe that all things are possible. I love you so much.

To my agent, Stacia Decker—you are never allowed to quit this job or move to Tibet in order to search out the meaning of life. If you do, I'm going to come find you. Your belief in me means more than I can ever adequately express. I am so lucky to have you in my corner. I'm also very lucky to have the entire team at Donald Maass Literary on my side. To Amy, Jennifer, Jen, Katie, Cameron, Charlie, and Don—thank you so much for your support.

To the wonderful team at Houghton Mifflin Harcourt for Young Readers—you are the best! Everything I write is made so much better by the amazing and tireless Margaret Raymo. I am beyond fortunate to work with such an incredible editor. I also would like to extend a huge hug of gratitude to my publisher, Betsy Groban, who makes me and every other author at HMH feel so special. To Rachel Wasdyke, public relations executive extraordinaire — you rock! Also, I would be remiss if I didn't give shout-outs to Candace Finn, Linda Magram, Lisa DiSarro, Taylor Foley, Emily Cervone, Meredith Wilson, Joan Lee, Carol Chu, and so many others who work tirelessly to champion my books. Much love to you all.

I also owe a special thank-you to Pete Bohan, who is not only an amazing marketing guy, but a great friend. Also, many thanks to the amazing Becky Anderson and her team at Anderson's Bookshop, Robert McDonald and the entire team at the Book Stall, and every bookseller and librarian who has championed my stories. This journey would be impossible without you.

Last, but most important: To each and every reader, thank you from the bottom of my heart. Each time you pick up a book, you make dreams come true.

Joelle Charbonneau began telling stories as an opera singer, but these days she finds her voice through writing. She lives near Chicago with her husband and son, and when she isn't writing, she works as an acting and vocal coach. She is also the author of the best-selling Testing series. Visit www.joellecharbonneau.com.

Don't miss the newest thriller
by Joelle Charbonneau:

TIME BOMB

Coming in Spring 2018!